THE LIGHTNING FIELD

By
MaryFrank Sanborn

The Lightning Field

© Copyright 2026 MaryFrank Sanborn

All rights reserved. No part of this book may be reproduced in any form or by any electronic or mechanical means, including information storage and retrieval systems, without written permission from the author, except in the case of a reviewer, who may quote brief passages embodied in critical articles or in a review.

Trademarked names may appear throughout this book. Rather than use a trademark symbol with every occurrence of a trademarked name, names are used in an editorial fashion, with no intention of infringement of the respective owner's trademark.

The information in this book is distributed on an "as is" basis, without warranty. Although every precaution has been taken in the preparation of this work, neither the author nor the publisher shall have any liability to any person or entity with respect to any loss or damage caused or alleged to be caused directly or indirectly by the information contained in this book.

This is a work of fiction. Names, characters, places, and incidents either are the product of the author's imagination or are used fictitiously, and any resemblance to actual persons, living or dead, events, or locales is entirely coincidental.

rev 26-0507

*"For us, there is only the trying.
The rest is not our business."*

~ T.S. Eliot

DEDICATION

To Girl Friends all over the world!
The women who support, inspire, and lift each other up.
We rise by lifting others!
From the bottomless center of my heart, I thank you all…
especially my own resilient tribe of Soul Sisters!
And to the power of the Divine Feminine,
whose qualities of Cooperation, Compassion, and Kindness
may yet save the world.

"The Invisible is Real."

Artforum, April 1980

*(stating some facts, notes, statistics and statements
concerning the real Lightning Field in New Mexico)*

CHAPTER 1

Fog—quiet, insidious, ravenous—the confluence of warm Gulf Stream waters and the icy Labrador Current, drifted southward and westward from the Bay of Fundy, consuming everything in its path: fishing boats, sea birds, buoys, everything but sounds and smells, which it returned like unwanted gifts.

There on one of a thousand fractal fingers extending gracefully into the sea, on a cliff in front of an abandoned Coast Guard station, a woman sat uncomfortably huddled in a canary-colored slicker, an oddly bright spot in otherwise colorless conditions. Her back was against a rough slab of granite, chilling her to the bone and numbing her toes. Her head was hunkered down into a woolly hat, the hood of the slicker pulled forward, concealing her face. Her feet, in tall yellow boots, splayed open, forming a V. Her eyes were focused on the black and churning Atlantic Ocean in front of her, but her mind was miles away.

Above and below the white noise of the waves was the mournful sound of a foghorn and the human-like scream of a seagull. But she was unaware of those too. She sat motionless as the salt spray slapped her in the face as the gray shroud swallowed the ocean, the cliffs surrounding her, and finally her yellow boots. She watched it all, uninvolved.

Tucked against the rock, she faced a narrow inlet where the waves slammed hard then whooshed into the slim channel with a rushing and then a sucking sound as they were pulled inexorably back to sea. In the opaque haze, she listened for the subtle differences in the swells, studying the waves as Papillion did when he made his great escape. But where was her escape? He at least imagined freedom at the end of his ride on that coconut raft. She could imagine nothing.

She took shallow breaths, an unconscious custom since childhood—dubious breathing skills that kept her alive, yet only half alive—as if she knew instinctively that breath was life, and she was afraid of it. Afraid to breathe too much, to feel, to invite too much in. Afraid that the gift of air might fill her with too much energy, cause her to fly up and out, make her visible when she knew deep within that she must not be seen, should not be known, that it was better to be quiet, hushed, silent. In the Far East, it is said that when a child is born, the lifespan is already predestined, not by years but by the number of breaths allotted.

She was afraid she was using up her allotment. Fast.

When a shiver of cold ran up her spine, she pulled her knitted cap tighter, tucking in loose strands of dark curly hair that had stuck to the salt on her face. Generally, she liked the fog, its insulation and the way it cushioned her against the rest of the world and kept her secrets. But she hated the accompanying cold, which caused her fingers to go numb and white. "Raynaud's," her doctor had told her—a circulatory condition caused by the constriction of blood vessels. She once read a psychological interpretation of the affliction as the desire to strangle something or someone. She had dismissed the information immediately as "New Age."

Hugging herself for warmth, she now balled her hands inside the matching milk-colored mittens and breathed into them through the yarn, trying to warm freezing fingers, then holding the mittens on her face so that only her azure eyes were showing. She had knitted the mittens, hat, and fisherman sweater that she wore under her slicker, taught to her by her mother when she was just six. It had been a rare intimate moment when her mother had placed long needles in her small hands and, with arms encircling from behind, helped her daughter form her first crude stitches. Knit, purl, knit, purl. Oh, look at all the patterns, glorious to her child's mind in their beautiful, infinite possibilities!

In Ireland, where her mother Faith was born, the women knit a family pattern. It was actually a grizzly way to identify their dead in case any of them fell into the sea and were pulled out much later. Faith taught her daughter the Cassidy family pattern, and also that of Carlisle, her entire lineage encoded in a weave, her DNA in wool.

The young girl took to it readily, for even as a small child she liked the idea of patterns and order and predictability.

Knitting provided the perfect retreat: a buffer for her loneliness, an occupation for her mind, a sense of accomplishment for her critical nature. All that was a comfort to her, especially now as the rest of her life was unraveling.

She was Clair Cassidy McKendrick—daughter of Faith Carlisle and Dan Cassidy, Irish immigrants. Wife of Blake McKendrick, WASP lawyer. Mother of Carl, twenty-seven, and Cassidy, eighteen.

And this was one of the worst days of her life.

Day after day can pass by without a ripple, then a butterfly flaps its wings in China and everything changes. A day psychologists might speak of as "synchronous," or astrologers might explain in the predictive daily transits, but whatever plan or non-plan, whether randomness or meaningful coincidence, it was one of those days in time when events collide and nothing is ever the same again.

⚡

Earlier that day Clair had stopped by the local knitting shop. The wind took the door as she opened it, causing her to nearly fall into the store. Above her, the tinkling bell sounded its merry message—*Visitor!* From the back of the shop, she heard Geraldine's chirpy voice calling out to her: "We're here!"

It could be a mass murderer and Geraldine would tell the intruder where they were. When Clair walked to the back, Flora, the older sister at eighty-three, declared, "Why, come on in, child, and get by the fire. You're soaking wet! You'll catch pneumonia!" These old women warmed her more than the fire.

They were all sitting around the wood stove, the sisters and Millie, their friend of fifty years. The sisters' Maine Coon cat Glory was also in attendance. The women all looked similar, full in the chest and low to the ground like hens and had all adopted a "uniform" of sorts that gave their short, stout bodies ultimate comfort.

But Clair had come to know that they were nothing alike and had unique and interesting backgrounds. She scratched Glory's ears on her way by and felt her heart ache momentarily for her own feline friend, Ragdoll, who'd died during the winter at age nineteen.

Clair could see that Geraldine was making a child's angora sweater, pink yarn with white bunnies on the front. And, as usual, Flora was telling her how to do it. And Millie was talking right over both of them as if she couldn't hear, which she probably couldn't since she had a habit of turning off her hearing aids and forgetting to turn them back on. Seated in their rocking chairs that were pulled up to the wood stove, they wore similar dresses that hung from shoulders to knees without touching them any place in between, long sweaters they had made, and spongy-soled lace-up shoes—just as if they'd consulted with each other that morning.

I'm wearing my baggy dress and hush-puppies. You too? Good!

The shop belonged to the sisters, but Millie was there so often she had finally brought her own favorite chair. She sat with an Afghan over arthritic knees. "From tennis," she'd told Clair, which surprised the hell out of Clair since she couldn't imagine Millie on a tennis court. In fact, it was hard to imagine any of them at other stages of their lives, although they talked of their former lives as girls. And the sisters also told of being mothers and, finally, widows. Throughout her time with the trio, Clair had really come to know them as they recounted stories from different times in their existence, which they relished telling.

The sisters had led more traditional lives, with long marriages and children. Flora had lost a ten-year old granddaughter to leukemia; Geraldine had outlived both her daughter and her son. Yet, refusing to be stagnant in their future years, the sisters had grown a successful business together that was still thriving in the small township where they lived.

But Millie! She was a renegade! Never married—although there was a hint of a passionate love affair, perhaps even with another woman. Clair wanted to know more, but kept her questions to herself when she sensed a reservation about this topic on Millie's part. She had gone into the Armed Forces though, traveled the world as a nurse and nutritionist, and didn't just play tennis, but was a champion. Now, in the closing decades of the three women's lives, they were tending the home fires and nurturing one another.

The women knitted all winter by the fire and sold the things they had made during the summer when the tourists came. In short order, they had discovered that Clair was a first-class knitter and had offered her a chance to put some things in the shop on consignment. Everything she gave them sold. And quickly. But when they asked for more, she faltered, slowing her production, for secretly she was afraid of joining them.

They are who I will become: sexless, a little senile, and endlessly making sweaters. She was afraid it would be the end of her, that she'd grow old and be one of them, never having had the life she wanted. And she didn't even know what that was.

"So, what are you in for today?" asked Geraldine. "Company or yarn?"

"Yarn today," Clair answered. "But company too," she added, suddenly realizing that they were her only friends.

She'd been in town only a couple of years, still very much the outsider. The townspeople, naturally suspicious of outsiders, were leery of the woman from Boston who'd bought the five sea-coast acres they'd hoped would become the town park; she was the woman whose husband never seemed to be around.

"I have news." Clair hesitated until she saw the tilt of the three very lined faces. "I'm going to have a grandchild," she blurted out, trying on the word *grandchild* for the first time.

They oohed and ahhed as she knew they would.

"My son called this morning with the news," Clair explained.

In fact, it was her daughter-in-law who'd told her. She and her son didn't speak very often, which saddened her.

"And what color yarn will you be wanting for this new arrival?" asked Geraldine.

"She wouldn't know that yet," scolded her sister.

"Well, this generation always seems to know what sex they're having," Geraldine shot back.

The sisters bickered constantly, but good-naturedly. There was always the sound of laughter at the shop, and Clair liked that. Sometimes it was the only reason she left her house, just to hear that sound.

"Yes, it's still too early to know," Clair said, though in her heart she thought: *Girl!* "The baby's not due until Christmas. I think yellow for now."

Yellow for the tiny embryo, my son's child, floating in the belly of its mother, tethered by a blood-filled cord.

When Clair left, several gulls were visible on the nearby rocks, heads tucked into their bodies, gray and white feathers ruffled. One occasionally opened its yellow beak, stuck out a red tongue, and screeched at nothing in particular. In the mist were flashes of light, like the giant lightning bugs she remembered catching as a child, and there were low rumbles in the distance that were growing closer.

"I want a divorce," he had said, during her second telephone call of the morning.

Heading for her car, Clair walked carefully across the lichen-covered rocks where bird droppings had splattered into ghostly shapes. The fog seemed to fold itself around her and she was beginning to feel panicky until she spotted her white Volvo station wagon, the only car in the lot. She beeped it open from a distance, hurrying as the rain started falling with an enthusiasm that Clair did not share. A porcupine startled her, waddling lazily by the roadside, but it was engaged in rooting for food in the pine needles and ignored the wet woman. As she got in, she quickly slipped off the rain slicker and tossed it into the backseat next to the bag of yellow yarn.

She turned the key and the radio blasted.

This is KGBH downtown Boston. Today's Sox game with Cincinnati is cancelled, folks, 'cause in case you haven't noticed, we've got ourselves a serious case of fog! Logan Airport's closed and traffic is slowed from here all the way up the coast of Maine. Land ho, them lobster boats, eh?

A quick twist of her wrist turned the radio off. While waiting for the car to heat, she revved the gas pedal to hurry it along. As she did so, she glimpsed herself in the visor mirror and pushed back the dark brown strands of hair under her hat. Touching cold fingers to swollen eyes, she managed to avoid looking directly into them in the mirror. She had read once that it was impossible to lie to yourself if you were looking into your own eyes. Finding that to be true, she skimmed her periphery instead; direct contact avoided.

⚡

"I want a divorce."

The words had shocked her. He'd never said them before.

Oh, she had known about the other women. There had always been other women and she had always looked the other way. It was an unspoken pact between them. He did what he wanted and she didn't ask. Men were men after all, and cheating was as old as time. The cliches abounded.

Ultimately they stayed together because it served them both. She could be Mrs. Blake McKendrick, an identity that suited her, with the status and safety of marriage, and he could flirt with all the women he wanted, but didn't have to get involved because, well, he was married. It served them both.

But this time he did get involved.

"I suppose you want to be with your girlfriend?" Clair spit out the words.

A friend from Boston had told her that she'd seen Blake with a young woman in a restaurant. The 'friend' had told Clair that the woman was beautiful and how adoringly Blake and the woman had looked at each other. Blake never could resist a beautiful woman. Ironically, Clair had been one of those women back in their college days.

"Clair," he sighed, his voice sounding weary, "we both know it's been over for years. Let's just end it."

"Easy for you to say." Clair's voice was rising in volume. "You have a whole other life." This knowledge that he was happy catapulted her to a fury. He was happy. Now she was screaming. She could hear herself out of control and hated what he brought out in her, hearing the echo of her own mother's rage.

"How old is she, Blake?" she goaded. "As old as our daughter?"

"Clair, stop this—you're just making it harder. And, no, she's not near Cassidy's age. She's thirty-eight … and, Clair, I didn't want to tell you like this, but," he hesitated, "she's pregnant."

He was saying other words, about them choosing not to have an abortion, and marrying the woman, but Clair's mind had turned off. A punch couldn't have surprised her more, and she slid down the wall to the floor. This was not what they had agreed upon. Her hands were trembling, her pulse coursing through her temples like something might burst.

"Have you spoken to your son yet this morning?" Her voice was weak.

Her breath. She had to catch her breath.

"Here's news: You're going to be a grandfather, Blake." She began laughing. "We're going to have a grandchild. Hey, his child and yours can grow up together!"

She could knit for both babies, she thought, dully. *Yellow sweaters with white angora bunnies.*

⚡

Clair inched the car through the fog, watching the whiteness part as she moved toward the main road.

I want a divorce.

Twenty-eight years next month. Or would have been. She had been thinking they might take a trip together, something to get them back on track, for he was insufferably right: There was nothing between them. Hadn't been for a long time. Maybe it was her fault for having ignored the other women? Maybe if she had confronted him throughout the years? But how could she, fearing the consequences as she had? Clair wasn't of his aristocratic world, only had him as her husband by accident because she had become pregnant. Now it had happened again, only he was choosing to marry this woman.

As she drove, a forest of pine, maple, and oak trees were dense on either side of the road. It was already the middle of May, but spring came late to this latitude. The maples, just getting their leaves, displayed a soft red fuzz on the tips of their branches. The road was one lane in each direction, one of the back roads not much used by the tourists who would be arriving in droves before long. In town, preparations were in full swing, repairs being made to sidewalks and shop fronts after last year's severe weather.

"*WELCOME TO SUMMER* 2000," banners announced throughout the small township.

"I want a divorce." He'd said that. After all these years.

As she drove, Clair felt a moaning coming from deep inside. As if she opened her mouth some guttural cry might escape, so she clamped her mouth shut, keeping the hurt and humiliation within. It was then that she noticed a dark shape on the road ahead. Driving slowly past, she looked down onto the body of a dead dog. Around its neck was something red which she thought for a moment was a bandana, then in horror, saw it was entrails.

Her empty stomach heaved and she stepped reflexively on the gas, jerking ahead and nearly slamming into a large yellow shape, which leapt at her from a pocket of fog. A yellow panel truck, red tail lights glowing like wild eyes. She slammed on the brakes, instantly starting to hydroplane on the wet black top.

"Jesus!" she yelled, grabbing control of the car and pulling off the road.

The windshield wipers were whacking back and forth on high, but still not doing the job. She felt her heart beat with their rhythm and turned them down, hoping to slow her own. She reached for her purse on the seat beside her and, in it, a small vial of peach-colored pills. Clair took one out and put it to her mouth but stopped when she noticed a huge forsythia bush in full bloom through the rain-streaked window, the first one she had seen in flower this season. The bush nearly dwarfed the weathered gray cottage crouched next to it. It had a porch on either side, one glassed, the other screened, and four windows with forest green shutters on either side of the front entrance. Around the door, the same shade as the shutters, hung a trellis that was draped with last year's vines, and upstairs were two dormer windows on either side of a red chimney. In the yard, hung a sign: *"Tea Leaves,"* and under that, *"Readings."*

Strange. I must've driven past this place hundreds of times. Why haven't I noticed it before?

After a moment's deliberation, she returned the pill to its case, turned off the engine in mid-wipe, and grabbed her slicker from the backseat. When she got out, she could hear the surf, its slow roll and long fizz, a sound she knew well, a sound that simultaneously soothed and urged.

CHAPTER 2

Clair opened a white wooden gate with an arbor overhead and stepped onto a lawn just beginning to green. She walked toward the front door along a serpentine path dotted with tiny purple flowers, not letting herself think about what a foolish thing she was doing.

Seeing a garden reminded Clair of how she had longed all winter to garden—to get in the dirt and dig. To plan and plant. She wanted to smell the rich moist soil, filled with worms as big as her index finger. She wanted the dirt under her fingernails, in her hair, smudged across her cheek. But the regional joke was that summer came on the fourth of July and left on the fifth, and she was beginning to think it was true.

She knocked once on the painted wooden door. When no one came, she tried a little louder and suddenly the door sprung open. To Clair's relief, an ordinary looking woman, not a witch, was standing there wearing a garden glove on one hand with dirt on the fingertips. In her other hand was a pair of scissors.

"I'm not sure why I'm here," Clair blurted to the woman. "I saw your sign."

"Well, of course," the woman with an accent smiled, opening the door wider. At her feet sat a golden-colored cat with long ears. "Come in out of the rain, and perhaps something will occur to you."

She was quite tall and slim, dressed in clothing straight out of L.L.Bean; corduroys, turtleneck jersey, cable-knit sweater, yet something about her was not of Maine. Her speech held no trace of the Downeast accent typical of this area; this woman spoke the King's English.

"I'm Grace," she introduced herself, extending her hand. "And you are?"

"Clair. Clair McKendrick."

"Please come in, Clair. Hang your slicker on the hall tree and I'll put some water on. It's a good day for some hot tea."

Several more cats who looked like smaller versions of the first one bolted in and began to wind themselves around Clair's legs.

"Hope you don't mind cats," Grace laughed. Sahu here has recently had a litter."

"No, I love cats," Clair assured her. "Sahu, did you say?"

"It's Egyptian."

"Hello, Sahu. You have beautiful children."

"So, Clair," Grace was arranging cups on a tray, "did you know your name means *bright, clear, famous?*"

"No. I only know that I was named for my father's dead sister," Clair told her, silently remembering that the other Clair had been handicapped and died young. "May I use your bathroom?"

Grace directed her down the hall to a room with a large circular skylight, an abundance of plants, and an aquarium with one electric-blue fish. Clair stood in front of the mirror and knotted her damp hair into a bun. Photographs on the wall were of Grace at different ages alongside a distinguished-looking man, who aged in unison with her.

When Clair returned to the kitchen, Grace led the way into a small glassed-in room adjacent to it.

"You have some lovely and unusual furniture," Clair said, commenting on several of the pieces she had noticed.

"My husband was a cabinetmaker. He made almost all the furniture in the house," she laughed, "I used to say, 'Stop, darling, we have no more room,' teasingly of course."

One side of the room was lined with a wall of cabinets—*probably made by her husband,* Clair thought. On one of the shelves was a foot-high statue of a seated woman with the head of a lion.

"I've seen that before," Clair observed. "At the British Museum … when I was on my honeymoon."

"Sekhmet, the Egyptian goddess of rage." Grace poured the tea. "She's the one who lets us know when enough is enough."

The opposite view in the room looked out over a garden in the process of being planted. Beyond it was a scene—

picturesque as a postcard—the foggy bay dotted with small fishing boats, seagulls flying above it in a flurry. Where was the dark room partitioned with glass beads? The crystal ball?

"I see you're a gardener too," Clair said, looking out the window and beginning to relax.

"Yes, I am, but hasn't it just been the worst year? So cold. I've almost given up, just focusing on my indoor plants." Her white hair was pulled back off her face and caught behind in a silver clip, but in spite of her hair color, she could have been Clair's age. Or sixty. Maybe even seventy? She looked youthful but, also, there was aging. She seemed light as a bird yet revealed a certain gravitas.

"I've never been to a …"

Fortune teller, Clair was going to say, but thought that might offend Grace, and so stopped.

"I didn't mean …" She stumbled on her words, but Grace ignored her awkwardness.

"Most people get a little nervous coming here the first time. Have you ever been to a psychic?"

"No, never."

"Not to worry," she almost sang. So Clair tried not to.

Settled in the greenhouse, the women sipped from glass teacups filled with an amber liquid. Three of the golden cats joined them on the overstuffed chairs while flames crackled in a corner fireplace.

"Was there something you had in mind, Clair?"

"Well, I …" Looking up at Grace, Clair struggled for the right words. "I guess I want to know if there's a chance to save my marriage."

"Is it a worthwhile marriage you're wanting to save, Clair?"

"Not really … not for a long time."

"Why, then, would you want more of a relationship that's unsatisfying?"

Clair didn't answer, but thought the question was a good one.

"I imagine you're wanting some of the clarity your name promises?" Grace's gaze was penetrating. "You're living alone in your home, and don't want to."

Stunned by the simple truth of the statement, Clair began to cry. A tissue box appeared on her lap, and she pulled out one tissue after another, piling up the damp wads.

"That's better," Grace assured her, when Clair had regained her composure.

Clair looked at her through red eyes, somewhat confused by the remark.

"Tears are a good place to begin," Grace clarified, then reached to touch Clair's hand. "They're honest, and if you follow them, they'll take you someplace." Leaning back in her chair, she added, "Clair, you're not as alone as you think."

"What do you mean?" Clair asked, feeling anxious and wishing she'd taken the Xanax.

"I sense a young man near you, very loving, protective. Was there a tragedy?"

Clair gasped. "My brother Patrick. Oh, my God! You see him?"

"I feel him, but yes, he's most assuredly here … and I sense you have the gift of sight too. Dormant but, yes, you have it."

Clair's eyes darted around the room hoping for a glimpse or a feeling of her beloved brother as she explained. "He drowned when he was eighteen. I was almost twelve. 'Trick,' I called him, was the most special person in my life." She reached for another tissue as more tears began to flow. "When he died, I lost my whole family, and we became like ice floes: alone, drifting, isolated."

"Tell me more, dear," Grace encouraged, as she poured more tea into Clair's cup.

Clair was grateful for the warmth of the tea, the fire burning in the fireplace, and this woman willing to listen. "The smile disappeared from my father's face and never returned. He began drinking, even more than he had. And my mother … she sunk into a deep depression, blaming my father for my brother's death. We were Catholic, but after that, and when President Kennedy was killed a few months later, my father vowed he'd never step foot in a church again. I guess after that we all lost faith." Clair's face contorted. She had worked hard to forget these memories, though painful fragments sharp as broken glass were always just below the surface ready to cut.

"I didn't know a person could hurt so bad. I physically ached for Trick after he was gone. He was the one I had turned to … for everything. Comfort, guidance, courage. When he died, I had no one, and I was never allowed to bring up his name."

July 13, 1963

A young man sits cross-legged on the peeling deck of a fishing trawler, his body rocking back and forth with the gentle rhythmic rolling of the sea. The motion is as soothing as if to a baby safe in the arms of its mother.

Everything's going to be alright.

But that isn't true

The air is laden with the smell of dead fish, fish that were caught and have since died, flopping and gasping, then gutted. The boy sits in the bloody evidence of thousands of dead fish.

How appropriate, he ponders, that he should die here too.

The day is beautiful, sunny and bright: white clouds almost stationary in a blue sky. Patrick listens to the clang of a buoy marking the channel. The sound is familiar and soothing, lulling him into a state of prepared readiness.

The boat belongs to Patrick's father. The two have fished these waters together since Patrick was a small boy barely able to keep his balance on the pitching deck.

But they will fish together no more.

Patrick squints into the bright sun, looking for one last time at the way the sunlight dances off the dark blue ocean. Reflected light sparkles on his red hair—his mother's hair, people say. The sixteen-year-old breathes deeply, inhaling the saltiness. He loves the ocean overwhelmingly, passionately, its fathomless depths, its abundance, its creatures. The life that he and his father ate and sold.

Eating fish or any living creature had sickened the boy—something unacceptable to his father— so his head was held back by his father's powerful rough hands and his throat was crammed full of the tender white flesh, his mother screaming, "Leave him alone!" in the background. Eventually he acquiesced, as he had learned he must.

Patrick picks up the can of gasoline beside his left foot, splashing the contents over himself. The liquid is still cool, not yet warmed by the sun's heat, but all the same, an acrid smell fills his lungs. Without hesitation, he reaches out with his boyish hand—not yet as big as it would become if he were to grow to full manhood—and picks up one of the

The fog had lifted some, allowing more sunlight to peek through the clouds. The kittens were "doing their yoga," as Grace called their stretching, with Sahu watching her young brood from an oversized pillow.

"It's painful to lose someone we love," Grace said, leaning forward in her chair to get closer to Clair. "Especially someone so young, who has their whole life in front of them. And Patrick sounds like such a sensitive young man. What a tragic loss … and, oh, Clair, that you had no support during that time, child that you were, is just unbearable." She laid her hand on Clair's. "I hope that you've been able to seek help since then."

"Not nearly enough," Clair confided with a wan smile. "He had wanted to be an architect, Trick … so, for years I thought I should be that for him."

"We sign on for something when we say yes to life, and we can't know how it'll play out. We just have to trust our soul's plan for us. Trick's life was brief. He didn't get to grow into the person he saw himself to be. But you, Clair, though you may be capable of it, your destiny is not to be an architect."

Grace rose and added another log to the fire, while Clair looked around the room, noticing a collection of agates in the windowsill—beautiful patterns, glowing in the light. And she heard wind chimes, tinkling from somewhere else in the house. She felt tension draining from her body and asked, "What kind of tea is this? I feel more relaxed than I've ever been, except on medication."

"It's my own special blend," Grace smiled. "I grow the herbs myself… if you'd like, I'll give you some to take home with you."

Clair recounted more of her story as the afternoon idled on: meeting Blake in college; her pregnancy and rushed marriage; their early years, three lost babies, her crippling depression. Then she told Grace about the phone call that morning. While she spoke, she fingered a gold band on her left hand, and another, encircled with diamonds.

Grace listened with attention, compassion evident on her face. Then, when Clair paused, Grace spoke with simple certitude. "You're an artist, Clair. Images are swirling around and through you, longing for release. The way out of your depression is through contact with your true nature, your art. Do you paint?"

Clair's eyes were wide when she looked at Grace.

"I'd almost forgotten, it was so long ago, but, yes, I did paint when I was a child. My brother told me I had a gift and he encouraged me." She reached for another tissue. "I haven't painted since he … well, for a long time."

"A drowning, you say?"

"Yes. He drowned."

"Clair, dear child, I think we both know it was more than that."

Clair looked into Grace's cornflower blue eyes, kind eyes. "You're right," Clair admitted. "It was more than a drowning. The truth is just so hard to accept."

"But accept you must, before you can heal."

Grace reached for Clair's cup, swirling the tea leaves left in the bottom. Next, she took Clair's hands and held them under her own around the cup, then closed her eyes. "I'm never sure exactly what might happen, but if you just relax, Clair, it will help the energies to come forward if they are so inclined."

Who were they?

Grace's eyelids fluttered, eyes rolling upwards as she inhaled deeply several times. "I see six golden lionesses walking together on a desert pavement."

What? Clair thought, confused. *What about my husband?*

"It is hot." Grace's face flushed, as if she might be feeling an extreme heat herself. "They pant, swishing flies with long tails, but find relief in the shade of a tree, the trunk coiled like that of a snake. They are a pack of sisters who hunt together, providing protection as they raise their young."

Clair wanted to interrupt, to ask what this had to do with anything, but the room suddenly seemed to supernaturally chill and goosebumps ran up her spine from her sacrum to the crown of her head. She looked toward the fireplace to see if the fire had gone out, but saw it was burning brightly. Then, Grace's body began to vibrate.

Perhaps she too was cold? Clair felt a knot under her ribs, a fat and gnarly boson's knot like her father might have tied. Her impulse was to leave, to get up and run, but Grace was squeezing her hands so tightly, she couldn't break away. But was it Grace? The skin of Grace's face had darkened visibly and, when she spoke, it was in a much deeper voice.

"I've been watching you." The cadence was more formal, measured, with no trace of Grace's lilting English accent. Clair's heart pounded, feeling a slight current of electricity coming through Grace's hands.

"Who are you?" Clair asked, terrified.

"I am the Source," the voice stated, speaking with complete authority. "I am the Awakener. The one who knows the way." Clair stared in disbelief as the voice continued in a litany of titles. "I am the Roamer of Deserts, the Ruler of Lions," then "it" opened its eyes, not blue like Grace's, but a startling liquid emerald shining in the dark, speaking directly to Clair.

"Do you know me, Daughter? I've come for you." Then it closed the green eyes, and when they reopened, Grace was back, her skin color returned to normal, her eyes once more the blue they had been before she closed them.

Grace released Clair's hands, leaning back in her chair, and smiled knowingly, her melodic voice returned. "You're going to a strange land, Clair, and there you'll find your pride."

"But what about my husband?" Clair asked weakly, already doubting what she had just witnessed.

"Tell him goodbye," Grace nodded. "And thank him."

CHAPTER 3

In the car, Clair rested her face in trembling hands for a moment, then fumbling the key into the ignition, pulled away, spraying sand on the white picket fence and delicate grape hyacinths just beginning to peek through the cold ground. The windshield wipers whacked with the same urgency as they had hours before, but the rain had stopped. She turned them off. A multitude of images and fragments of the afternoon's conversations all vied for her attention as she negotiated the narrow road. *You see, don't you? I'm watching you.* At the moment she didn't want to dwell on any of them. Home. She needed to get home where she could think about what had just happened. Lions, deserts, craziness! What did any of that mean?

Tea leaves! How absurd! Blake would laugh at her foolishness.

⚡

The couple had decided to buy a second home far from the city, to enjoy now and retire to later. His preference was Cape Cod, where his friends were—the men with whom he played golf and tennis and sailed. Clair harbored the fantasy that it would be where she and Blake would welcome their children and, later, grandchildren, for holidays. The task of looking was relegated to her—a terse announcement from Blake that thrilled her.

"You find it. I don't have time." And though she had not intended to look at homes in Maine, when the broker heard what she was looking for, he suggested a drive to the "Bold" Coast, as it was called.

Two massive fieldstone columns came into view, marking the driveway to her home and she slowed her approach, noticing ominous clouds still lingering in the darkening sky. A feeling of relief overcame her as she passed under the old gate with the familiar metal scroll of letters: *Harbor House.*

The property reminded Clair of the Daphne du Maurier novel, *Rebecca*, a romantic gothic, read when she was a teenager. The sound of the gravel under the tires was oddly pleasing, as well as the graceful trees and ancient rhododendrons hovering like ghosts in the shadows. The sea was visible from everywhere.

The original property had included a small chapel with a stained-glass window depicting a ship in a stormy sea. Adjacent to it, the remains of a family cemetery were surrounded by a ring of towering beech trees. In the graveyard were two large headstones: husband and wife. *He* had died at sea, *She* shared a birthday with Clair. Five small brass plates marked the graves of their children—the same number as she and Blake would have had, if all their babies had lived. The broker was a good salesman—showing Clair its tragic history was just the right enticement; she had learned to be at home in tragedy.

Harbor House next belonged, the broker had told her, to an industrialist back in the 1920s. The New York gentleman had bought up hundreds of acres of oceanfront, but the property went into probate while his heirs squabbled over money. Finally, it was sold, piece by piece. The piéce de résistance, up for sale that very day, was five acres, including the remains of the main house, badly damaged in a fire years before.

"Don't expect me to spend much time in the boondocks, Clair," her husband warned when she showed him the property. "This is just too far away from my life in Boston. And my friends on the Cape."

And maybe that's when their lives had really begun to separate. He had been gone from her for a long time, and she had accepted that. But when she insisted on that house—a forceful side of her that didn't often emerge—perhaps then she left him too. And so the place, *Harbor House*, began to change her.

During the year of making sometimes daily drives to the site, she separated from their life, from the people she found tiresome, from her gracious "helpmate-and- hostess" veneer, from dates of round robin tennis and endless gossipy lunches. Instead, finding a boldness in herself, she came to Maine—the "bold" coast, the boondocks—through all kinds of weather, learning the seasons and the light, dreaming of what might grow out of the remains and rubble. When her vision for the place was clear, she hired an architect to draw plans from the sketches in her mind's eye. In so doing, she felt as though she was creating something alongside her brother.

She imagined that living in the house would be the ultimate experience—a grand, sprawling estate on various levels, a million dollars' worth of stone, glass, and rough timber. She soon discovered that it was the planning and building that had been the most satisfying. She had enjoyed being with the men who built it, men who worked with their hands. To none of them was she "Mrs. McKendrick. " Instead, she was: "Hey, Clair, toss up that hammer."

She wore work clothes, not worrying about the condition of her hair and nails. To her surprise, she developed muscles in her arms. But instead of creating a home, a haven, as she had hoped, she'd run to the edge of a cliff and, with her dreams as dead as her three lost children, felt her fingernails grasping the rocky embankment, clinging to a life that was once hers.

⚡

On the long winding drive, she passed the swimming pool where nobody swam, the tennis court where nobody played. Yawning open with her car's approach, the garage door revealed row upon row of unopened banker's boxes, a toothy grin along the back wall.

The sea was the salient feature of the house, visible from most of the ten rooms. A view intruded everywhere. Clair had kept color to a minimum to let the ocean, with all its moods and manners, decide that for the house. On some days it was green, on others brilliantly blue, but often it was fog-bound, gray or dark. Clair couldn't decide whether the ocean was affecting her or was it her affecting the ocean? The exception to the neutral colors was a large painting taking up one whole wall of the living room, all but vibrating with brilliant cadmiums, deep dark cobalt blues and black.

"What in the hell is that, Clair?" was Blake's reaction when he saw it. His taste in art tended toward landscapes and scenes of the ocean, the etchings of Winslow Homer perhaps. Clair had a broader interest and liked to purchase from the artists themselves. And because she had the wherewithal and interest, their home was filled with a collection of handmade items: paper boxes with linen hinges, unusual pieces of pottery and glass, handmade furniture, paintings. It gave him the high ground, freely able to criticize her purchases when he disapproved of her taste.

"I bought it in a gallery in SoHo," she explained. "It spoke to me."

Clair walked through the house, comforted by its perfect order. She needed everything in its place at home, otherwise she felt agitated, so she kept it that way herself. Always tidying, cleaning, vacuuming. The housekeeper had quit months ago for lack of anything to do.

Today it smelled strongly of narcissus blooming in a dozen clay pots. And though it had been months, she still missed being greeted by Ragdoll—the straggly kitten that had wandered into her life after she'd miscarried the year before Cassidy was born. She had been alone that day, hemorrhaging and nearly bleeding to death on the tile floor of the bathroom. After calling the paramedics, she had sat in the darkening puddle, rocking the lifeless body in her arms until they arrived seconds later.

Blake had been out of the country.

The highest point in the house was the master bathroom. Clair walked in that direction, ignoring the blinking light of the phone and the unopened stack of mail on the kitchen counter. She knew she should eat, but had no appetite, even though she'd had nothing all day. Her greater need was for warmth and comfort.

She turned on the tub faucet, dropping in several scoops of sandalwood bath salts, letting the steam envelop her in a warm mist. Rock-encased, surrounded on three sides by glass, the tub looked out over a walled garden with a private beach and further to the open ocean. Turning off the lights and dropping her clothes in the hamper, she lit several candles on the rim of the tub. Catching sight of herself flickering in the full-length mirror, she surveyed her body—some would say it was too thin with small breasts, the incision from Cassidy's Caesarian birth a mocking smile on her lower abdomen.

Cassidy, the precious daughter who'd lived. Born on Valentine's Day—a gift of pure love.

"'No!" was her first word at ten months. "Do it myself!" was her first defiant sentence before she was two.

Cassidy was born with a spirit of independence and rebellion foreign to her mother. Her infant fierceness was legendary in the McKendrick household, Blake began calling her Butch Cassidy. Her attitude may have been like a bulldog, but she looked like an angel—a heart-shaped face, as if verifying the date of her birth; dark ringlets; eyes, pale green to golden depending on the light; rosy cupid's-bow lips.

But she wasn't what she looked like nor was she the daughter her mother had expected, so by the time she was six, she dressed like Madonna and fought her mother, who tried to put her in gathered smocks and Mary Jane's. At thirteen, when Cassidy started menstruating, she saved her allowance and got a tattoo of a bleeding pomegranate on her abdomen. When Cass was fifteen, Clair found a bag of marijuana in her room.

When confronted, Cass declared, "I'll smoke grass if I want. You can't stop me!"

Clair was often embarrassed by her daughter's appearance— hair, often various colors, and once even shaved clean off for some protest. Her pants were baggy, dropped low, inches below short T-shirts. And every time she returned home, it seemed that some new body part was pierced or tattooed.

"Why don't we go shopping together," Clair would ask, "and let me buy you some things?" But Cass disliked buying new clothes, not wanting to support the fashion industry whom she considered demeaning to women.

However, she'd made good grades in school. All her teachers agreed that she was a brilliant young woman, although "disruptive" to the other students—a rabble-rouser. A sympathetic teacher once took Clair aside to say, "Cassidy is naturally rebellious but a strong leader. People like her and follow her. She'll be just fine when she realizes that she doesn't have to live at such an extreme edge. Give her room to express herself, Mrs. McKendrick. The world needs people like Cass."

Cassidy was appalled by the conservative politics of her father and by the attitudes in her private school—the push toward a business career that overlapped with contacts for later, the old boys' club, which had begun building in those early years.

"It's wealth and power in the hands of the few. It's criminal! All humanity is related. We are all brothers and sisters!" she would declare with a stomp of her boot, bought in some Army/Navy store.

Cassidy, a warrior in a world unfamiliar to Clair, was as appalled by her mother as Clair was by her daughter.

"How could you have been alive in the sixties," Cass challenged, "and not have supported an end to the Vietnam War? I would have been at every protest march in the country."

Clair's tone was defensive. "I was on a scholarship, Cass, and unlike you I had a job. Plus, I had to keep my grades up or lose my scholarship and my chance for an education. You're overlooking what was happening in my life at the time."

"And now you live in this exclusive, isolated world," Cass shot back, not listening, "and let your husband diminish your whole being."

The remark, and the venomous tone in the way it was delivered, felt like a slap. Cassidy was witness to the truth of their relationship. In fact, both children were, at least until they were packed off to prep schools. And Cass was right—Clair did live in a world of comforts, with few real worries, and she had sacrificed everything, including her own identity to remain there. Until now.

I want a divorce.

What would Cassidy and her brother Carl think about this?

And as for Carl, his happy news about becoming a father would be overshadowed by his dad's announcement of his own child's arrival.

Carl, her first child. Her son. An "accident." Not the best reason to come into the world, and maybe he knew that.

1973

Clair and Blake have been advised to keep the pregnancy secret even after they marry, at least for a couple of months, which bothers Clair who wants to share the joy she feels. They are living in the small guesthouse on Blake's family's estate. He leaves for work early and comes home late, leaving Clair with nothing to do and only her mother-in-

law to talk to, which means being talked down to. Lucky and Jim have already married and moved to a Naval base in California, and though she and Lucky talk occasionally, their lives have taken them in different directions, and they just have less in common.

"Abruptio placenta" is the separation of the placenta from the uterine wall. When it's completely torn away, the mother can suffer a life-threatening hemorrhage, and the fetus is also in jeopardy, denied an essential supply of oxygen and nutrients. Clair's abruption is a foreshadowing of the many blood sacrifices that Clair will make for motherhood. Blake's mother rides in the ambulance with Clair; Blake arrives after the birth.

But when her baby is placed in her arms for the first time, wrapped snugly and safely in a little blue blanket, his tiny face bruised from the length and trauma of his birth, Clair's heart fills with love. She names him Patrick Carlisle McKendrick, despite pressure from Blake's family who have another name chosen in honor of some esteemed ancestor.

But as much as she loves her new son, Clair doesn't trust herself as a mother. She doesn't know how to soothe his heartbreaking cries and feels helpless and unprepared. But the other Mrs. McKendrick, Blake's mother, is more than willing and ready to take over the mother duties while Clair's postpartum anxieties are dulled by a pharmacy of various drugs.

Lowering herself into the deep tub, Clair felt the tension of the day—Blake's news, Grace's strange predictions—began to ease as she leaned against a plastic pillow Carl had given her as a Christmas present last year. She smiled. He knew his mother.

Carl was quiet as a child, not a lot of friends, a voracious reader. In that way, he reminded Clair of her own brother. Oh, how Trick would have loved being an uncle to her son! Clair did enjoy reading to Carl, snuggling with him on his bed at bedtime. It was the one sweet way that mother and son could relate. There were so many times she was sick, either from being pregnant or recovering from a miscarriage, making the times she could spend with him constantly interrupted. He continued through the years that followed to turn to his grandparents for the stability he wasn't getting from his parents.

At school he excelled in sports but also in writing. One time, Clair came across some creative essays he had written in college as an English major before going into law. The stories were wonderfully creative and she thought perhaps he might have a career in journalism. But he followed his male lineage and entered the law firm his great great-grandfather had founded. She was proud of him—he had become a man, taken charge of his life, and now he was going to be a father.

She wondered how Carl would take his father's news. Once again, Blake would have another interest instead of him. Even Carl's child would not measure up because Blake would have his own.

In the glow of the candlelight, she gazed down the length of her body through the water's distortion and her own. Her body. Blake must be repulsed by it. This new young woman must have a beautiful body, swelling with his child. She imagined Blake's hands on this woman's full breasts and soft curves. Images of the two of them together swirled in her mind, taunting her. How long had it been since he'd touched her with any tenderness? Since he'd desired her?

Finally, to break her obsession, she grabbed the handle of the scrub brush and slammed it hard on the surface of the water. Splat! Drops ran down the window and snuffed out one of the candles. Looking in that direction, Clair saw something reflected in the glass—a face? It didn't make sense. She was three stories high. But, still, she thought there was something.

Leaping from the tub in a gush of water, instinctively crossing her arms over her breasts, she ran through her bedroom and into the dark hallway.

I've been watching you.

Water dripped from her body, and she shivered, but not just from the cold.

I've come for you.

Panicked, Clair ran naked, wildly turning her head left to right, all the way to the other end of the house, but when her wet feet hit the kitchen tile, they slid out from under her and, in slow motion, she glimpsed her feet, ankles, and knees rise in the air. Twisting, like a cat, she turned instinctively to catch herself and came down hard on her left side, taking the full impact of her body weight on her wrist. The shock reverberated up her arm, wrist, elbow, shoulder.

"Unhhhhhh!" she screamed with pain. "Ow! Owwww! Owwwww!"

Lying still on the floor, trying to catch her breath, she was afraid to move, feeling cracked and broken and watching her left wrist through tears as it began to swell. Aside from the pain, what she felt was humiliation.

"You idiot!" she shouted at herself. "Running from a phantom!" *There was no one at the window. You got spooked from a splash of water!* "You're such a fool!"

Right arm in support, she inched her way up the wall and stepped carefully through the kitchen, throwing a dish towel on the floor to dry her feet, testing wobbly legs. Passing the window, she caught sight of herself. *Pitiful.* She was pitiful and deserved to be abandoned by her husband and hated by her children.

Returning to the bathroom, she removed a towel from the hook and tried to dry her body off using only her good arm. Then turning the flood lights on outside, she looked into the illuminated darkness. There was no one. Of course. The drop was twenty feet.

"Clair, you've got to get a grip," she said out loud. *No, it's okay. I'm okay, it's just the day. Too much has happened. I'll take something and go to sleep.*

Her wrist continued swelling, turning an angry dark color, and she shook two Percocet's from the amber vial by her bedside. Using the one good hand, she pulled on flannel pajamas, wool socks, and a cashmere robe. With the pills in her pocket, she walked back to the kitchen. Across the room, she noticed the blinking phone showing two messages, but before checking, she added water to the kettle and turned on the blue flame.

"Clair, pick up!" Blake's was the first call. Then a hesitation. She could hear him breathing. Hard. Grace had said, *Thank him? Never!*

"Okay. Have it your way," he said, in his usual beleaguered tone. "I'm trying to be reasonable, but maybe it would be in your best interest to get a lawyer."

A second call followed the first. "Clair, this is Grace." Clair froze. "I'm calling to let you know that you left your purse here, dear."

She hadn't even noticed. *I must have written Grace a check and put my bag on the counter.*

"Fortunately, you're listed in information. So, your purse is here and you can call me about coming by. I hope you're alright, Clair. I know we opened up quite a lot for you this afternoon. Here's my number: (207) 214-1979."

Returning the phone to its receiver, she glimpsed an envelope with red cowboy hat stickers on it in the pile of mail, and shuffled it out of the rest, at first thinking it must be for Cassidy. But in the left corner was the name "Lucky Miller" and a New Mexico address. Her old friend!

Waiting for the tea to steep, she struggled to open the envelope, holding one end down with her elbow, then shook out a white card along with a pile of confetti, consisting of tiny cowboy hats, boots, and pistols.

The card read: "Let's Party!"

Stone Head Beach
July 13, 1963

The day is sunny and bright, white clouds stationary in a deep blue sky. Clair Cassidy and Lucky Miller have spent the afternoon together at the beach, something they do nearly every summer weekend so Lucky can see a boy who she has a crush on. His name is Jim. He's sixteen years old and a junior lifeguard. Jim goes to Exeter and when he graduates, he says he's going to Harvard.

Lucky is beautiful, especially in the summer when her skin turns golden bronze and her waist-length blonde hair is a thick lion's mane down her back. This year she's grown taller, much taller than Clair, who thinks her friend looks like a Greek goddess. Lucky, two years older, has breasts now, and curves in her body that magically appeared this year, causing Clair to feel childlike and envious, eager for a sexy swelling of her own thin body. In previous years, they've fit together, mirroring one another, but Clair can feel their lives separating and the loss makes her sad.

Lucky turned thirteen the week before—had a big party—and since then always applies lipstick called "Orangeade"—especially if she thinks she might encounter Jim. Her two-piece bathing suit is orange too, orange with white stripes, which Lucky bought because she wanted to match Jim's lifeguard suit.

Clair's father insists, "Absolutely NO to lipstick."

She wishes she was older. She wishes her hair was golden blonde. She wishes she had breasts and would tan to a bronze glow in the sun. Instead, her hair is wavy, sometimes uncontrollably, and the same dark brown as her father's, though now she's noticed strands of white mixed in along his hairline. Her skin is fair, like her mother's, causing her to blister and peel if she's exposed to the sun for more than an hour, so she wears some of her brother's hand-me-down T-shirts over her bathing suit.

Clair does have pretty blue eyes though, everyone tells her so. "Oh, your eyes, Clair! They're beautiful." She has looked at them in the bathroom mirror when she knows she won't be barged in on and has seen that her eyes are indeed a sky blue, but a white ring encircles the black center, which at certain angles makes them opaque.

While Lucky and Jim talk, Clair sits under the beach umbrella drawing in her sketchbook. She always carries a pad and pencil, humming as she draws. In her sketchbook are images of boats and birds, rocks and feathers, waves, people, anything that grabs her attention. She draws her brother Trick over and over, awake and sleeping, finding his face so interesting, its angles and edges, the depth of his eyes. And she draws Lucky, when Lucky will hold still long enough. The one Lucky did hold still for—because Lucky's the one who insisted on the drawing—was a nude.

"Artists always sketch nude people, Clair. If you're going to be an artist, you simply must. And I will be your model."

Clair doesn't keep the nude drawings in her book, afraid that her parents might find them. Instead, she tears them out and gives them to Lucky, who says she will put them in a locked box in her closet. Clair simply knows that Lucky will give the drawing to Jim.

Sitting crosslegged, Clair sketches a flower that has just blown onto the towel. It's a simple daisy, a favorite of Trick's, and she wonders where it came from. Suddenly, she stops drawing and looks up at the open sea. A split second later she sees a bright explosion.

"Whoa!" exclaims Jim, as the three teenagers jump to their feet.

Clair knows most of the boats in the harbor, her father being a fisherman with a boat of his own—but with all the flames and smoke out on the horizon, she can't see the boat clearly enough to recognize its owner. Abruptly, she feels a sickening flash in her mind and takes off at a run, yelling to Lucky, "Take my things—I'll get them later!"

When she arrives home, Clair sees a police cruiser and two other cars in front of her house. She notices the front door is ajar so she climbs the steps instead of going around to the back like she usually does. She hears the sound of crying as she climbs—her mother's weeping, but increasingly louder in volume. Sobbing, moaning and, below the level of her mother's whimpering and wailing, a chorus of hushed voices she doesn't recognize.

She pushes the front door all the way open and stands snug against the adjacent wall, as if pinned. Her eyes dart back and forth in the room—her father's empty gaze, her mother's head thrown back, mouth agape. A neighbor, still in an apron. Father McNamara, their parish priest, somber. Clair looks down at her feet, seeing she still has sand on her shoes, but doesn't remove them, although she knows her mother will be mad that she's tracked in sand. She can hear her mother now: "Get those shoes off before you come into this house!" But Clair remains riveted to her spot, face draining of color, and she wonders if her mother will ever notice any sandy floors again.

Father Mac reaches out and tries to contain Ma in his arms as she rants, raves, and thrashes about, yelling, "It's your fault! If you had just let him be! If you had only let him be himself! My son! My son!" She seems to be shouting at her husband, who sits stoically as if he suddenly turned to stone.

With every ounce of her being, Clair wishes she could fade into the faded wallpaper. Silently, she pleads, praying, "Please God, let me be somewhere else."

In fragments of conversations, Clair hears the name of her father's boat, the Emerald Isle, and the words "fire" and "drowning." She watches her mother break loose from the arms of the priest and lurch to the floor, crawling to the feet of Clair's father, who sits not flinching, even when her mother pounds the floor in front of him and then begins pulling at her own hair.

"It's all your fault!" She screams over and over again.

Father Mac finally notices Clair, sees her terrified look and takes her aside.

"Oh, Wee One!" he says sympathetically, in an Irish brogue that sounds like her grandmother's. Now he puts his arms around her as he had her mother and, with much sadness in his voice, says, "Our Patrick has had a terrible accident."

But Clair already knows.

CHAPTER 4

With teacup in one hand and letter tucked under her arm, Clair retreated to her bedroom to see what Lucky was partying about now. Logs were laid in the fireplace and she struck a long match along the bricks, lighting the newspapers and "fat wood" underneath the logs. Flames jumped into being when the fat wood caught, casting a golden glow in the room. Sitting in the chair nestled close to the fire, she read:

> Howdy, Cowgirls!
> Alex, Clair, Jesse, and VJ!

The letter was a computer print-out decorated with red cowboy-boot stickers. And Clair noticed that Lucky had alphabetized the list, so as not to play favorites. That was Lucky.

> My foot's in the stirrup.
> My pony won't stand.
> Goodbye, old buddy,
> I'm leaving Cheyenne!

Lucky always had a way of expressing herself that made Clair laugh, and she smiled in spite of her pain. She took a sip of the tea along with the two pain pills from her pocket. Swallowing, she read:

> I've been trying my damnedest to get out of
> this, but there seems to be no suitable
> alternative, sooo, I've decided to turn fifty
> after all! And I need myself some witnesses
> for this here grand event. I've chosen a place
> that's special to me—I'm not telling where—

but I want you all to come and be my guests
for three days of merriment in July while I
crumble into old age before your very eyes! I
promise I'll put on a good show, better even
than my performance of karaoke at the
Brush Creek Saloon last month—and THAT
was something to behold!

The destination is casual so dress
accordingly. And the gift I want from each
of you is just to be there. Oh, and one other
thing: Bring something to bury, something
symbolic of what you're ready to let go of,
and what you want to plant in its place.
And anything else you'd like to share.

Instantly, Clair thought that what she'd like to do is bury a hatchet in her husband's head, let go of him, and plant him head down. She imagined herself saying, "Also, I'd like to share that my husband's girlfriend is pregnant." *What would Lucky's friends think of that?*

Let me know if you can come (you'd better,
Clair Cassidy!), so I can make final
arrangements (and you're welcome to come
and stay in Santa Fe with me and Max,
either before or after the event. We would love
it!).

Lucky had invited her out west many times, but Clair had never gone. She had only met Max one time, back when Lucky and Max first got together, eventually becoming Lucky's life partner after Jim was killed.

"I'm just not a big traveler, Lucky," Clair had told her each time, which was true, but also it was excuse-making, and they both knew it.

The invitation was signed "Hasta luego!" Whatever that means, Clair thought—and there was a red lariat sticker next to Lucky's name.

Lucky is celebrating and my life is falling apart. I can't go, Clair decided. When she was growing up, Clair's mother wouldn't allow parties; too much confusion, she said. But Clair remembered Lucky's parties, legendary, as far as teenage girl's parties go. And she remembered the kindness of Lucky's mother, who would always remember Clair's birthday on September 13th and have a cake for her. Clair would invariably throw it up though—as if the gesture, like the cake, was more sweetness than she could bear.

Clair fingered one of the red cowboy hats, rubbing the silky texture with her index finger while she sipped her tea, thinking about how parties and new people made her feel uncomfortable.

I'm sure they're all ranch people, she told herself, like Lucky and Max, though Max was also an artist, a painter. I doubt I'd have anything in common with Lucky's friends. I'd like to be there for Lucky but, with what's going on with Blake ... I just can't tell Lucky that I've failed at the only thing I've ever done with my life—getting married and having children.

Seized by a sudden ray of hope, she added the thought, *Cassidy's graduation is in June, then she's off to Europe. July is just a big blank. I could go.*

You're going to a strange land, she heard in her head and remembered the disembodied voice.

New Mexico did seem strange, but as far as she knew, it didn't have lions.

Or did it?

With her good arm, she managed to get another log on the fire, then crossed the length of the room to the bed, feet cushioned by the wool pile carpeting. The bed was a white-washed pine with song birds and ribbons carved into the headboard—*what was she thinking when she chose that! Must have been her inner Cinderella.* She pulled back the down comforter to reveal white Egyptian cotton sheets and stacked the antique English-lace shams stuffed with pillows neatly on the empty side of the bed.

<h1 style="text-align:center">1963</h1>

Holding her throbbing wrist in the air, Clair pulled down the pajama bottoms to view the bruise spreading across her left hip like a dark purple stain. On impulse, she walked to the liquor cabinet in the library and poured a finger's breadth of Irish whiskey into a glass.

"May you be settled in heaven before the devil knows you're gone," she said out loud—her father's favorite toast.

Taking a deep swallow, she returned to the bed, easing in carefully and laying on her right side. A pot of fragrant paperwhites in full bloom rested on the nightstand atop a stack of unread books. Surrounding the books were framed photographs—pictures of a happy family, carefully selected. One was of her and Blake in Italy with the children. Clair had just found out about one of Blake's affairs and was wearing her best fake smile so as not to ruin the family vacation. Another, in a sterling silver frame, was of their wedding.

When she and Blake met at a college mixer, besides falling head over heels, she saw him as a way to escape her mother— he was her knight in shining armor, the prince who could rescue her from a life she wanted to forget. He would be the one to give her the fairytale existence she imagined.

She hadn't planned the pregnancy six months later, but when it happened, she believed it was her destiny to have this man and their child. Blake's mother Margaret completely took over when they told her the news of Clair's condition. Surprising Clair, Margaret was quite reserved about it, saying, "Well, you two seemed to be in a bit of a hurry."

She'd only spoken to Clair's mother once, saying "tisk-tisk," what naughty children we have, and how many people do you want to invite to the wedding? "Of course, we have quite a list what with Malcom's business acquaintances, so we'll pay for the whole thing."

Margaret made a few phone calls and within days had the Ritz Carlton secured. She took Clair to lunch, then to Bonwit Teller for her wedding dress and to Bradford Bachrach for her formal wedding pictures. At the photographers, Clair threw up her Welsh Rarebit, barely missing her Belgian lace gown. But vowed to herself and God that she would make him a good wife, give him well-behaved children, and healthy breakfasts and dinners by candlelight after the children were fed.

London Honeymoon
1972

Clair and Blake are at the British Museum, Clair's first time. She marvels at seeing the Great Court and its breathtaking glass and steel roof, thinking how much Trick would have loved the architecture.
She loses Blake in the Egyptian Collection and, with panic setting in, pushes her way through hordes of tourists,

head swinging left and right, trying to glimpse his tall frame in a navy blue blazer. When she comes to a flight of stairs, thinking that he might have moved on, she begins to climb, her breathing more labored with every step, heart pounding. Alarmed for the baby she is carrying in her body, she stops to rest for a moment. Despite all the crowds, the stairwell is unusually empty. While leaning against the wall, she hears a low volume hum coming from the landing above. Resuming her ascent, she sees the head of a stone lion crowned by a solar disk. Once in front of the stone statue, she sees that it is that of a woman. There are four life-sized statues of them in all. Regal. Powerful. Alone in the room and transfixed, she has an irresistible compulsion to touch one. She reaches out her hand slowly towards the curled fingers of one of the statues. As her fingers come into contact with the stone, she feels the child in her belly quicken for the first time.

Leaning back on the stack of pillows on the bed, taking slow deliberate breaths, the pain in Clair's wrist lessened and with the ache subsiding, images of that afternoon with Grace again rose from her subconscious. "I sense you have the gift of sight too."

Hadn't her grandmother said something like that to her as well? Getting up, she shuffled across the bedroom to her closet. She and Blake had separate closets with hers the size of a small bedroom—odd for a woman who was hardly ever out of sweatpants. Most of her clothing was from a previous life.

Grace had said, *"Thank him." Could it be that she could find a life without him, she wondered*—without realizing that she had already been doing just that.

The closet was well-organized so Clair found the box she wanted without any trouble, tucked behind a rack of shoes. The box was marked "Mother," in black magic marker—and contained the few items that Clair had collected of Faith's life.

The box was awkward to carry with one arm so she slid it across the floor by pushing it with one foot. At the bed, she grabbed one of the side handles and, one-handed, hoisted it up, making room for herself to sit alongside.

Peering into the box, she felt a malaise come over her, remembering the day she packed it, two years ago now, after the sudden death of her mother at seventy-seven. It was painful to see what was left of a life after being reduced to a banker's box. Inside were the few things precious to Faith—a scarf her mother had knitted that Faith took to wearing as she aged and was always chilled; a flowered tin box, with some things inside that Clair hadn't bothered to look at then; a dozen or so photographs.

Clair noticed that one of the photographs was of Faith and Dan when they were young before they'd even left Ireland, a black and white, that someone had hand colored. Dan was wearing a woolen vest and cap. Faith's hair—her best feature—was full and fiery red. Clair didn't know if the person who painted the photograph had used some artistic license or if Faith's hair had truly been that bright. Clair didn't remember it that way. To her, her mother's hair was dull and streaked with silver. The young couple in the picture were smiling, her mother, shyly, Dan's arm was protectively wrapped around her waist. You could almost hear him saying, *"This here Lass is mine!"*

In another picture, Faith was seated with Clair in her lap, Clair then about two years old. The "Wee One," was staring straight at the camera and wore an expression that was more pensive than a two year old should have. Several pictures were of Patrick, of course, her mother's favorite child. *You can tell when you are not,* she couldn't help thinking.

Clair opened the cloisonné tin box, removing a monogrammed linen handkerchief that held a small stone in the shape of a cross on a thin gold chain.

Ireland, 1961

News arrives that her grandmother in Ireland is close to dying. Clair has never met her, though gifts have arrived throughout the years: a hand-knitted sweater in a soft blue color, a four-leaf clover pressed into a slim volume of poetry by William Butler Yeats, marking the poem, "A Prayer for My Daughter." In pencil, her "Mamo," as Clair calls her, has written, "For my dear granddaughter, Clair." Sometimes, as Clair holds the book, she thinks about this woman who lives so far away.

With news of Mamo's imminent dying, a trip is planned by Faith to take Patrick and Clair to Donegal County, to meet and say goodbye to a woman Faith has rarely spoken of with much affection. "We just never did see eye to eye," Faith explains to Clair. "But she is my mother and deserves final respects from her only daughter."

Mostly when the adult Clair thinks back on that time, she remembers the excitement of her first airplane ride. It was two years before Patrick died, the year before everything changed, so the world still held possibilities.

Clair also recalls walking with her grandmother. "Walk with her slowly," her mother advised. "She's old and frail and will break something if she falls."

Clair obeys, holding tightly to Mamo's hand as they tread through the lush green of the countryside, passing a small stone house in a field with a wall surrounding it and a flock of sheep on the road. Her grandmother soon steers them off the road onto a trail through the forest with damp weeds and a heavy cover of trees blocking the sunlight.

"Off the roads, Child, you get to see the fairies," she smiles at Clair, crinkling bright blue eyes like Clair's own. Mamo speaks of fairies and forest creatures as if they are real. "I can see 'em, and so can you if you look careful-like."

When Clair looks at her grandmother and sees the twinkle in her eye, Mamo doesn't seem old or frail. Her voice almost sings with joy as she coos, "Ahhh, Wee One!"

"People think I'm dying, Girl, but it don't trouble me none 'cause I know I'm not. Oh, I'll let go this old body, leave it behind," she laughs gleefully. "God knows I've worn it out some. But, Wee One, never live in fear of that silly notion that we die and are gone forever ... life goes on and on. Thar' plenty more adventures a-waitin'!"

Clair is mesmerized by her—and the joy with which Mamo views her world—and she wonders what happened between her mother and Mamo.

"You can see, can't ya, Child? I know ya can. It's a lineage, having the sight. My own grandmother had it too ... skips a generation, it does ... that's why your dear mother won't understand. Always thought I was daft! But that's okay—you'll see." She hesitates, then goes on with eyebrows knitted together. "Girl, ya may see terrible things ahead, but don't ya ever be afraid ... everything in the whole universe has a purpose. We just don't always understand it at the time."

Until now. All these years later.

At the time, Clair thought, she wouldn't have questioned her mother. There would have been no point. She remembered her old feelings of uselessness. Her mother had the final word, even in matters of her own life.

"I know what's best for you, Clair, I'm your mother," she would say, and that was that. But now, in this moment, as Clair's fingers closed over the stone cross in her palm, she recalled how she wanted to snatch it from her mother, how she wanted to shout, "No, it's mine! Mamo gave it to me!"

She wished she could have been brave enough to do that.

Didn't her grandmother say that she's stronger than she herself knows? And didn't Grace say exactly the same thing this afternoon?

A month later word came that Mamo had died in her sleep, though Clair knew the truth. Her grandmother had merely left her old body behind as she said she would, so Clair didn't see any reason to feel sad.

Was what her grandmother told her true? Did she have some sort of sight? Had her own mother been afraid of it? She turned off the lamp on the nightstand and, with just the fire lighting the room, fingered the stone and sipped the bitter whiskey. She had hoped she might sleep but after an hour, then two, passing, she got up and opened the French doors to the terrace. The sky had cleared and the stars were twinkling in the black night. She took a deep breath, grabbing the brass handles of the door with her right hand for balance.

The terrace was where she went on the nights when she couldn't sleep—the first step before giving up and driving the coast roads until it was daylight. It was quiet now, except for the ocean—she could hear it tossing and pounding the rocks. Often, in the morning, the whole beach would be rearranged, even the steps leading down might be buried in feet of new sand that within days would be gone again. She noticed that nothing is permanent and yet didn't take it in deeply. The nature of everything is change.

Letting go of the door, she moved toward the railing but found that her trajectory was off a little.

"I'm drunk," she thought to herself with amusement. My father's daughter.

Closer to the edge, she inhaled the salty fragrance of the sea and felt the cold stones through her socks, which reminded her of Dante, the Italian stonemason who'd laid the stones and also sung to her.

Opera arias, in a beautiful tenor voice. Still unsteady on her feet, Clair leaned into and over the railing, looking down onto the beach. *Such a craftsman he was, and how he had flirted! "Bella," he called her, and "cara mia."* He told her she should eat more: "Mangiare, Señora!" Often he'd offer to share his lunch—sausages, smelly cheeses, olives, crusty sticks of bread—which normally Clair would have never done, but she had a special feeling about Dante, and so accepted gratefully. As she watched, the waves pounded the beach below.

What if I were to fall? No one would know. Until I washed up somewhere along the coast.

CHAPTER 5

A couple of weeks after "the strange day," as she called it, Clair was in her bedroom, mindlessly listening to the Prairie Home Companion on the radio and awkwardly folding a pile of towels, made difficult with the cast on her left arm. Garrison Keillor was describing some charming scene, although Clair's attention was somewhere else. To her dismay, mostly still on Blake. He hadn't visited since his big announcement, but he had informed both of the children by phone that he and their mother would be divorcing. Clair had to admit to herself that her dream of having "the happy family," was harder to let go of than the reality of Blake himself. While they were together, though, it had remained a possibility. Now, she had to come to terms with that dream never happening.

The truth was she always knew deep down that as a couple, she and Blake were never going to last. Now it was here. Kind of a relief in a way.

The phone rang for the first time all day, and the abrupt sound startled her. Reaching across the bed, she knocked over the stack of towels and watched them tumble, gray and white to the floor. "Shit!" she swore under her breath just as she picked up the phone, then into the receiver, "Hello?" in a raspy voice.

"Well, shit to you too." It was Lucky.

"Oh, Lucky, my goodness, hi, and sorry. I'm glad it was you instead of someone else hearing that."

"Get a lot of calls from strangers do you?"

"I meant … oh, it doesn't matter. Actually, I don't get many calls at all."

"Sounds lonely up there in those woods."

"Yeah, a bit," Clair confessed. "It felt better when I was involved in the building project."

"Sounds like you need a trip, girl! Did you get my invitation?"

Clair immediately felt guilty. She hadn't wanted to say no to Lucky, so had simply put off calling her back.

"I did, Lucky … and I'm really sorry that I haven't gotten back to you. Wow, can you believe it … fifty … how did we get here?" She wanted to blurt out the truth about Blake, but didn't have the courage to speak it yet.

"Never mind the guilt trip … and you've got two years to go, so treat me with some respect. You're coming, right?" "I'm … thinking about it."

The truth was that she couldn't bear to take part in Lucky's lucky life when hers was in such shambles.

"Don't give me that, Clair Cassidy," Lucky jumped in. "You've promised too many times. You're coming! You *are* coming. I absolutely will not take no for an answer."

Clair laughed at Lucky's familiar persistence. How many times had she been coerced into doing something that she didn't want to do? Lucky had the power of persuasion and never doubted that others would follow.

"Well, since you put it that way, I guess I'll come."

The decision was made, but Clair knew she could always change her mind, give an excuse. She'd done it before.

"So, what's happening out there?" Lucky asked. "Still freezing your butt off?"

Clair wanted to tell Lucky about Blake, the afternoon with Grace, her broken wrist, and the terrible dreams she'd had since then, but instead, she sidestepped. "Oh, you know, it's been one of those years … so cold you wonder if spring is ever gonna come."

"Excuse me, Clair, but I have to interrupt." Lucky's voice took on an urgency. "I'm watching the most incredible sunset and this is a place famous for sunsets. It's transcendental."

Lucky used far-out words like "transcendental."

"Where are you?" Clair asked.

"I'm sitting in my backyard on a chaise lounge."

Clair tried to imagine Lucky's yard. She knew about sitting on a lawn chair here in Maine or even the Cape, but she couldn't picture what it would look like in New Mexico.

You're going to a strange land, said the voice she'd heard that day.

"Just a minute, Clair," Lucky said, then muffled the phone and yelled, "Max!" over the sound of a motorcycle. "Get your head out of that motor and look up."

Clair thought of Max, Lucky's "partner," as she called him. The ranch hand who showed up and never left. It was odd to think of her with him when, to Clair, she would always be Jim's wife, although he had been dead for twenty-five years. Recalling Max from pictures Lucky had sent over time, he'd seemed a little dangerous with his craggy face and cowboy look.

Clair couldn't really understand what Lucky saw in him. He was so different from Jim, who was such a golden boy, so heroic, so perfect for Lucky. Yet, Lucky seemed happy with Max and, more than that, she seemed crazy in love with him. Pictures she'd sent showed them on horseback and hiking in some godforsaken place, and naked in a river. Lucky had actually sent a picture of them naked and smiling. They were always smiling.

"Clair," Lucky's voice sounded breathless, "it started a few minutes ago just as I was dialing. Now the whole sky is lit up pink and purple and red and the edges of the clouds are rimmed in this brilliant light."

Clair tried to imagine color in her mind. It had been so long since she'd seen anything except gray and shades of gray that just the thought of pink was kinder than she could remember,

"Hey, if you lose me, figure Los Alamos just had a meltdown! Fuck!" Lucky burst out. "Now the sun's below the horizon and the rays from it are reaching back like psychedelic fingers all across the sky." Her voice dropped and got whispery. "And now everything has just gotten so quiet. Honestly, Clair, there's not a sound in the whole valley. Not a dog barking, no birds twittering, it's as if the whole world is in a state of heightened awareness." Clair noticed the revving motorcycle had stopped too.

"Are you saying all this just to get me out there?" Clair teased.

Now it was Lucky's turn to laugh. "Yeah, it's just a trick. Actually, it's gray and dull and I just ingested a button of peyote."

Lucky's call forced Clair's hand.

"I'm going to New Mexico," she told the women at the knitting shop.

"Where?" Millie asked.

"New Mexico … out west. My friend is turning 50 and I'm going to her party."

"Don't drink the water, Hon," Flora warned.

When Clair told Grace, her response upon a moment's reflection was, "New Mexico, ah, yes, there is something for you there. Find your pride, Clair, dear."

She and Grace had seen each other a couple of times—once for tea and once for a walk along the coast. The day that Clair had gone back for her purse, Grace insisted on taking her to the hospital. "This," she said, examining Clair's arm, "is at the very least a bad sprain. I'm going to drive you to the emergency room."

While waiting to be seen by the doctor, Clair asked, "Grace, will you fasten this necklace around my neck? I found it last night in a box of my mother's things."

"Of course." Grace extended her hand to receive the necklace, then turning it over and taking a closer look, she asked, "Do you know what this is, Clair?"

"No, not really. I only know my grandmother gave it to me when I left Ireland, but my mother took it off me on the plane. This is really the first time I've seen it."

"It's a Fairy Stone—see the unusual shape? It grows like that. It's a crystal … very special. I'm glad you're wearing it. You'll grow in the shape you're intended to … with some help from your dear departed and quite magical grandmother."

There was no need to tell Blake she was going. They had hardly spoken even at Cassidy's prep school graduation the following week, the first time they were all together since the news broke. In spite of everything, Clair wanted the day to be special for Cass, so she hoped that she and Blake could bury their hostility and put their daughter first, which they did manage to do. Carl and his wife, Jules, had come, Jules glowing and just beginning to show a baby bump. At the end of the day, when Clair walked them to their car, she linked arms with her son and his wife, "I am so happy for you! And I promise I'll finish the sweater for him or her, as soon as this bothersome cast comes off."

She also learned that Blake's new woman turned out to be a celebrity, the anchor woman for a Boston news station, causing Clair even more private humiliation. She wanted to throw a napkin over her head and just walk out of the room and hope to never see any of them again.

Blake was overly formal. He never even asked about the cast on her arm. Cassidy won the art prize, and after a few days at home, was off to Europe with friends—her graduation present— two months in Europe with a backpack and a rail pass. In the fall she would enter the Museum School in Boston. Her life was just beginning.

School of the Most Precious Blood February 1964

The art teacher Mrs. Crane is Clair's favorite. Mrs. Crane and Mrs. Spelling, the gym teacher, are also the only teachers who aren't nuns and come in once a week. The two-hour art class is after lunch on Wednesdays, and Clair can barely eat, so excited is she to get through the lunch period and into the art room.

Clair shows up early every week to help Mrs. Crane set up the materials needed for each student. The school provides the basics: posterboards and paints and colored chalks, but often Mrs. Crane brings in more exotic things, like Japanese papers and tubes of glorious shades of water colors and oils. Clair wants to lick the paint as it oozes from the tubes and to slide the chalks and charcoals over her hands and up her arms. She feels a singular pride when she walks home knowing that her face is spotted with the colors of her palette of the day. When Mrs. Crane gives her extra paints and brushes, Clair leaves class dizzy with delight.

At home she generally sketches in pencil and charcoal, although Trick had bought her a small box of watercolors with money he earned working at Mr. Gibbons' drugstore.

Trick hangs several of Clair's paintings in his room, encouraging her to do more.

"You have a gift, Clair. From God."

Her parents don't say much one way or the other but, once, Clair caught her mother looking at some of her paintings, though nothing was said.

Trick buys Clair a used copy of *Artists of the Early 20th Century*, and Clair falls in love with Matisse, Picasso, and Chagall. Each night before going to sleep, she thumbs through the book, sometimes reading about the artists and their lives, but mostly just looking at the images they created. When it is time for lights out, she tucks the book—her Bible—securely back in its box on her nightstand.

Sometimes, her mind saturated, Clair has dreams. On the following Wednesday, she tries to paint what she has seen in them. Frowning with concentration, and then with a burst of clarity, of confidence, she begins to paint in a rapture—shapes and colors, forms and configurations, perfect in symmetry.

Clair has terrible nightmares after Trick's death—sounds and screams, the ocean on fire, blackening flesh. And Trick is always trying to get back to her, crossing vast oceans, caught in violent storms, wild waves as high as skyscrapers.

In Mrs. Crane's class on a day in February, Clair picks up a brush and paints in a white heat as if she is possessed. A force is inside of her, beating at her edges, wielding the brush—both terrifying and wonderful. She loses all awareness of the classroom. It is only when she stops that she realizes Mrs. Crane has excused the others and that school is long over.

The painting is a horror. "I don't want it," she exclaims, pushing it away when Mrs. Crane suggests she take it home.

"Clair, sweetheart, I understand it may frighten you now, but it's raw energy, truth wrought big. You must keep it. You'll understand it better when you're older and a great artist."

Clair keeps the painting but pushes it to the back of her closet.

It is the season of Lent and she vows to give up painting forever.

CHAPTER 6

"Welcome on board flight 1023 to Dallas."

Clair crossed the threshold of the DC10, paused briefly, repeating the secret words her brother had told her on their first flight—words that he promised would keep her safe. She had learned those and other superstitions that she relied on in an unsafe world and carried them into adulthood. Just in case. If she didn't say the words at just the right moment with one foot on the plane and one in the boarding tunnel, the plane would crash. She was almost convinced. Clair's other secret weapon for feeling safe and relaxed was Xanax, and she had swallowed the pink pill an hour before boarding.

Three flight attendants, two women and a man dressed in smart-looking gray uniforms with maroon-and-black trim, stood in the shadow of the curved silver doorway.

"Good morning, good morning!" they said, in voices too cheery for that time of day. Then, "Greg," his name tag said, stepped forward.

"I'll put your bag in the overhead for you, Mrs. McKendrick." He had noticed her cast.

"Oh, thank you … I'll just tuck my purse in it before you do." She smiled up at the very tall Greg " … otherwise I'll just end up kicking it around on the floor.

⚡

Lucky had insisted that Clair get the first flight out.

"If you take that one, you'll be in early enough for us to get where we're going."

"And where is that?"

"Now, now, I can't spoil the surprise. Just make sure you take the early flight."

Wanting to fit in with how she assumed Lucky's friends would be dressed, Clair thought about wearing jeans and buying some cowboy boots but settled on an off-white linen suit she'd found in her closet and paired it with a white sleeveless top, allowing her cast to fit through the armhole. She added the expensive Hermes scarf that her husband had given her after he'd confessed to one of his many affairs.

The whole trip was only for three days—she hadn't committed to staying on after the party—so she'd packed a couple more outfits and Lucky's birthday present into her carry-on.

⚡

Clair adjusted herself in the first-class leather seat next to the window, strapped on the seatbelt, and took a couple of deep breaths. She nervously checked her watch, awkwardly positioned on her right wrist because of the cast on her left. It was six in the morning; departure was in thirty minutes. The ground crew was busy loading the luggage—probably searching it for valuables, according to a news show she had recently seen on television and felt relieved that she had her one bag tucked securely in the overhead compartment. Clair couldn't believe she was on her way to New Mexico. Albuquerque, a word she couldn't even spell until recently.

In the cabin other passengers were making their way to the tourist section. Clair watched them and couldn't help wondering if she would be sharing some exceptionally dire fate with these strangers that would bind them together forever as a tragic statistic.

"Can I get you some coffee, Mrs. McKendrick?"

The flight attendant was about Clair's age.

"Yes, please, with cream and sugar." She was glad to see the change in airline policy where women could keep their jobs as they aged. There was a time when they hired only thin, attractive, young women who were fired if they gained weight or got married. A book from the sixties had famously portrayed them as party girls with loose morals.

58

As the fog rolled in from the harbor, buildings appeared and disappeared on the Boston skyline like a mirage. Clair hoped the visibility was clear enough to fly.

No one had sat next to her yet. *Maybe no one will.* She disliked making small talk that seemed obligatory. Taking several more deep breaths, she rubbed the stone cross dangling at her throat, at once feeling a sense of calm.

The power of the pink pill had emboldened her thoughts.

Just before the doors closed, a man wearing tortoiseshell glasses slipped into the seat next to her. She glanced at him and nodded hello. He nodded back the same greeting.

Good. We're both nodders.

The flight attendants performed their safety routine, then the engines revved and Clair felt pressed back into the seat as the plane accelerated and lifted off. She watched out the window, as the airplane climbed through the dense fog before coming into the light of the sun, always shining, just sometimes not visible.

The man sitting next to her was dressed in a light-colored suit, nearly the same shade as her own, a bit crumpled, the way linen looks, and a blue polo shirt. On first glimpse, he looked to be about her age. When he took off his jacket and gave it to the flight attendant, she noticed he was wearing a lapis bracelet around his left wrist, deep ultramarine blue beads with smaller silver ones in between, forearms sparsely covered in dark hair.

After a while, a harmonic ping announced the seatbelt sign was off, and the flight attendant came around with moist towels. She handed one to Clair with little tongs.

"Would either of you care for something to drink?" She was young, with fair hair pulled into a simple ponytail, exposing a pretty face.

The man deferred to Clair.

Embarrassed to order the Bloody Mary she wanted this early in the morning, she reined in her reckless whim and instead answered, "I'll just have more coffee, please, with cream and sugar."

"Orange juice and coffee, no cream, for me," the man requested.

He had his laptop out, earphones on, and was staring intently at the screen.

Clair opened the New Mexico magazine, featuring an adobe-style fireplace on the cover, that Lucky had sent to her for the flight. In the tourist section, a baby was crying and someone coughed.

The attendant returned with their beverages and said, "This morning we have Eggs Benedict or a ham-and-cheese omelet. Both served with hash browns."

The man ordered the omelet. Clair wanted the Eggs Benedict, but worried about being able to cut it with her arm still in the cast, so ordered the omelet as well. She thought how relieved she would be in a week or so when the cast would come off. It had been such an inconvenience. So many simple things she couldn't do—like zip her own pants, tie her sneakers, open jars!

She adjusted her tray and magazine, pleased that the flight was smooth—the pilot had said it would be "clear sailing" all the way to Dallas—so she relaxed, watching the clouds scattered below. Then, putting on her earphones, she closed her eyes and listened to the heartbreaking closing aria from *La Traviata*.

Farewell to the happy dreams of the past.

Everything is at an end.

Breakfast arrived. Clair returned the earphones to the seat caddy in front of her.

"Are you leaving home or returning?" the man asked pleasantly, spearing a bite of omelet.

"Oh, I'm actually traveling to see an old friend in Santa Fe for her birthday."

He had an attractive face. Etched jawline.

"Must be a special friend or a special birthday to have you go all that way."

Resonant voice.

"Yes, we're childhood friends."

"Ah, nice—old friends." Then he laughed. "That kind of came out wrong … didn't mean you were old."

Clair laughed too. "I understood what you meant. I'm not insulted."

"Santa Fe, eh?" he continued. "I'll be there myself in a few days. I haven't been before but heard it's quite a unique place, adobe architecture and all. I'm an architect so I like looking at buildings. Ad nauseam, so I've been told," he chuckled.

"I worked with an architect from Boston a few years back when I built my home. He was from Bates and Bates."

"Yes, of course, I know Greg Bates. Must be quite a home. They build only the best."

She felt embarrassed, as if she were name-dropping but didn't know how to correct it, so simply said, "He did a nice job."

She found she wanted to tell him that it was really she who had designed the home, not Greg Bates, though he did make the drawings.

"My style is a little less, how shall I put it?" he said, putting down his fork. "Grand? That is, when I do homes at all. Lately, it seems I've been attracting more public projects." He named a couple of buildings, including the addition to the museum where she had worked as a docent.

"I know that room very well," she exclaimed. "I love it. So light filled and such an unusual use of space."

"Glad you like it." He seemed genuinely appreciative. "I wanted it to contain but not intrude on the art."

Suddenly, she felt like she knew him in some intimate way, having been inside and loving a space that had first been conceived in his mind.

"By the way, I'm Ben," he smiled, offering his hand.

"Clair," she said, lightly grasping his right hand and looking into clear gray eyes. Suddenly, an image flashed in her mind. Him. In a desert? The image was oh so brief, disappearing, like a dream, before she could grab hold of it. He was saying something but still reaching for the flash, she hadn't heard what he said.

"I'm sorry, what did you say?"

"What happened to the other one?" he said again, pointing his chin toward her cast.

"Oh, this," she lifted her arm. "Nothing too exciting. I slipped in the kitchen. The thing was though, I made it worse by not going to the hospital right away."

"Why didn't your husband insist?" He had noticed her ring.

She hesitated, not knowing quite how but suddenly wanting to say it out loud.

"He wasn't there. Um, we're separated, actually getting a divorce." She wasn't used to the words and they came out awkwardly.

"I'm sorry, it's none of my business. I apologize for asking."

"No, it's okay. It's probably good that I say it. Makes it real."

Ben put down his fork, giving her his full attention.

"It's recent," she told him, fingering the ring, "the split. I guess I just haven't come around to taking this off yet."

"Long-time marriage?"

"Nearly thirty years."

"Well, you must've been a child bride," he quipped, smiling, but followed it with, "I'm sorry, Clair, it must be hard. There are a lot of dreams tied up in thirty years. Many memories."

His eyes never wavered from hers.

"Yes."

"Hurts like hell, doesn't it?"

"Yes, it does. But it was overdue. I stayed much longer than I should have."

Do I really feel that?

Her mind flashed through many of the moments, the opportunities, when she should have left. So many moments: the regular shouting matches that would cause him to storm out, not returning for days; his blatant affairs; his total lack of interest in her; and his growing infatuation with younger and younger women. And the worst, her own total lack of interest in herself. The black depressions. More and more pills.

"What kept you there? Kids?"

She held his gaze.

"Fear," she said at once, surprising herself with the suddenness and surety of her answer. "I guess I was just afraid to leave. Afraid of what I'd have to face alone."

She couldn't believe herself, telling a stranger things she hadn't even known until he asked.

"Sometimes safety and security are poor substitutes for joy," he replied gently.

Then the two strangers returned to eating. Clair gazed out the window in between bites, but mostly unmindful of the clouds, thinking instead about the odd image of this man in her mind. What was it she saw? She reached for it, but it was like flailing around in the fog. Nothing to grab. She'd had a glimpse but now it was gone.

After the trays were taken, Ben picked up the conversation as though it had never stopped. "So, what's on your bucket list in Santa Fe?"

"I won't actually be in Santa Fe. Once I land in Albuquerque, we're going someplace else for her birthday. She didn't say where because it's a surprise."

"The birthday girl surprising her guests," he observed, nodding approvingly.

"I like her style."

Clair noticed his bottom teeth were crowded, but his smile was wide open.

"Are you going to Albuquerque too?" she questioned.

"No, I'm getting off in Dallas, making a stop to see my kids. My ex-wife lives there now, remarried … see? I know about divorce from experience."

Clair returned his wan smile in kind.

"But I'll only be there for a couple of days …" he continued. "I'm seeing them between their tennis and music camps. Kids are busy these days! I don't get to see them all that much since they've moved."

"How old are they?"

"Eighteen and sixteen. Two incredible daughters, the blessings of my life."

"I have an eighteen-year-old daughter too. She's probably in Italy right now, her graduation present."

He whistled. "Lucky girl!" he exclaimed.

"She wouldn't always agree with that. Teenage contrariness."

He nodded, knowingly. "After my visit though, I'm doing something I've always wanted to do. Promise not to laugh?"

"I promise."

"I'm renting an Airstream and taking a drive through the great Southwest."

"Wow, a real adventure."

"Yep. When I was young, I went on a trip around the country with some buddies, in a VW bus … had such a great time. Of course, we were drugging quite a bit back then," he laughed. "But I want to capture that feeling again … freedom, independence, youth maybe. I've been too locked down for too long." His face suddenly looked sad, but the crinkling around his eyes showed well-worn grooves, identifying the sadness as temporary.

Here is a man whose face is etched by laughter.

She enjoyed watching the expressions on his face, the way he reached for just the right word to describe his feelings. He was easily sharing these feelings with her, fairly unique for a man. She imagined him young and free, bandana around hippy-length dark hair. Now though, his short crew cut was mixed with gray. Signpost of what's ahead.

"Must be a midlife crisis," he admitted. "I'm turning fifty soon … but I'm not ready to hang up my boots just yet."

"I'm going to a fifty's party too—my friend's."

"How 'bout that … but you, you can't be near fifty. I wouldn't believe it."

"Close enough," she sighed. "I'll be forty-eight in a couple of months. But tell me more about your adventure. I want to hear."

"Well … I'm planning on a loop around the Southwest … Santa Fe, Grand Canyon, Utah. The whole area had such a profound effect on me the first time I saw it. Now I'm ready for my own revolution!"

"It sounds like fun," she said, surprising herself, because it did.

"There's an outdoor opera in Santa Fe. I've got tickets to *The Marriage of Figaro* next week."

"Really? I'm an opera fan too," she offered, delighted. "I listen to opera all the time. In fact, I was just listening to *La Traviata*."

"You're kidding! Me, too, though I prefer the not-so-tragic."

"Ah, but isn't that the point?" She smiled, astonished to meet a man who enjoyed opera. Blake tolerated it, but had finally just quit, insisting he had business whenever she had tickets. To her, it was pure magic.

"Maybe you should stay longer and meet me there?" he winked.

Could he possibly be serious or did his eye twitch?

"Ladies and gentlemen, this is Captain Gordon from the cockpit," came a honeyed-southern accent. "Those of you on the left side of the plane have a beautiful view of the mighty Mississippi. We're still at our cruising altitude of 40,000 feet, and the seatbelt sign is off. We're expecting a smooth flight, but I'll be turning the sign back on when we begin our descent into the Dallas Fort Worth airport. 'Til then, enjoy the flight!"

Ben pushed his seat back to the most reclined position and rested his head, turning it toward Clair.

"That's a very unusual piece you're wearing around your neck."

She reached reflectively for her grandmother's talisman.

"It belonged to my grandmother," she replied. "I was told it's a Fairy Stone."

"I've heard of them. They're found in just a couple of places in the states, but around the world as well."

"Maybe Ireland, where my grandmother lived?"

Now they were both leaning back in their seats, sometimes staring straight ahead, sometimes tipping their heads toward each other, like they were lovers in bed … maybe an imaginary pizza box between them?

"I always thought it would be fun to travel in one of those RVs," she said thoughtfully, again surprised at her own comment. "They look so comfortable with little kitchens and baths. They're decorated rather poorly, but I suppose that could be changed."

"You any good in the kitchen?"

They both laughed, and looked toward each other, holding a gaze that was a bit too long for strangers on a plane.

How might it be if she were free to do such an outrageous thing? Take off around the country? And what might it be like to be with someone who laughed a lot?

"I plan to use the time to think about what's next for me," he continued. "I've thought about moving, leaving Boston … more than leaving Boston really, I'm thinking of leaving my profession."

He leaned his head toward her in the headrest. "I don't know why I'm telling you all this," he confessed. "The idea is new to me, not well thought through yet."

"I once read that architecture is like frozen music. Your addition at the museum is like that. Why would you want to give up your profession? Something in which you clearly excel?"

"I think I'm ready to try something else, I suppose. You know, before it's too late. I got into architecture to please my father. It was a family lineage. What I wanted to be was a sculptor. An artist. My dad's been dead for several years, and one day recently it dawned on me that I didn't have to please him anymore. That maybe I was entitled to the rest of my life. My kids are financially secure, and I don't have any responsibilities right now, other than to myself."

"Huh! And I wanted to be an architect," Clair confessed, with a little grin.

"Really?"

"Yes, but I wanted to do it for my brother. That's what he wanted for himself, but after he died, it was a way to, um …"

"To live his life for him?"

"Yes, now that you say it."

"Funny, isn't it, how we live for other people?"

"I don't even know what I really want. I used to draw and paint. Recently I've been reminded of that time."

The folksy voice came on through the loudspeaker. "We're coming up on Dallas, folks. The weather is 88°. Going to be a hot one today. Passengers going on to Albuquerque, please remain on the plane. We won't be on the ground for long."

"Wow, that was a quick trip," Clair commented, wishing it could be longer. *When have I ever wished a plane ride could be longer?*

"Would you excuse me, Ben? I think I'll use the lavatory before landing."

"Of course." Ben released his seatbelt, lifted the armrest, and stepped to the side, allowing her to rise.

Standing side by side, Clair had to lift her gaze to look at Ben, staring down at her now from his new six-inch vantage point.

They stood that way for a moment until Clair finally said, "Um, Ben, I need to open the overhead."

"Oh, sorry, let me get that for you."

"I just need …" she said, reaching for a zippered pouch in her bag's zipped pocket, "… this." Smiling shyly at Ben, she made her way forward a few steps to the lavatory, passing two of the flight attendants who were busy securing things for the landing.

Oh, my goodness! she thought, closing and locking the door. She took a deep breath, feeling strangely like she needed extra oxygen, and looked into her own startled blue eyes. I just felt like a teenager!

What is happening?

She washed her hands, put on some moisturizer, combed her hair and dabbed lip color from a tiny pot. After smoothing her clothes in the cramped space, she dabbed on a little perfume and arranged her hair as best she could, given the cast.

Returning to her seat, she noticed her fellow passengers for the first time, just a dozen or so in the first-class cabin, mostly men probably on business trips, she thought. Ben rose when he saw her coming—he had his jacket on now—and raised his eyebrows, questioning whether she wanted to open the overhead again. She nodded and he opened the overhead for her so she could return the pouch to her bag and slide back into her seat.

"Nice perfume," he commented, with an exaggerated sniff as she went around him.

Gawd! I hope I didn't overdo it!

The flight attendant announced the descent, picked up Clair's glass, and asked that they put their seats in an upright position.

"I hope you have a good visit with your friend," Ben said with sincerity, nodding his head.

She looked toward him. The baby in the back began to cry again and someone coughed. The sun shot a shaft of light through the window. She didn't respond, but nodded, mirroring him.

"When are you returning to Boston?" He asked.

"Tuesday, late. I'll stay in town overnight before heading back home."

The curve of his mouth.

"Short visit."

"Yes, short. My friend wanted me to stay on, but I probably won't, though I may change my mind."

The straight bridge of his nose.

"Hey," he exclaimed suddenly. "No one has signed your cast yet. May I?" He reached for a marker in his briefcase. "It's the law, you know ... you have to have it signed."

She started to protest but relented when he lifted her left arm and slipped his right one underneath.

"I need to do it this way," he explained, "so it will be upright for you to see. Don't look until it's finished."

She laughed. "I promise!" and turned her attention to the view out the window, then wondered what in the world he was doing, as it was more than signing his name.

"Oops," he chuckled, when the plane hit some air turbulence. "I'll have to incorporate that bump." She laughed.

And then they were on the ground, taxiing to the terminal.

"Just a minute more."

She wanted to spend these last few minutes looking at him, but she had promised not to look until the drawing was finished. When the plane came to a halt, he said, "Okay, done! I hope you don't mind—I got a little carried away."

She glanced down and saw a drawing, but then quickly looked up at him, because now he was standing and reaching for his bag in the overhead. He was leaving.

Wait! Wait!

And then a stampede of people was behind him, pressing to get on with their lives.

"Clair," he said warmly, extending his hand, but suddenly he was swept away by the pressing crowd.

After a moment, Clair looked down at the cast.

The drawing was just a sketch, but Ben managed to capture a little scene that brought a smile to Clair's face and heart. It was an Airstream trailer in a desert landscape of cactus, along with the winged roofline of the Santa Fe Opera House.

Underneath the drawing, was a phone number, and a question: "See you in Boston?"

CHAPTER 7

Departing Dallas, the plane ascended through puffy white clouds that shadowed the ground below with various shapes like puzzle pieces dropped and scattered by a naughty child. The clouds thinned, and soon disappeared. In their place as far as the eye could see was an uninterrupted view of pale blonde desert. Occasionally, a distinct line was visible through the surface, reminding Clair of how she used to drag a stick through the hard packed sand of Stonehead Beach as a child, tracing her name again and again: *Clair, Clair,* as if in the cursive shape she might come to know herself.

1961

It's a cold winter morning, and Clair is bundled like an Eskimo—a scratchy woolen scarf her mother made tied tightly around her neck along with blue mittens and a matching hat. She comes to the beach to escape the inevitable Saturday morning fight between her parents, usually about her father's drinking the night before.

Further down the beach, she sees the shadow of someone, sun behind them so that their shape dances in and out of the sun's disk. The figure is running full tilt, whinnying like a horse, several dogs trailing behind. Not trusting the dogs nor the whinnying person, Clair watches as the long shadow reaches her seconds before the girl does. Coming alongside each other, the girl and the shadow both stop. The girl is wearing a pair of jeans, blue Keds, and a maroon sweatshirt with "Harvard" printed across it in white letters. Her cheeks are cherry red, the long braid that had bounced as she ran now resting calmly on her shoulder.

"Got a Kleenex?" the girl asks. "I've got snot running into my mouth."

The seat that Ben had vacated was now filled by an older man who told Clair that he'd been bumped up from economy when they ran out of seats. "My lucky day!" he exclaimed loudly. "First time I've ever flown first class." He was not staying in Albuquerque, however, just renting a car and driving straight to a place called Roswell for a UFO convention.

"I was stationed in Roswell fifty years ago. I tell you, somethin' happened there. Somethin' no one likes to talk about. Now, I hear there's talk of alien bodies and spaceships … I just want to see for myself what in tarnation is going on."

Clair nodded politely, just as if she was paying attention.

⚡

Usually, Clair and Lucky's meetings on the beach are after school, Clair still wearing the navy blue uniform of Saint Jude's, the patron saint of the impossible. The girls search for special shells, swinging long ropes of seaweed like lariats or chasing the birds along the shoreline. One stretch of beach has several deep caves accessible only for a few hours at low tide.

"Come on, Clair! Don't be afraid. I promise you won't get hurt or lost. The cave's not that deep. I've been in it millions of times."

"I don't want to, Lucky. I'm afraid."

"Don't be a chicken. Nothing is going to happen."

"My mother said kids have been lost in those caves, and then they get eaten by fish and crabs."

⚡

The old guy, George, droned on, hardly pausing for a breath.

He must have lungs the size of airbags. "Excuse me, George," Clair interrupted. "I need to use the lavatory."

George didn't offer to help so Clair opened the overhead on her own, but when she did, she did a doubletake. The place where her bag had been, alongside Ben's, was just an empty space.

Surely, it was there. It probably slid into the back part during takeoff.

"Ma'am," she interrupted, as the flight attendant was pouring a drink for a passenger, "I'm sorry to bother you but my bag … I can't find it."

"Okay, Mrs. McKendrick, don't worry. We'll find it. You're sure you didn't check it?"

Clair's eyebrows raised an inch. Blue eyes glared in disbelief. "Check it? No! The young man, the steward, put it up there when I came on board." Clair frowned, lifting her cast, showing her why. "I opened it during the flight from Boston to Dallas. You saw me, I stood right here. The man, the other passenger stood with me."

"Alright, let me have a look."

Bethany, the flight attendant, shined her small pen-light around some of the passenger's feet. "So sorry, so sorry. A passenger has lost something."

"Ma'am, please, I told you it's not on the floor," Clair. "You're not going to find it there. It was in the overhead bin."

"Mrs. McKendrick I know you're upset, and I'm sorry, but when we get to Albuquerque and everyone is off the plane, we can take a good look," Bethany assured her. "I'm sure we'll find it. Sometimes it might be another passenger who thinks it's his bag but notices and puts it down somewhere else." She shrugged her shoulders. "We'll find it."

Back in her seat Clair began going through her memory of all that was in the bag. *Lucky's present, all my clothes, oh, my God, my Xanax!* She began to breathe more rapidly, feeling she needed another Xanax right this minute. But all the while, George talked about being a state park employee, working at Mammoth Cave in Missouri, going on about bat guano and darkness.

Stop! Stop! Clair wanted to yell.

"I was the conductor of a little train. My favorite part was taking people into the cave then turning out the lights." He went on gleefully, like a small boy pulling a prank. "Oh, that really got 'em spooked!"

"Really? Might that not have frightened the children?" Clair accused him, feeling angry.

Not listening, he continued. "Why, in the Carlsbad cave, you can walk all the way to the bottom yourself, no train, ninety stories below ground! That's equal to the height of the Empire State Building." He was almost reverent when he spoke the word "cave," as if he was speaking of the Vatican or Versailles. As if when he stood, he would have to genuflect on stiff old knees to pay respect.

He quieted down once the upscale breakfast arrived, thrilled to receive such grand treatment.

"Man could get used to this," he crowed, pushing up his sleeves, ready to dig in.

Since Clair had eaten on the last flight, she declined her breakfast, choosing water instead.

George fell asleep after the meal, and in the respite, her own situation seized hold again. Her bag represented a lifeline—her home away from home—the few things that grounded her. With no identification, no money or credit card, no clothes or makeup, not even her glasses, she felt adrift. The muscles of her shoulders and neck tightened. *Calm down,* she admonished herself, as she felt her heart beating quickly, blood coursing through her temples.

I can't go! How can I go without anything? Lucky will have to understand.

1963

"Well, do you think nuns shave their hair off?"

The two girls are riding their bikes to the beach one day after school. Both have green bookbags in their baskets. Lucky is shouting the questions at Clair as they weave closer then farther apart.

"Of course not. They just pull it back." Clair gets impatient with Lucky's misinformation about the nuns. Some days she thinks she herself might have a calling to enter an order—a "vocation," as the nuns call it—and she doesn't like it when Lucky teases about the nuns.

"I heard one got caught styling her hair so they all got punished for it. Now they have a barber visit every couple of weeks or so and, under penalty of death, they can't reveal what they look like without those hats on ..."

"Habits," Clair corrected.

The flight attendant came by to give Clair a claim form to fill out, *"in case you need it,"* but without her glasses, reading such fine print was a strain, especially with the plane bumping and shuddering. Stuffing the form in the seat pocket in front of her, her gaze drifted out the window to an emptiness, the likes of which she'd never seen. Stark. Isolated. Like the moon. She remembered that she'd read somewhere that in the Southwestern desert you could see General Patton's troop maneuvers still etched onto the surface of the land.

A resonant "ping" sounded to indicate the seatbelt sign had come on.

"Ah, folks, we'll be landing in Albuquerque shortly, but there's always some bumps around the mountains. Please secure your seatbelts and we'll be on the ground in just a few minutes."

Soon the plane descended, slow and bumpy like they were driving on a dirt road.

"Up there to the north are the Sangre de Cristos mountain range," she heard another passenger say, "in Santa Fe."

The landing gear dropped and the heavy plane rocked side to side. Clair saw a muddy river, squat houses, cars on the highway, and a small outcropping of city buildings.

She said goodbye to George and wished him well at the ET convention. Then, with nothing to gather, she sat until the plane was emptied out.

Several of the crew began searching through the first class section, but nothing was found. The bag was gone.

"The airline is very sorry, Mrs. McKendrick. We'll do all we can to get your bag back to you. Another passenger probably turned it in already." His face looked sincere. "When you get inside the terminal, give your form to the attendant in baggage, and they'll help you sort it out."

Four women were standing in view of Clair's emergence from the tunnel doorway, one with a camera in front of her face. Clair, who was walking just ahead of the flight crew, spotted a blur of motion and noise, then saw a cowboy hat waving furiously. It was Lucky, one arm holding the hat and waving it like she was riding on the back of a bull. Suddenly, Clair felt herself being grabbed, spun in a circle, and nearly lifted in the air, coming to a halt with Lucky's long braid resting on Clair's shoulder.

"So, what? You were sitting in the back toilet?" Lucky was wide-eyed. "Jesus, Clair, you're the last person off the flight. I was beginning to think maybe you'd changed your mind. And what in the hell did you do to your arm? Motorcycle racing again?"

Clair had to laugh. It was her same old friend, and she was very happy to see her.

Lucky was wearing jeans, a red-checked sleeveless shirt, cowboy boots, and holding a big hat. She looked so alive! Clair felt matronly by comparison, immediately wishing she had worn something else.

"Lucky, I can't go," she whispered.

The other women were standing a short distance away, waiting while the two friends greeted each other.

Clair heard the click of a camera in the sudden silence.

"What do you mean you can't go?" Lucky questioned, the smile falling off her face. "Clair, you're already here."

"Someone took my bag from the overhead in Dallas. I can't go further. I have nothing with me."

"Is that what you were doing with the crew?"

"Yes, and I have to fill out this damn report and hand it in."

"Oh, Clair, that sucks. I'm really sorry." Lucky was guiding her toward the other women as they were talking. "Come on, the others have been dying to meet you."

"Everyone," Lucky announced. "Here she is! The ever enigmatic, Clair. But no joke, guys, her bag was stolen in Dallas. We're gonna have to deal with that first."

The tallest woman in the group hadn't waited for Lucky's introduction, but stepped forward to give Clair a bear hug, pulling her close to a rounded body. Not expecting such familiarity, Clair awkwardly hugged her back.

"I'm VJ," the woman stated, "and don't worry about your bag, Clair. Between all of us, we'll have anything you need."

"This is Alex," Lucky said, introducing a second woman, who had beautiful bone structure, direct gray eyes, and sunglasses on top of her head, holding back pale-blonde hair.

Alex hugged Clair more gently, mindful of Clair's cast. "I'm so glad to meet you at last, Clair, Lucky has talked about you so much through the years."

"And this is Jesse."

Jesse, the one with the camera, had very short mahogany-colored hair capping her head and sticking up here and there at odd angles. With the camera no longer blocking Jesse's face, Clair noticed a tiny gold stud on one nostril. Her body-hugging jersey and pants didn't quite meet at the waist, and there was a gold ring in her navel, reminding Clair of her daughter.

"Welcome to the Land of Enchantment." Jesse hugged her with surprising strength.

"Clair, having your bag stolen doesn't mean you can't come," Lucky chided. "What good would it do to go home? It's not gonna bring your bag back."

Clair felt herself being carried along with the tide of them as if she was a leaf on their surface.

"Let's go do the paperwork and then get out of Dodge."

"And we can make a stop if you like." It was the blonde woman, Alex, speaking. "We can get anything you might want."

VJ added, "I told Clair we'd probably have everything she might need." VJ had strawberry-blonde hair streaked with silver, wore loose-fitting dark pants, a big white linen shirt, and over that, an unbuttoned plaid vest. Around her neck was a mother-of-pearl triangle hung on a silver chain.

Clair's eyes were taking in the various people passing by. She felt as though she had stepped onto a movie set. Men in cowboy hats and boots; women, too, in Western garb, heavy silver belts over long pleated skirts. She spotted an impressive bronze sculpture of a Native American with bird wings extending from his arms.

"Lucky," Clair pulled her aside, with one last ditch effort. "I take medication for anxiety. I need it."

"Oh, Clair, you'll be fine," answered Lucky, ignoring her plea. "We're not gonna do anything that would make you anxious. And besides, we have plenty of tequila with us … we'll just get you drunk."

At that moment, Alex moved closer towards Clair and Lucky. "I'm sorry," she interrupted, looking concerned, "but I heard that you're on medication, Clair ... and Lucky," she chastised, "this is not something to wave off."

"I'm sorry, Clair," Lucky offered, looking contrite, "I didn't mean to ... oh, you know me ... I have a tendency to want to rush forward."

"I happen to have some Xanax with me," Alex assured Clair. "I'm a therapist and pack for any and all emergencies." She smiled. "And, Clair, it's nothing you have to keep secret from this crazy group!"

All the women seemed to have formed a circle around Clair, and as she looked at each of their faces, she felt more at ease in their sisterhood. Then VJ confirmed what she had said earlier. "See? Between all of us, we do have just about anything you might need ... but we can make a stop if you'd like."

"I think I'll be alright," Clair said, taking a real breath and feeling that to be the truth. "Thank you."

With the necessary papers filled out, and Clair assured by airline security that they would find her luggage, the women left the terminal and stepped into the sunlight. Without sunglasses, Clair squinted when she stepped out of the sliding doors and into the clear air. She had never seen the sun this bright! It was like turning on a spotlight in the middle of the dark. She wanted to shield her eyes with her hands to prevent them from being seared. And it was hot, like an oven hot, but when she touched her face, her skin was dry as paper.

"I have an extra pair of sunglasses in the car," Lucky offered, placing her cowboy hat on Clair's head, "but this'll help."

She slipped her arm merrily through Clair's as they walked, a gesture from girlhood that tugged at Clair's heart. Arriving at a big blue Suburban, Clair noticed several bumper stickers on the back fender: "Free Tibet"; "Cowgirls Are Forever"; "Visualize Whirled Peas." It took Clair a moment to grasp the last one, but when she did, she smiled and took the front seat next to Lucky.

When they were all strapped in, Lucky said, with a shit-eating grin on her face, "So! Want to know where we're going?"

CHAPTER 8

"Don't keep us in suspense anymore," someone yelled from the back seat in a mock pleading tone. "Tell us!"

"Okay, okay," Lucky said, her voice raised, but holding onto the suspense. "Let me get onto the highway, and then I'll tell. But first Clair has to tell us about her arm … 'cause I'm sure it wasn't motorcycle racing, like I first suspected."

"Yes," the women chimed like a chorus. "What happened?"

"Well, you're right, Lucky … *not* motorcycle racing … you know I gave that up years ago," Clair teased back. "I'm afraid it was nothing glamorous. I just slipped and fell in my kitchen and broke a couple of bones in my wrist. The cast is due to come off very soon."

"And what's the drawing on the cast?" asked Jesse.

"Oh, nothing, really," Clair answered, feeling suddenly embarrassed. "Some man I sat next to on the plane insisted that it was mandatory that he write on my cast."

As they drove, Clair looked around at the peculiar-looking city, no high-rises, no cloverleafs of traffic, no frantic pace. Like a dream or waking up in an unfamiliar landscape where you can't quite get your bearings.

She remembered the prophecy from the afternoon at Grace's. *You're going to a strange land.*

"Those are the Sandia Mountains behind us," Lucky stated to Clair, who craned her neck back to get a look. "*Sandia* means watermelon. That's the color the mountains turn in the setting sun."

Lucky negotiated a curve in the road and then settled in on the highway.

"This is the Mother Road, Clair."

"The what?"

"Route 40, the old Route 66, you know, get your kicks on Route 66."

"Oh, yes, I remember that song."

"So here it is, ladies," Lucky announced, turning in her seat to address the group in a way that made Clair want to grab the steering wheel. "About twenty-five years ago, an artist by the name of Walter De Maria wanted to build a vast land sculpture in a place that attracted lightning."

Clair didn't like the sound of the word *"lightning"* attached to where they were going.

"For years," Lucky continued, "De Maria looked for just the right spot, wanting it to be one of the most struck places in the country. New Mexico won because of the large amount of empty land and the lack of people."

"So, where are we going?" asked a voice from the back.

"We're going to the Lightning Field in Quemado, about 150 miles away."

Clair's stomach knotted.

Alex was immediately leaning forward over the front seat. "Lightning!" she exclaimed. "How archetypal. Uranus rules lightning, the great awakener. Oh, Lucky, how exciting."

I am the awakener, the voice had said.

"I remember you talking about this place," said VJ. "Didn't you and Max go there once?"

"We did, but I don't want to tell you anymore, so you can all be surprised."

"How often does lightning strike?" Clair asked warily.

"I'm not sure of the statistics, but July holds the best chance. New Mexico has its monsoon season in July and we get some pretty wild storms. Let's hope for the best."

Clair was sure they were hoping for different outcomes when it came to the lightning, but she felt good about the outcome she wanted with the weather so hot and dry. She noticed a sign for the Petroglyph National Monument and then nothing. Only vacant undulating land, dotted with scrubby brush, dizzying in its emptiness.

"This sure isn't Kansas, is it, Toto?" Lucky joshed, as they came to the top of a rollercoaster-like hill.

Clair looked out on a grand moonlike vista, but in technicolor. Red land dotted with green under a bright blue sky.

But the thing that seized her attention were the clouds—dazzling pure white, hard-edged and popping from the azure of the heavens, like the 3D movies she'd seen as a child while wearing those red-and-green glasses. She watched one cloud morph into the profile of a mermaid, whose hair reached out in long tentacles, and another as it formed into a huge open-mouthed fish swimming across the sky toward a smaller one until the smaller was consumed.

"So, Clair," it was Alex leaning into the front seat again. "Lucky told us that you're married with two kids, right?"

"Yes, that's right. My son Carl is twenty-eight and Cassidy is eighteen." She wanted to steer the conversation away from any talk of her marriage. "How about you, Alex?"

"Me, too, married, but just one child, a daughter. Same original husband though, like you, I believe. But we've had a few breaks along the way."

"What do you mean?"

"We divorced, then, years later, got back together."

Clair had turned to face her, noticing Alex's slight southern accent and a flowery scent.

"It's been rather crazy … getting married again after being apart, but we still don't live together. Greg's a surgeon with a practice in Atlanta and can't leave yet. And I have a practice in Santa Fe as a psychotherapist and can't leave either. So, it's been thirty years … but not really," Alex laughed.

"Alex just finished a doctorate in mythological studies," Lucky told Clair.

"Oh, how wonderful!" Clair interjected, impressed and feeling a little intimidated.

"Yes, I'm hoping to have my dissertation published someday. But there are so many possibilities, aren't there? Greg and I also would like to move to Italy at some point. He's been a closet painter for years and wants to live where so many of the great masterpieces were created."

The land was an unusual pallet of colors, soft browns and sage greens against a background of intense bright-blue sky.

"The taller bushes are actually trees, pinyon pines." Lucky pointed toward several in the landscape. "Its nuts were a staple food for the Native American and Hispanic populations.

"What were the very large trees back by the river?" asked Clair.

"Oh, those are cottonwoods, my favorite. In the fall they turn bright yellow."

Even as a child, Lucky had known the names of things—trees, birds, flowers, anything in the wild.

"Nearly everything here turns yellow in the fall—cottonwoods, aspens, chamisas—fall is the season of yellow."

VJ yelled from the back, "And they're accompanied by the sacred aroma of roasting green chile."

A chiming of unanimous agreement rang through the car.

Clair looked from horizon to horizon, left to the south, north to the right. To see so far was dizzying.

"The only way to see this much expanse back east is on the ocean," Clair mentioned, with a healthy dose of awe.

"In fact," Jesse said, "all that you see was under an ocean during seven different epochs of planet earth. Seven! The planet is eight billion years old, but humans, who have been here so briefly, think they know everything."

This began a conversation among the four, with Clair mostly just listening, that glided easily from the history of the world to Schrodinger's cat, from astrology to aging parents to a daughter's wedding … and a couple of recent films. They also discussed the First Amendment, prisoners' rights, and reincarnation.

Clair added a comment from time to time, just enough to not be rude, but it was hard to join in, as they were like a well-oiled machine. Throughout the discussions and chattering, Clair studied Lucky. She was older, yes, but still her effervescent self. *Had it been maybe five or six years since they'd seen each other?*

Lucky had come back east to help her parents in their move to Florida. Clair had taken the opportunity to invite Lucky to come for dinner in her and Blake's large Tudor home in a suburb of Boston. Blake, being his charming self, drank too much and flirted with Clair's friend right in front of his wife. Lucky fended him off with style, of course, never indicating "what an asshole your husband is!" Then the women went out to dinner by themselves and Clair did something she hardly ever did: She let down her guard; let herself be honest, be vulnerable. She cried.

"We'll stop at a place down the road and have some lunch," Lucky announced. "Are you hungry, Clair?"

"Not too, I ate on the plane."

"Are you enjoying the views?"

"Views? It's so empty!"

"Most of it is private land. Belongs to the Native Americans or to BLM.

"Big Lonely Mermaid?" Clair joked, more relaxed now and remembering the cloud mermaid she'd seen.

"Ha-HA," Lucky intoned, looking at her knowingly. Clair had always spotted mermaids in the sky when they were children. "But, actually, out here in the west, it's the Bureau of Land Management."

At a place called Mesita, the palette of the landscape changed. Crumbling houses were sitting in the shadows of towering red rock cliffs and, in the distance, Clair spotted a small white church with a cross gleaming in the sunlight. At a pull-out with a sign broadcasting *"Scenic* View," were shacks displaying jewelry and rugs and, beyond that, a sign for *the Blue-Eyed Indian Bookshop.*

Ahead, the shape of the land changed again, softened, and betrayed darkly- sculpted openings worn into surrounding cliffs. Clair heard the camera click from the back seat. At Acoma Pueblo was a sign for a casino. The parking lot was full of cars, though wild horses roamed through it.

"Well, it looks like Ralph Lauren might have waved his magic western wand around here," Clair grinned, then asked, "What's 'kachina' mean?" She'd seen it on the casino sign.

"Spirits," answered Lucky, "messengers between the worlds. The men of the Hopi tribe in Arizona carve the roots of the cottonwood trees into figures embodying various spirits. In the past they were made as dolls for the children so they could learn the tribal stories. Now tourists have to wait sometimes years to be on a list to buy one. At a very hefty price, I might add. But, oh, they take your breath away, they're so energetically powerful."

Outside of Grants, she saw the first thing that looked familiar since she'd arrived: a billboard advertising "the golden arches." New Mexico wasn't the moon after all! They passed a white cross on the side of the road draped with faded plastic flowers.

Lucky turned off the main highway at a sign reading: "El Malpais," and indicated 117S to Quemado. For a few miles, Clair had been seeing some very black rocks on the side of the highway and now saw miles more of them covering the landscape.

"This is an ancient lava flow," Lucky told them. "'El Malpais' means bad country. All the native tribes have a legend about it. One is that hot black lava-blood flowed from the eyes of the blind Kachina, KauBat, because he was angry with his sons, and now the whole state is dotted with volcano cones. One north of Santa Fe is supposed to have blown debris as far west as the Pacific Ocean and as far east as Ohio."

On the left were very high cliffs. In front of one area that looked like a cathedral was a broken-down corral made from wood and tires. One loose boulder looked as big as an ocean liner. The cliffs were light in color, scarred and scored with deep grooves and trees that poked out here and there. Etched into the surface were shapes resembling figures and faces, perfectly carved profiles of grotesque-looking gargoyles with open mouths, spires that towered like giant phalluses along vulva-like caves.

Seeing one formation that looked like an eerily familiar face, Clair turned to Alex, "What did you mean when you said the 'Great Awakener?'"

Alex released her seatbelt and slid forward. "I was talking about the archetype of Uranus."

"I don't know what that means … archetype or Uranus, except that Uranus is a planet."

"Well, in astrology the planet Uranus is sometimes associated with Prometheus from Greek mythology, the Titan who rebelled against the gods and gave fire to humans. So, there's an association with lightning, of it being the creative spark, radical change, rebellion, risk, waking up … very cool things like that."

On the right was a hellish scene, miles of tar-black rock as far as Clair could see, fold-after-fold like pulled taffy. Some were fractured into smaller jagged pieces, some covered with a green-colored lichen. Throughout the landscape were dwarf trees scattered alongside spiky cactus of various sizes. They passed the Ranger Station, but not a single other car, so Clair was surprised when Lucky said they'd pull over soon for lunch.

What kind of restaurant would be out here in this godforsaken place?

In another mile or so, Lucky pulled off the road in an area marked "Public Wash."

CHAPTER 9

Clair put her hands on her hips, relieved to be out of the car, stretched backwards, then side to side to ease the tension in her back and shoulders. She had been up for twelve hours, seated for most of it. The air was hot but pleasantly so, with a savory fragrance.

"Sage," Lucky identified, when she saw Clair sniff.

Clair was beginning to feel better, settling in among Lucky's friends, who seemed genuinely welcoming.

Besides the fragrance of sage, Clair heard a humming coming from every direction like crickets but much louder.

"What's that?"

"Cicadas," VJ told her. "Aren't they incredible? We've had them in Santa Fe this year too.

"I think they have a seventeen-year cycle underground," Alex commented, "before emerging to lay eggs and die, their life purpose fulfilled."

Boston
1982

Cass is a year old, and Clair is in a serious depression. The joy of giving birth to a live baby after three miscarriages is soon overshadowed by the roller-coaster ride of a surgical menopause caused by the removal of both her ovaries, performed after Cassidy's birth.

The constant hormonal fluctuations are so debilitating that her doctor suggests she see a psychiatrist while they try to find the right combination of hormones and drugs to ease her symptoms: interrupted sleep, heart palpitations, chronic anxiety, and day and night sweats that leave her drenched and in despair. Clair calls it her descent into hell.

Family and friends whisper in hushed circles and wonder if she could die.

"Lunch will be ready soon," Lucky hollered, pulling a cooler from the back of the Suburban. "Take a break … look around, Clair. You don't see this in Maine."

"Actually," Clair answered, "When you said we were stopping for lunch, I thought we were going to a restaurant."

Lucky burst out laughing. "No restaurants around here, my naive friend."

Moving closer, Clair whispered, "Lucky, I have to go to the bathroom … and I really should call about my credit card."

Lucky nodded. "Do you have your flipper phone, Alex?" she asked.

"I don't think I brought it, Lucky, and besides there wouldn't be any service out here."

"Don't worry—you can make a call when we get to Quemado," Lucky told Clair reassuringly. "We'll be there in just about an hour. As far as peeing, no prob, find yourself a bush. Tissues are in the driver's door."

The thought of peeing outdoors didn't appeal to Clair in the least, and her mind continued to grumble as she stumbled over the rocky ground, holding up her pant legs and trying to find some privacy.

"Watch out for cactus," Lucky yelled, just as Clair spotted a spiky cluster at the toe of her canvas espadrilles. "And leave no trace … bury the tissue."

The toes of her shoes were dusted with the paprika color of the ground. Bending over, she tried to wipe them off, but the attempt just smeared the dust, making it worse. In her bent-over position, Clair noticed something climbing through the cactus needles. Leaning in, she spotted a tiny bug, golden and green, iridescent wings folded along the body. The insect was making its way through a forest of long silver needles crowned with delicate pink flowers like tiny cups. Each cup became a requisite stop for the bug, who sipped from each miniature chalice.

Mesmerized, Clair stared into a universe unto itself—cactus blooms, providing sustenance in the wilderness for a tiny traveler. Clair was struck with the fact that this would be going on whether she was witness to it or not. This small spiky cactus.

This outlandishly-attired bug. These tiny flowers, this world. She could have just as easily stayed back in Maine, never aware of the existence of all these microcosms. For a moment, she felt awe.

Walking further along the side of a cliff to assure some privacy, Clair looked up at the cliffs towering several hundred feet above her, blocking the sun and casting a cool shadow. She looked furtively around to make sure that Jesse and her camera weren't close by. Unbuckling her belt and sliding her pants down, she felt her legs being wobbly after so much sitting, so with the fingers of her broken arm, she grasped a slim branch for support. With her good arm, she tried to keep her pants out of the way of the pee splash. Then without warning, goosebumps raised on her arm and the back of her neck, causing her to shiver involuntarily. She felt like she was being watched, but didn't want to look where her eyes were drawn. Finally, turning her head slowly in that direction, hoping it would be Jesse, what she saw instead of a camera lens was a face etched in the rock cliff ten-feet high, deep eye sockets darkened by the high angle of the sun.

I'm watching you.

She wanted to run, but couldn't, fastened as she was to the ground by a stream that she couldn't stop. Suddenly, from the bushes, out popped the biggest rabbit Clair had ever seen. The long-haired thing was as surprised to see the peeing woman as Clair was to see it. Snap! sounded the thin branch supporting her balance, and over she tumbled onto her knees, letting out a yell as she caught herself with the good hand flat on the ground.

Alex spotted her first when Clair made it back to camp.

"Taken up mud wrestling, have you?"

Clair brushed herself off as if it might help. "I fell over," she confessed, shrugging her shoulders and managing a weak smile.

"Oh, honey!" sympathized VJ. "And, look, you've torn your shirt."

Sure enough, on her left shoulder, an inch-long jagged rip.

"You must've caught it on something when you fell."

"Hey, Lucky? Clair?" said Alex, working on the food prep. "Why don't you guys take a moment? You haven't had any time alone together. We'll get lunch ready and call you when it's on the table." And with that, she shooed them away.

Clair followed Lucky to a couple of side-by-side rocks, just right for sitting.

"Gotta hand it to you, Clair," Lucky cracked. "You're hardly here any time at all and already you look like you belong."

"I'm a mess," Clair said, defeatedly, as she surveyed her pant legs. "And I've probably embarrassed you in front of your friends."

"Are you fuckin' kidding me? It'd take a whole lot more to embarrass me in front of those crazy chicks. Don't think anything of it, but tell me, are *you* all right?" Lucky looked at her with a growing concern on her face. "Is it your bag?"

"No, it's not that … yes, I'm concerned, but … it's just …"

She wanted to blurt out the whole awful story of Blake and the divorce and these strange things that had been happening. She wanted to let it all out, all that wasn't right about her life ... but she couldn't find the words and was afraid that if she started to cry, she'd never stop. Mostly, she never wanted to cry in front of Lucky the Brave.

"It's nothing really, you know. I didn't sleep well and had to get up really early. I'm tired and, yes, worried about my bag, and not having my medication. I'm sorry, Lucky. I don't want to spoil your party."

"Stop!" Lucky held up her hand as if in traffic. "You've got nothing to be sorry for, so stop apologizing. Don't you know how happy I am that you came?"

The two old friends leaned in for a hug, bridging the distance between the rocks where each sat, and heard a camera click.

"Jess is such a stealth," Lucky laughed, in bemused tolerance of her friend's passion. "Consider yourself forewarned. But really, Clair, I know it's hard for you to be away from home. I'm the one who's sorry that I was so insensitive about your bag and medication. If you really need it or if you'll feel better having something other than what Alex has, we'll make some calls and find a pharmacy or something."

"I'm good … it's all okay," Clair assured her, hoping that was true. "But I have been dying to share one thing." She smiled and waited to see Lucky's face. "I'm gonna be a grandmother!"

"What? Whaaaat? My God, Clair, I can't believe it. Well, I hope you're talking about Carl, not Cassidy?"

"Yes, Carl and Jules"

And Blake and Prudence, she wanted to add.

"Oh, Clair, that's so great! When?"

"Around New Year's."

Both babies are due around New Year's. Two little diapered New Year babies.

"Come and get it!" VJ called out.

A blue-and-white checkered tablecloth draped the tailgate of Lucky's Suburban. On it were containers of portobello mushrooms, roasted red peppers, grilled chicken, sourdough bread, goat cheese, and oil-cured olives, alongside plastic plates, utensils, and spring water.

"Wow!" Clair exclaimed, stunned by the feast that had appeared and suddenly feeling ravenous.

They balanced plates on their laps, Clair mostly listening as the women talked about sacred spots and vortex energy centers—New Age ideas in which Clair didn't place too much trust. But she did *feel* something about this place, that if she had to name, would come close to the word *reverence.*

"When I first came here, I remember thinking," Alex told them, "that places have a feeling-sense to them, just like people. New Mexico, and maybe most of the Southwest, has this deep feeling of ancientness."

"It's a lot older than just the culture," Lucky added. "The dinosaurs roamed this land for 165 million years. Max and I have found their bones, and many other fossils … why, this area is where the first amphibians crawled out of the muck and evolved as mammals!"

Lucky jumped up all of a sudden. "Okay, ladies! We gotta get going. We have to meet someone at two."

They passed fewer than a half dozen cars during the next seventy-five miles, the distance to Quemado. The lava disappeared, and in its place were open pastures with windmills. "Those bring up water for the cattle," Lucky volunteered.

A couple of drivers gave a little finger wave without lifting their hands from the steering wheel. Lucky did the same. Clair didn't see any telephone wires, but there were miles and miles of fencing, along with dips and swells in the straight road. The yellow centerline became mesmerizing, and with her belly full and the others talking quietly in the back, Clair closed her eyes and must have dozed off, for suddenly, her body lurched forward with tremendous force, held back only by the seatbelt.

"Jesus!" yelled Lucky. "Is everyone alright?"

"What happened?" Clair asked, looking around.

"A deer," Lucky answered. "Came out of nowhere. Sorry to startle you awake."

The area now was more mountainous, the trees thicker and taller. They passed a school bus stop and telephone wires came back into view, as well as a few scattered rundown houses.

"Well, did you have a good rest until that rude awakening?"

"I'm surprised I fell asleep so fast."

"People are generally sleepier here. It's the altitude … not a lot of oxygen."

"Hey!" Jesse yelled from the back, "we're here!"

Quemado was just a short strip of storefronts a few blocks long. At the intersection where they turned right was the Sacred Heart Church, small and white, with a double arch and a cross on top. The sign showed there was one mass a week, Sundays at 9 a.m. In the parking lot sat a Christmas tree made out of deer antlers, a faded red- ribbon star on top, looking like it had been there for many years. Beyond the church, was a cemetery, and completing the scene was a bright blue Chevron gas station sign.

Lucky drove slowly down the main street and pulled in at an angle in front of a plain white concrete building.

"This might be it. I'm not sure, but it's one of these." She looked around.

"Oh, it can't be!" exclaimed Alex, sitting forward on her seat. "It looks abandoned."

The building was two stories with oddly-shaped windows placed in a random fashion. The plaster was falling off in big clumps, showing gray underneath the dingy white. Two doors flanked each other, but no sign indicated they were at the right place. Next door was a liquor store and, next to it, a bar and café, both of which looked closed.

"The reservation said a white building on the east edge of town," said Lucky. "This has to be it. I remember being confused when I came with Max."

"I could ask my pendulum," VJ volunteered.

Across the street was the chuckwagon restaurant with a full-size chuckwagon sitting on top of a flat roof, advertising steaks, burgers, and the world's largest salad bar.

"That looks closed too," said Jesse.

"Why don't we drive through town and just take a look?" asked Alex.

Lucky backed out and began the drive to the other end of the town, a journey of less than two blocks. There was a small grocery store, a convenience and hardware store, several abandoned buildings and a couple of rundown motels.

"It looks like a ghost town," Lucky commented. The others voiced their agreement.

Clair was feeling nervous. This was not anything like she thought it would be.

"This isn't where we're staying, is it?" she asked nervously.

"Oh, no," Lucky assured her. "Someone is supposed to meet us here and take us to the place."

For a moment, Clair was relieved

They returned to the building and got out of the car to a furnace blast of heat.

"My pendulum says this is the place." VJ was dangling her necklace watching it sway between her fingers.

"I really should try to call the credit card company," Clair said.

"Maybe there's a phone inside," Lucky suggested, trying one of the doors. It opened.

The others followed her into a space, cool and dark, like a cave.

It took a moment for Clair's eyes to adjust to the light but when they had, she saw they were in a small bare room with a desk and a cabinet of some kind, but no phone.

"Let's go find a phone, Clair," VJ offered. "There's bound to be one somewhere."

VJ pushed open the door to the saloon and the two women surprised a trio of men sitting at the bar, beer bottles in front of them, bartender leaning in. They were smoking cigarettes and the smoke curled above them like thought-forms. The four simultaneously turned when Clair and VJ entered.

"Buenos Días, señor," VJ said to the bartender. "Tiene algún teléfono que podamos usar? Por favor?"

"Si, señora," he replied, pulling a rotary phone from beneath the bar and placing it on top.

Clair wanted to wipe it off before touching it but refrained. She did hold it lightly in her fingers though and kept her mouth away from the receiver while she waited for an operator to get her an 800 number for American Express. "Raindrops Keep Fallin' on My Head" played in direct competition with some lively Spanish music on the bar radio. Out of the corner of her eye, she stared in fascination at the three black-haired men, their backs to her. All were dressed in dusty jeans, well-worn boots, faded printed shirts, and straw cowboy hats pushed back on their heads.

VJ had wandered closer to the men and began a conversation in Spanish. Soon they were all laughing like good friends.

Clair was eventually told by a computer voice that due to unusually busy circuits, she would have to call back later. Frustrated, she remembered an 800 number Blake had for out-of-town clients and dialed it. Waiting for the machine to pick up, she caught a glimpse of herself in the mirror over the bar. No wonder the men stared when she came in. She was a mess! Her hair was uncombed, shirt torn, pants and shoes spotted with red dirt. And she had dressed so carefully just hours ago!

The machine cued her to leave a message: "This is Clair McKendrick," she spoke clearly into the machine. "I'm in New Mexico. My American Express card has been lost and I can't reach the company. Someone there might want to handle this."

She hung up, satisfied.

On the short walk back to the white building, VJ, who had been witness to Clair's level of frustration, said, "Trouble getting through?"

"Years of it."

Without saying anything, VJ put an arm around Clair's shoulder and squeezed.

"VJ, what was it that you were doing with your necklace when we pulled up at the building?"

"It's my pendulum," VJ answered, holding it out from where it hung between pendulous breasts.

"You said it told you we were in the right place?"

"A pendulum is just a tool that attunes you to a deeper reality. It can help you connect to one's inner guidance. I ask it questions."

"Like directions?"

"Yeah, like that," VJ smiled, with a dawning awareness that this was not in Clair's wheelhouse. "Everything from asking if we were at the right place … to the direction of my life."

Clair was gazing at the full-size chuckwagon sitting on the building across the street.

"And you trust it?" she asked.

"Well, you know, it's just a way to talk to my inner guides and I do trust them. But that's a relationship that has grown through many years."

"Success!" VJ announced as she and Clair re-entered the building.

"This is definitely the place, we're just a little early," Lucky said. She and Alex were sitting on top of the desk, Jesse nowhere in sight.

"There're forms here we have to fill out before going out to the Field." She held out a clipboard she'd picked up off the desk.

Clair took it from her next and began to look through the pages. Visitors were thanked for coming to Walter De Maria's the Lightning Field but, as she read, phrases like, "for insurance purposes," and, "for your own safety," and, "the presence of wild animals," began popping up. This did *not* sound good. The one happy note was that photography was not permitted.

I wonder what Jesse will think of that?"

Jesse reminded Clair of Cassidy with her small but muscular body. Clair had noticed that Jesse also had two visible tattoos, one on the back of her neck, and a second around her left ankle. She thought about her daughter briefly, where she was, how she was, before returning to the paper in hand and what wild animals might be native to the area. In that moment she heard a car pull up, a door slam, and a clinking sound as the door to the room swung open showing a backlit shadow in a cowboy hat filling the frame of the doorway.

"Howdy, ladies," the shadow spoke. "I'm Clete. I'll be driving you out to your quarters."

The beat-up Chevy Suburban was similar to Lucky's model, only older and splattered with red mud just like Clair's pants and shoes. She was beginning to understand that despite the heat, white was not a good choice of color for New Mexico. After loading the coolers and canvas bags of food, luggage, and even a bag of knitting with the needles sticking out—which Clair wondered about—Jesse boldly put her camera bag right on top. The other three climbed in the back while Jesse held the passenger door and said, "Clair, you'll see more up front."

"What's the other guy look like?" Clete asked with a grin, when Clair slid across the bench seat toward him. It took her a moment to realize he was inquiring about her arm.

"I had a fall," she said, not meeting his eyes.

"I broke mine last year," he continued, stretching out his right arm, opening and closing his fingers. "Took its time healing … probably because I've broke it two other times. Hazards of cow-poking."

He had an easy laugh, so Clair smiled ruefully and nodded.

"I'm due to get my cast off next week. I hope it's healed properly."

Clete removed his sweat-stained hat, revealing disheveled auburn hair plastered to his head. "Yeah, those docs know what they're doing. You'll be just fine."

The tone of his voice was soothing, oddly reassuring, so she believed him.

Clete placed his hat on the dashboard, then swung the car out of town with a smooth twist of the steering wheel. After a few miles, he took a right without warning onto an unmarked dirt road, dust flying.

"Too much breeze?" he asked his passengers, as he picked up speed.

"We're good!" was the consensus.

The other women were talking and laughing, speaking loudly in order to be heard. Clair had half turned in the seat so she could join them, but finally gave up and focused her attention on the backs of Clete's wide hands on the steering wheel. The veins were visible underneath very tanned skin. His fingers gripped the wheel as the car bounced and slid over the dirt road. Two of the knuckles of his right hand were skinned and had bled recently.

"So how long have you been the caretaker of the Field, Clete?" It was Alex leaning over the seat.

"Bout as long as it's been there," he turned to face Alex, and Clair almost grabbed the wheel. *Not again! Please! Eyes on the road!* Clair thought. "Began building in the late '70s."

"You live nearby then?" Alex continued questioning.

"Yep, got a ranch close by, me and my gal. We raise Arabian horses and rescue wild Mustangs."

"My partner and I have a couple of horses," said Lucky, joining in the conversation.

"They're fine animals. Been around 'em all my life," Clete nodded. "Ladies, out there are the Sawtooth Mountains."

"The what?" Clair asked.

"The Sawtooth," he repeated, "those are the Sawtooth Mountains."

She looked past the square angle of his face at an empty landscape ringed in the distance by a ridge of mountains.

"They're beautiful," she responded, captured more by his face than the mountains. She felt this surprising need to draw him.

"What does the town name "Quemado" mean?" she asked.

"Burning, hot, fire, somethin' along those lines."

He careened the truck over the mud road, never slowing for holes or curves.

"Been some rain," he observed.

"Does that mean lightning?"

"Maybe."

But Clair was hopeful since there wasn't a cloud in the sky. The color was a cerulean blue, the color you would paint the sky in your imagination, and entirely even from horizon to horizon in one long, sweeping saturated brushstroke, not a deviation or a break anywhere. A perfect blue sky.

They bumped along for another thirty minutes through a countryside that seemed to stretch as they entered it. Suddenly, Clete applied the brakes and the car came to a complete stop, throwing people forward abruptly and bringing all the chatter in the car to a halt.

"Coyote," Clete said, pointing to the right.

Twenty feet in front of them, a thin, shaggy animal, looking like a sad gray dog was crossing the road.

"The Trickster," Alex said, quietly.

"Are they dangerous …" Clair started to ask before being interrupted by Lucky.

"Clete, are those the poles I'm seeing way in the distance?"

"That's them. Good spottin'."

At first, Clair couldn't see what they were talking about, then noticed a consistent line of what looked like thin scratches of white in the emulsion of a photo negative.

"The poles!" the others cried out.

"And there's the cabin," said Clete, nodding in the same direction.

Clair saw a small brown building in the distance, looking like a matchbox in the land surrounding it.

Oh, my God! What have I done?

CHAPTER 10

The log cabin was crudely built, with a pitched and shingled roof, slightly collapsed in shape and looking like the victim of an ill wind that had caused it to land hard in the middle of nowhere. Along the roofline, two red chimneys stood alongside a line of lightning rods—a miniature version of the hundreds of them in the Field.

Clair felt uneasy, knowing the group was about to be left here, but made an effort to smile and join the others in their enthusiasm.

Getting out of the car, she noticed the three-foot-wide wooden deck that wrapped around the perimeter of the house and a pile of stacked firewood next to the door.

Doubtful we'll be needing that in this heat.

Then, turning in a circle to take in the expanse, she felt shocked to see nothing that resembled civilization in any direction, which made her feel as disoriented as if she were on a merry-go-round. Nothing was recognizable.

"Charming, eh?" quipped Lucky, wearing a big smile.

Not the first word Clair would have chosen to describe the scene. She was thinking of something more like "appalling" but, if pressed, she would have to agree that there *was* something oddly magical that she was beginning to notice. And perhaps even feel?

Clete opened the back of the car, reversing the task of less than an hour ago, pulling out coolers and canvas bags along with luggage of various sizes, and handing them on to the others as if they were passing water buckets to put out a fire.

"I do have to warn you about one thing," he said, slamming the tailgate. "There's a snake that's been seen by a couple o' folks."

Clair, holding a drum that Clete had passed to her, froze. *Snake?*

"So be on the lookout."

"Is it dangerous? Will it come in the house?" she asked warily.

She had only seen an occasional garden-variety snake, but even those were enough to startle her. A chicken instinctively knows the danger of a chicken hawk.

"Nah, snakes generally stay away from people … but …" he hesitated, picking up the cooler, "it's a rattler, Clair, so you wouldn't want to git yourself bit."

"What should we do if we see it?" She was surprised he knew her name.

"Chances are you won't."

"Like what? Fifty-fifty? Seventy-thirty?"

He laughed, but then realizing her genuine concern, he put down the cooler and looked at her. "Look, there are plenty of mice and rabbits, so it stays well-fed, but if you see it anywhere, just call me on the radio and I'll come kill it."

"Radio?" Her voice had raised an octave. "There's no phone?"

"It's a shortwave. I'm going to show you how to use it. Just be careful where you walk."

Clair stepped up onto the deck quickly, deciding not to leave the cabin until he came back to get them. She followed him and the others into the kitchen and was instantly greeted by a buzzing sound.

"Sorry about the flies," Cleat said, managing not to sound particularly apologetic.

An electric stove was beneath the window to the right and beyond it, facing her, was a sink beneath more windows. Both were alive with flies, hundreds, buzzing and banging against the screen. Clair's flesh crawled.

"Been an infestation this year. Wet spring," he explained. "I can bring you some spray, but to my mind the spray's worse than the flies." He offered up a red plastic flyswatter. "But this works."

"We'll survive," Lucky assured him, joining them in the kitchen.

There was a roll of paper towels hanging under the window and next to it a bottle of liquid soap. A glass pitcher of tea was on the counter, wrapped in plastic and glowing amber in the sunlight. Everything else was the same wood as the outside of the cabin, the floor, the ceiling, the crude cabinets, and a small table on the left. On the table was a bowl of fruit: green apples, oranges, some grapes, all covered tightly with plastic wrap, which relieved Clair, what with the flies.

Clete opened a couple of the cabinets, showing them where the dishes were kept. Then lifted up one of the counters. "The secret cabinet," he announced. It was loaded with cereals and jams, whole wheat bread, coca, sugar, various kinds of tea, and boxes of cookies and crackers.

"'Course the eggs, bacon, coffee, casseroles, and salad fixings are all in the refrigerator."

"What kind of casseroles?" VJ asked.

"Lasagna and chicken enchiladas."

"You make those, too, when you're not rounding up wild mustangs?"

He laughed out loud, revealing deep smile grooves on each side of his mouth that made long cracks in his cheeks. He winked at VJ. "Yeah, didn't tell you, but I'm also a chef."

In the freezer were several candy bars—Baby Ruths and Snickers. "In case you get a hankerin'," he smiled.

Still standing in the kitchen doorway, Clair looked through a large room and out another door to the outside where the others were now headed.

"C'mon out, Clair," Lucky yelled. "Ya gotta see this!"

"I'm coming … Clete's just going to show me how to use the radio."

She followed behind him, noticing the way his shoulders strained against the cloth of his printed shirt. His body was dense. She had seen his belt buckle earlier, big and brass, announcing him a champion bull rider and imagined him with long legs gripped tightly around a bucking animal, hat in the air, mouth yahooing, like it was nothing at all to hang on.

"So, you're not from around here," he said, not really asking a question, more stating a fact.

"No, Lucky is. Well, from Santa Fe. I'm from Maine."

"Never been. But I was in New York one time. Oooo-weee! Wouldn't want to live there. Way too hectic."

"Where are you from?"

"Pie Town born and raised … down the road a piece."

He turned down a small hallway, Clair following. It was hot and stuffy in these close quarters, but at least there were no flies.

"So, here's the shortwave." He pointed to a table in the corner with what looked like a portable radio on it. "It's real simple … see that button there?"

She leaned in. "Yes."

"Just press it and holler. I'll come a-runnin'."

She grinned. "Okay. I'll count on that."

"What are you two doing?" It was Lucky, with Jesse and Alex trailing behind.

"Clair here was interested in a crash course in shortwave. I told her a snake's been seen, so keep an eye out. If you do see one, this here is how to get me. Pronto."

The main room included a large table, six chairs, a wood stove, and three uncomfortable-looking rocking chairs.

"You'll find your way to the bedrooms and baths, pretty self-explanatory," Clete said, "but let's head outside for now, and I can answer any questions you might have."

"Who's this young lady?" VJ asked, picking up a mangy cat, a mottled golden color, very dusty, with eyes that matched the shade of her fur, and tall ears.

"She's whoever you say she is," he declared. "She was brought out to mouse this season … does a fine job, too, so she's well regarded, but no one as far as I know has given her a name."

"That's terrible!" VJ proclaimed, then addressed the cat who was now cuddled on her ample bosom. "We'll find you a name, girl, don't you worry. Is she fed and watered by anyone?"

"Yes, ma'am, every day. There's cat food in that secret cupboard, but mostly she catches her own dinner. She's a pretty independent gal."

"We'll christen her in the meantime," said VJ. Lucky reached out to scratch the kitty's ears.

"Any questions about the field before I leave you to it?" Clete asked. "You probably know the statistics of the place from the brochure … four hundred stainless steel poles in a grid pattern "a mile times a kilometer." You're welcome to move around and through the whole field, if you like. It's especially pretty at sunrise and sunset, so be sure to notice."

With that, he hit his cap on the side of his leg, causing a tiny dust storm.

"I'll see you ladies in a couple of days."

And he was gone, just like that. Leaving them alone.

In the middle of nowhere.

Walking back to the kitchen, Clair saw Clete's dust trail disappearing down the road. She pictured Blake the last time she had seen him, driving away in his silver sedan after Cassidy's graduation.

How foolish Blake would look here, she couldn't help thinking, *with his sweater draped over his shoulders like some aging preppy.*

"Okay, ladies, let's get settled," Lucky proclaimed, "then reconvene on the portal." Lucky pronounced it "por-TALL."

"What do you mean by 'portal?'" Clair questioned.

"Oh, sorry, Clair … 'portal' means a covered porch in New Mexico. Let's meet there when everyone is settled in."

"Lucky, you take the single room in the front," offered Alex. "You're the birthday girl."

"That would be great … that's the room Max and I stayed in years ago."

"And Clair," Alex added, "how about you and I bunk together?"

"That'll work," confirmed VJ. "Jesse and I will take the other."

While Alex was in the bathroom, Clair, having nothing to unpack, decided to clear the room of some of the flies. When she entered the bedroom, she saw the bag of knitting sitting on the chair next to Alex's overnight case. So, Alex was the knitter! It pleased Clair to have something in common with her. The loud buzzing from the flies reminded her of her mission, and she grabbed a flyswatter conveniently hanging on a nail and headed for one of the windows, soon quite engulfed in a disgusting cloud of dust and dead flies. Suddenly, her vision was drawn outward beyond the flies, beyond the screen, to the Lightning Field itself. *Was that a large, tan-colored animal out there?* But as she tried to focus further, the poles grabbed her attention.

Were they rearranged?

Before she could rectify that unlikely possibility, movement in her peripheral vision changed her focus again, and she swatted out, reflexively, missing. It was a fly, but it had flown into and was trapped by a saucer-shaped web. Clair stopped her backstroke with the swatter and listened. The fly protested with loud intermittent buzzing. Within seconds, a large golden spider parachuted from someplace above, swooping silently down on the ill-fated insect.

Startled, Clair stepped backwards, but curiosity drew her in. Watching in fascination, she saw the spider begin to spin the fly into a tight cocoon. Moving in even closer and wishing she had her glasses, Clair watched morbidly, wondering what it might feel like to be bound in such a way.

The spider had a fat body like a plumped-up pillow. The hairy legs were striped with brown, its back revealing dimpled markings resembling a cat's face. The web itself was a beautiful orb, about the size of a frisbee, fastened to the window frame by threads as fine as baby hair. Holding its dinner with its front mandibles, the spider finished wrapping the still-buzzing fly, then bit into the doomed passenger until it was deathly quiet. Carrying the package like a sack of groceries, the victor swiftly climbed the web to hide out in a small crack in the wood frame, as the poles appeared to rearrange themselves again.

⚡

"I read that the technological world is being shaped primarily by men," Lucky was heard to say as Clair approached the kitchen where the others were now gathered. "The number of women in that field has actually dropped in the last ten years."

There have to be ways to engage young women," VJ exclaimed, "It's crucial."

"Yes," Alex agreed, "Otherwise, once again, only men will shape the new technology."

"And the world," VJ added sardonically.

Clair stopped at the kitchen door, unsure how to join in. She knew virtually nothing about the tech industry. *Why, I can barely use my answering machine!*

As they were talking, Lucky and VJ were emptying one of the two coolers and the large canvas bag. Out of them came a sundry of things like rabbits from a hat: wine and beer, sparkling water, champagne, candles, French bread, cheeses, and even flowers!

"Wow!" Clair reacted.

"Lucky didn't want us to starve," said VJ, grinning.

"They provide meals, but not party food," Lucky assured the group.

1963

"Come on, Clair!" Lucky shouted from the road. "Get your bike. Hurry up! I've got lunch for both of us!"

Clair knows it will be different fare than the eternal peanut butter and jelly sandwiches her mother makes. Mrs. Miller always surprised the girls with something unusual, like ham and Swiss cheese with dark bread and grainy mustard. She'd add fat sour pickles in a separate plastic bag so that the pickle juice wouldn't wet the bread, and potato chips in another bag to keep them crisp.

Eating was way more fun when Lucky's mom made their lunch.

"So, what's all this in the second cooler?" Lucky questioned.

"Well, we couldn't have a birthday party without cake and champagne," sparkled VJ.

"Awww, you guys!" Lucky blew kisses to them into the air.

"Heads up, Lucky!" VJ shouted, as she began tossing lemons and limes to her. "Put them in the fruit bowl, will you, Birthday Girl?"

VJ tossed the fruit to Lucky so quickly, Lucky couldn't help but drop a few. "Hey! Hey!" Lucky protested, laughing with all of them. Clair stooped to pick up a lemon that had rolled towards her feet when, all of a sudden, the cat jumped out of one of the paper bags, making her yelp, which caused more laughter.

"We've got to name that cat!" VJ declared. "Let's think of something good."

"Hey, where's Jess?" someone asked.

"She'll join us in a few," answered VJ. "She said she was going to meditate."

Clair crossed the room and began looking in the cupboards for some kind of vase for the flowers. VJ was at the small table arranging some green apple slices alongside crackers and grapes around a mound of blue cheese on a blue tin plate. Clair watched enviously as the three ladies moved around each other with familiar rhythms, like sisters at Thanksgiving, talking and laughing, knowing just what to do. She felt like she was in the way, although she was pleased she had found a tall glass that would work for the flowers.

"What can I do?" Clair asked.

"How about you take the beer and opener out to the porch," suggested VJ. "We'll join you in just a minute."

Happy to have a task, Clair grabbed the beer and opener and went through to the rickety porch, putting the beer down on the bench that was positioned against the wall of the cabin. She stood up and looked around at where she was, peering out at the Field and noticing that strange feeling she had whenever she looked at it.

You're going to a strange land.

She felt a shiver remembering that afternoon at Grace's. How could Grace see so much from a cup of tea leaves? *This* was a strange land, as strange as any she'd seen. Strange and beautiful. And hot, as Grace had predicted.

The field looked different again. She could see that the rearranging she thought she saw in the poles came from their polished surfaces. Some now seemed invisible, reflecting what was around them like a mirror and masking their own existence. Grace had also seen lionesses in the tea cup, and though Clair had seen a deer and a coyote around, she was certain there were no lions.

Her lips felt dry, and she licked them, but the moisture didn't last more than a second. Feeling her mouth dry as well, she picked up one of the beers, opened it, and took a sip from the longneck bottle. She couldn't remember the last time she'd had a beer, but this one tasted icy cold with a hint of lime.

"I like beer," she proclaimed out loud, surprised.

When she returned the bottle to the bench, Clair was jolted again by the sudden materialization of the little cat. The cat was a bit like the poles, appearing and disappearing without notice. At this moment, Kitty was sitting upright, a posture of calmness, and exuding an elegance that was more disarming than her out-of-the-blue appearances. Staring intently at Clair with golden eyes, the cat's pupils displayed fine vertical black lines in the light of the day.

I bet she's covered in fleas, Clair thought, wanting to reach out, but hesitant.

"Anyway," Clair said, as the cat climbed into her lap unbidden, making Clair's decision for her, "you'd hardly qualify as a lioness."

With her inner architect engaged, Clair studied the lines of the porch. Eight feet wide by twelve feet or so, the boards nailed width-wise were shiny with age. The roof was supported by three weathered gray posts and covered the deck, which had a single step all around, under which rocks had been jammed at random. The porch faced south, but on the west side, there was an extension of a narrower deck that began on the other side of the cabin.

Must be newer, she gauged. Probably added recently.

The cabin did have a certain "charm," as Lucky had said—in a rustic Ralph Lauren sort of way. *The others would be out soon,* she thought, deciding to bring out a couple of additional chairs from the house.

"Sorry to disturb your slumber, Kitty, but I'll be right back."

In the dining room she noticed several decks of Tarot cards on the table along with some books.

"I put those out," Alex said, coming in from the kitchen. "Thought we might try them later."

Alex was a curiosity to Clair. She seemed so wise and rational, and then put out fortune-telling cards! *She and Grace should meet,* Clair thought, but instead changed the subject. "I saw your knitting bag in the bedroom, Alex. Maybe later you could show me what you're doing? I'm a knitter too. In fact, I had some with me, but it was in my bag, of course."

"Oh, I'd love to show you. Lucky told me you're an expert knitter. I'm not very good at it; in fact, it's a mess right now."

"I'd be happy to help."

"Great, but first I'll help you get the chairs outside."

As they were placing the chairs on the porch, the screen door kicked open behind them, and Lucky emerged carrying the tray of apples and cheeses, along with a sundry of other treats, and with VJ behind her.

"Beautiful, eh?" Lucky nodded, looking around.

"The poles look different, don't they?" observed Alex, looking outward toward the field, hands on her hips.

"I thought so too," answered Clair. "Must be the reflective surfaces."

"One of the artist's intentions, I imagine," Lucky agreed, placing the tray of food on the floor.

Clair was squeamish about both the cat going after it and possible germs from the floor and dearly wanted to pick the tray up and place it on the stool … but didn't.

"Maybe you could talk more about that, Clair," Lucky said, then to the others added, "Clair's an amazing artist."

Clair was delighted to hear her friend's description of her but felt immediately intimidated since she hadn't created anything in a very long time.

"Well," she said, not wanting to disappoint Lucky, "I've never envisioned a land sculpture, but first the artist would have searched for the perfect site for his vision. In this case, it's a place where lightning strikes are plentiful and dazzling, and no one can be harmed."

She looked around at where they were, absorbing the landscape in all directions. "But every choice would be in service of 'The Vision'—the reflective material of the poles themselves, the changes in the time of day, the quality of light, the weather. It wouldn't just be when or if lightning strikes."

"And don't forget the isolation factor," Alex offered. "Bringing people way out here."

"To give them an experience of *'Be Here Now,'*" Jesse added, coming around the corner of the house. "An opportunity to reduce all the daily distractions and just be present."

"Yes," Clair agreed. "The artist brings us here, and in doing so, forces you to slow down. Even gives you a focal point."

"It's like a meditation," Jesse agreed, nodding her head and directing her gaze to the poles.

"So, the poles are arranged in a grid shape," Lucky said, "of one mile times one kilometer, four hundred of them, twenty-to-twenty-two feet high, depending on the topography of the land." Then she added, "And they're honed to a point on the top."

"Like a giant bed of nails," VJ suggested.

"When I came here the first time," Lucky confessed, "the poles were kind of scary to me."

"You? You were scared?" Clair exclaimed.

"In what way?" asked Alex.

"They seemed threatening. You know—like soldiers marching, advancing."

"Masculine energy puts up big poles and launches missiles and rockets," said Alex, catching on.

"And the feminine?" asked Clair.

Alex looked thoughtful. "'The feminine receives, connects … and it's the place from where we emerge … caves, tunnels, grottos … uteruses. Do you feel different visiting this time, Lucky?" Alex questioned.

"I do," Lucky responded, nodding her head. "Now it's as if the poles have taken on a godly presence. Here they are—unchanged. The world is different, my life has gone on, the sky is swirling above, and yet here they are, the same. I see them now as something to count on … to return to … something consistent and stable."

"Like those statues on Easter Island," proposed Jesse. "Someday we'll all be gone and these will still be here."

"Well, that's a cheerful thought," VJ laughed, lighting up a rolled joint. "What do you think, Clair?" she asked. "We're used to this desolate landscape, but it must be quite a culture shock for you."

Clair was shocked, but it was more that VJ was smoking marijuana than the landscape of New Mexico. She recognized the smell from her daughter's clothes.

"It is certainly wide open," she answered evasively, remembering a volatile encounter with Cass the previous year after finding a tin of marijuana in Cass's closet.

Maybe you should try it, Mom, it might help you to loosen up. Expand your mind.

Looking to clear her thoughts, Clair sidestepped again. "I met this man on the airplane today," she said, "who told me about this place called Roswell. He said there had been a coverup in the 1940s, where an alien spaceship had crashed."

Holding her breath, VJ gestured toward the others with the joint, which Lucky reached for, saying, "It's interesting when you think it wasn't more than a few miles from where the first nuclear explosion was detonated a few years before. If I was an alien, I'd come to find out what all the noise was about."

"Zeus hurling lightning bolts in the form of the atomic bomb," Alex declared.

"So, Clair!" It was VJ. "We know some of Lucky's history from her own unique perspective," and at this, she smiled at Lucky, "but tell us your side of the story."

Hey, kid, wanna see something cool?

"Well, we met on the beach," Clair answered, remembering. "I was about seven or eight; Lucky, two years older. She showed me a dead shark."

"I did?" asked Lucky, surprised. "I don't remember that at all."

"*I'll* never forget it. You wanted a tissue, because you had snot running down your lips, your phrase, not mine," Clair laughed. "And then you asked if I wanted to see something cool. You took me to the beached shark and poked at the poor dead thing with a stick. It was disgusting."

"I was a sick child. I apologize."

"Assuredly, you were curious."

The sun came out from behind a cloud, and Lucky pulled the brim of her hat forward to shield her eyes.

"She looks just the same," said Clair, like she could hardly believe it, "only bigger, and she always had that great hair."

Lucky, eyes squinting in the setting sun, smiled warmly at her old friend, as she ran circled fingers down the length of her braid.

"Mine was naturally curly and out of control," Clair continued. "frizzing and tangling; I was so jealous! Lucky's locks became my barometer of what hair should look like, thick and straight."

"Yours is straight now," observed Alex.

"And mine's not so thick," added Lucky, pulling at some strands that had escaped her braid.

"Mine's straight now 'cause I blow it dry," Clair added. "Oh yeah, and my brush and dryer were in my suitcase. Can I borrow someone's?"

"You can grab anything you need from my suitcase, roomie," volunteered Alex, adding, "Hair is kind of our first persona, isn't it?"

"And our first agony," grinned Jesse, "I'm with Clair. I never thought mine was right. I was always chopping at it." She laughed. "Still am." She scrunched her pixie cut with both hands, giving her head a shake.

"I love your haircut," Clair remarked. "I wish I could wear mine that short."

"You can," answered Jesse. "All you need is scissors!"

"Besides wanting to choose our own clothes," said Alex, continuing. "it's our hair that begins to separate us out as young girls: how we wear it, whether it's straight or curly, long or short. It's a big deal in our young personas."

"I must admit," said VJ, "I always had a lot of vanity about my hair. I got a lot of attention because of the red color, and I'm a smidge sad as I watch the luster fade and gray strands appear." She mock-cried.

Clair thought of all the arguments she had with Cass over Cass' hair, especially after she became a teenager.

That girl! Sometimes she'd come down to breakfast at two in the afternoon, and it was blue or purple or bright red. Once she even shaved it completely off. The child was just born to shock.

"I was probably wrong ... trying to control my daughter Cass," Clair confessed. "I tried to shape her into how I saw her or wanted her other than how she is. She's not me," she admitted. "And yet she is going to art school in the fall. So maybe a little like me."

"Oh, Clair, that's great!" enthused Lucky. "You hadn't told me." Congratulations! Museum school, I bet. And she'll be lucky if she inherits any of your talent."

"Getting back to your story about Lucky, Clair," encouraged VJ, as she offered Clair the joint, "tell us more."

Not since college had Clair been confronted by that offer, and she stared at the acrid-smelling object presented to her, confused as to what to do. She didn't want to offend Lucky's friend, and she didn't want to embarrass herself by exposing her inexperience.

"Maybe later," Clair refused, holding up her hand, and then returned to VJ's question about Lucky. "Well, we went to different schools. Lucky was at a nonreligious private school while I was at the Catholic one. But there was something between us right from the start ... a connection ... I suppose."

"Yeah," Lucky agreed. "After that meeting on the beach, we were together most of the time. It was the height difference that was the strangest. I was tall for my age, while Clair was this tiny person, filled with this outrageous talent. She amazed me with her natural gift in drawing and painting. What she did was so professional-looking! And she was just this little squirt. I admit it, Clair—I was jealous of your talent."

"Why, thank you, Lucky." Clair put a hand to her heart, genuinely touched. "Well, ladies, you won't be shocked to hear that Lucky was definitely the wilder of the two, pushing me to do things I was afraid of, which were plentiful. And she loved all animals: horses, dogs, cats, even squirrels. I couldn't have pets because my mother was allergic to everything, so I had my first relationships with animals because of Lucky."

Remembering those times, those years, that first connected them, the two women smiled deeply at each other, their faces radiant. They both leaned in for a big hug, with a sprinkling of tears. After a moment, the others joined in.

"AWWWWWW, this is beautiful!" Alex said, as Jesse snapped a picture.

"And I adored her family," Clair sniffled. "Especially Lucky's mom. She was the best. Anytime they could include me, they did, for dinners, even vacations. Her mother was such a character, too, hysterically funny, and more of a mother to me than my own. Really, she was great! And Lucky's dad too. I can safely say that I spent more time at their house than my own."

"What was your family like?" asked Alex, with concern on her face.

Clair sighed. "Literally dark. My mother kept the blinds drawn during the day."

"I remember that," Lucky chimed in. "It was always like night."

"It was because of her headaches; the light hurt her eyes. I know now she was also in a severe depression, but I didn't know what was wrong as a child. I only knew that at Lucky's house her mother was always cracking jokes and talking to us."

"Do you know what your mother was depressed about?"

"She lost a lot of babies, for one. So, postpartum depression for sure. And then when I was eleven, my brother drowned. She never recovered from that loss. But the odd thing was that I followed right in her footsteps, losing babies and battling my own depressions."

"Then, by high school, we didn't see much of each other," Lucky admitted. "I went away to boarding school, you see, and once we got to college, we hardly saw each other at all. Clair called me when she was getting married, and she came to my wedding, but it was only after Jim was killed that I went back home and we became close again. It was Clair who encouraged me to write down the stories I was telling the boys."

"My son loved her stories about horses and adventures. It wasn't such a big deal. All I said was to write them down."

"It *was* a big deal. Writing at the time gave me some purpose, a way out of my grief. I was grateful. I kept asking Clair to come out and visit when I moved to New Mexico, but she never would."

"Things kept coming up."

"Yeah, I know."

You don't know the half of it.

The women were sitting on and off the portal, the food mostly eaten, pushed to one side, their feet arranged in a circle. VJ's legs were straight out in front of her, ankles crossed, the nameless cat purring in her lap and kneading VJ's belly contentedly. But when VJ kicked off her sneakers and her feet were visible, Clair did a double-take.

"Your feet!" she exclaimed, "They're so ... *what was the word?* ... decorative!"

Across VJ's toes and continuing along the instep to the heels were graceful swirls forming a complex lace pattern.

"Thanks," VJ said, pleased. "It's called Mehndi, a henna tattoo. It can last about three weeks before it fades away. I first learned about it from my daughter when she came back from India. I've been playing around with it for years. Glad you like it."

"You do this yourself?" Clair moved closer in for a better look at VJ's feet.

"Yup! I have my kit with me too. I had thought the birthday girl might want a special design for her fiftieth, but I can do you too."

"Oh, yes, please. I would love it!"

I would? she thought, surprising herself again. *I didn't know that ... but it seems that I would!*

Suddenly Clair realized that she could hardly *wait* to be tattooed in henna.

⚡

If the five women could be seen from a higher perspective, say from a bird's eye view ... like from the perspective of an eagle, a *golden* eagle, resting high on some warm thermal air ... if a bird like that happened to look down while slowly circling in wide arcs, its view of these women would be a continuing shifting and changing of their positions; a leaning in and a leaning out, a sway, a rhythm, like a choreographed dance, which of course it was on some cellular level.

The women were aware of this subconsciously in the way that any group in sync dances and sways, just as in the way that a group of women living together will eventually menstruate in rhythm. But they remained unaware of the exquisite beauty of their dance as reflected in the eye of a soaring eagle.

CHAPTER 11

The sun dropped lower in the sky, lighting the edge of the mountains like a piece of lace trim, hastily sewn. Earlier, the Lightning Field was almost too bright to look at, but now in the dimming light, the colors softened. The poles had rearranged themselves again, this time with each one lit up, all four hundred shining tall and straight, from the ones in front to the slivers at the farthest edges. Clair tried to count them, a diversion from a conversation the others were having about a topic with which she was unfamiliar—but the polls became mirages in the heat waves, so she kept losing track and had to begin again. She could hardly look at them, though, without a strange buzzy feeling engulfing her.

"Earth to Clair!" she heard Lucky say.

"Oh, sorry, what?"

"I asked, 'Do you need a refresher?'"

"Oh, thank you, no, I'm good. I just need to use the bathroom."

On the way Clair noticed the dining table was filling up with various art materials—watercolor paper and paints, a sketchbook, pencils and charcoal sticks—and several decks of cards adorned with picturesque illustrations. Alex must have put the cards there, as she had mentioned she would.

Clair liked Alex, her warmth and refinement, her soft, Southern gentility, and also some quality she couldn't quite define that reminded her of Clair's new friend Grace. One of the decks, *Animal Medicine Cards,* a pretty shade of blue with a yellow lightning bolt on it, caught her attention. On impulse, she picked up half the stack and turned it over. Staring back at her from a circular shape in the middle of the card was a rabbit with brown eyes, white whiskers, and long ears.

Hey, you! Clair laughed to herself. *You were in the bushes where I peed.*

From the bottom of the circle hung several totems: a feather, a lock of hair, a bone, and what looked like a piece of coral. Underneath the deck was a book. Clair opened it and thumbed through to the number "30," the card of the rabbit. It read: "Scared little rabbit, please drop your fright. Running doesn't stop the pain or turn the dark to light."

She read that Rabbit people are afraid of tragedy, illness, disaster and, well, of just about everything it seemed. And in their fear, they call to themselves the very fears that teach the lessons they want to avoid. The takeaway was: *"What you resist, will persist. Stop worrying."*

Well, she had really pulled the rabbit out of the hat, hadn't she? Because she knew that what the card said was true. She had battled fear all her life and had felt ashamed from the deepest part of her being, hating her fearfulness, and herself for being embodied by it. She longed for the kind of courage Lucky had demonstrated throughout the years.

In the bathroom, she turned on the light above the sink and looked at herself in the mirror. Her face was a little flushed from the beer and her hair was a mess. *Needs a good brushing,* her mother might have told her. The flies were quieter now that the heat of the sun had gone from the window.

She looked down at the tear on the left shoulder of her shirt and sighed. *Oh, well! Guess they're new gardening clothes. Maybe it will finally be warm enough in June so that I can plant.* She wondered what gardening would be like in these harsh dry conditions but couldn't imagine it. *How do people live here?*

The others had said she could use their things, so seeing a brush in one of the cosmetic cases, she picked it up and cleaned it, tossing the blonde hair into a wicker basket under the sink. As she brushed through her brown hair, she thought of Clete, feeling admittedly intrigued by this bull-riding cowboy. Not many of those in Boston.

There was a knock on the door.

"I need to get some soap when you're finished in there. No rush," came VJ's voice.

"It's okay, I'm done."

Clair headed back outside, instantly noticing a pitcher of water and a basin of water sitting in the middle of the women.

"This little girl needs a bath!" VJ stated emphatically, adding "You'll thank me later," to the cat.

"Hey!" Jesse grabbed for the soap, "That's my ten-dollar bar of soap!"

"Ever heard of sharing?" VJ reprimanded. "Guys, look, she's one of those six-toed cats! You're special, aren't you, gal?"

"Polydactyl," Clair added. "Earnest Hemingway cats. He loved them."

"We could name her Earnie?" suggested VJ.

"Noooo," everyone chimed. "Not Earnie."

"Alex," said Lucky, "Give her a mythic name. Something that resonates."

"How about Persephone?" volunteered Jesse. "Wasn't she kidnapped and forced to live in the underworld just like this poor little girl here?"

Alex thought for a moment, and then said, "You have to earn the mighty name of Persephone, doing the work in the Underworld, but how about Kore, pronounced Kory. She was the daughter of Demeter who was kidnapped by Hades and taken to the underworld. It's then that Kore then becomes Persephone, the guide to other souls, and takes her place as queen."

"Kore, it is!" the women happily agreed.

While VJ and the others continued washing and soothing the newly-dubbed Kore, Lucky leaned in to talk to Clair. "So, the drawing on your cast … you said the man sitting next to you did it? Quite elaborate, isn't it?"

"It sure surprised me when I saw it. We had spent some time talking during the flight … he mentioned recreating a time in his youth."

"Could he be the one who stole your bag?"

A lightning strike right at that moment couldn't have surprised Clair more.

"Ben? Oh no. Definitely not." He couldn't have! He wrote his phone number on my cast. Look," she lifted it so Lucky could see.

"Could be a fake number?" Lucky shrugged. "Look, I'm not saying he did it. It's unlikely, but it also could have been … Ben."

No, it couldn't be Ben. He'd said, come with me.

But seeds of doubt began to grow in her imagination, planted by a well-meaning gardener.

Suddenly, a white bird flew out of nowhere beneath the eaves, and Kore's eyes fixed on it, tail swinging rhythmically from under the towel. The bird kept aiming for a particular spot under the roof overhang that was cleverly hard to reach.

"She must have a nest there," Jesse speculated.

The bird's wings were spread wide like the fingers of a fan, resting on the small currents of air. Jesse aimed her camera upwards, capturing the flight. Kore jumped out from the towel, clearly done with all this bathing business, and left the company of the women for parts unknown.

The Mythology of Kore

Demeter was one of the Olympian gods, sister to Zeus. She was the only one who heard the cries of the early humans struggling to find enough food who felt compassion for them. She came down to earth and made the soil rich, invented grain, and taught people cultivation. As an archetype, she embodies the longing for the natural world of regeneration. And as consort to her brother Zeus, she produced her only child, a daughter named Kore, which means "seed" or "maiden."

Demeter was deliriously happy with her beautiful child and the whole world flourished accordingly, since Demeter was the goddess of all things growing and abundant harvests.

One day while Kore was out picking narcissus flowers, a bolt of lightning flashed and the earth cracked open! Riding through the crack in his ebony chariot pulled by six midnight-black horses came the Lord of the Underworld himself: Hades. He was instantly seized by Kore's innocence and beauty. For the first time, he was overcome with passion, grabbing the terrified and screaming young maiden in his powerful arms, and driving his black horses back into the crumbling tunnel from whence he came.

When Demeter heard of this, she was filled with despair and rage at the loss of her only daughter and, in a final desperate act, she threatened nothing less than the

Clair had leaned her head against the rough post, watching monstrous white clouds form over the distant mountains, a fine line of white along the rim. *Is that snow on top of those mountains?* As she listened to the story of the lost daughter, she found herself thinking about the winter morning when Cassidy was born two months premature. How ecstatic she'd been, even through the haze of drugs, to finally have a daughter who lived. Cass looked not much bigger than a cocktail shrimp, fragile and translucent, and Clair remembered how terrified she was to leave her lest the infant slip away like her two sisters.

"The Demeter/Persephone myth is such a terrible one," said Jesse, "full of kidnapping, rape, and separation."

"Yeah, but that's actually the point of the story," said Alex, with growing excitement. "It's only because of all those terrible things that Kore, the girl, becomes her true self as a woman. The difficulties had to happen because that's her fuel. The oyster needs the grit to make a pearl. Kore must be taken from the mother or the daughter will never become herself. It looks cruel, but it's necessary, psychologically, that is. The abduction and going down into the dark Underworld are really a deepening process. And, ladies, keep in mind, these are all metaphors. We're not saying that women need to be kidnapped and raped! This is an inner process."

Clair was trying to sort through these ideas, applying them to herself and Cass when Alex interrupted.

"I can tell you how it works personally," she added.

She had everyone's attention.

"I have an only daughter, Olivia. We were extremely close, and maybe closer than what was healthy for us, especially after her father and I split. We were everything to each other."

Clair was beginning to feel uncomfortable, her back aching after a day of sitting. Standing up, she took a breath, put her hands on her hips, and leaned back, left and right, stretching her cramped muscles.

"Well, as the story goes," Alex continued, "my daughter was abducted. Well, not really, but she ran off with this young man who was very involved in drugs and who knew other dark areas of life. She became obsessed with him and I lost her. For a while."

1998

"But, where are you going?" Clair nearly begs Cassidy on the phone.

"I don't know," Cassidy answers sharply. "For a ride. Maybe to California."

It was summer, school over, and some boy musician who Cass met at a mixer two months before now wanted to head cross country, Cass along with him.

"Control your daughter!" Blake decrees.

"Cassidy, please. We don't even know this boy."

As Clair talks, she paces the bedroom, the long cord following her like a pet snake. Her hands shake and she has trouble catching her breath. Periodically, she stops and bends forward, trying not to faint.

"What are you gonna do? How will you live?"

"We'll manage, Mother ... he has a plan."

"Will you call us, let us know how the trip is going? Check in once a week?"

"I can't put myself on your schedule. I'm not going to camp. I'm not going to send postcards, and I'm not gonna call every Sunday night."

She does call, though, for a while, but each time is more traumatic, until finally Blake hires a private detective who

"I can relate to that in myself," said VJ. "I was an only daughter and my mother completely possessed me. I couldn't make a move without her. I mean, I love her very much, but I also wanted my own life. I eventually made my break, leaving with a group of hippies. We drove around in a VW bus to other campuses, protesting the war in Vietnam, smoking pot, having sex. Broke my mother's heart, but it needed to happen."

"Often it's the sexual awakening that separates the mother from the daughter, observed Alex. It's the one place she can't go along—to the underworld kingdom of Hades."

"The pomegranate, the juicy crimson seed full of sexual energy, that's what finally separates the daughter from the mother's jurisdiction," added Jesse.

"And also," said Alex, "that's when the father becomes more important, and helps to break the mother's bond, teaching his daughter how to be effective in the world."

Just then, Kore pushed the screen door open, nosing back onto the porch. VJ let out a gasp, the first to see her. "Look!" she said, rising and taking a deep bow, "My queen."

Kore's fur had dried and the transformation was remarkable: the dusty, matted fur was now silky smooth and lustrous.

"Maybe we should get the casseroles in the oven," Lucky suggested. "It must be close to seven."

Clair checked her watch and was surprised that Lucky was correct. It was seven o'clock—nine to Clair—though the sun was still very present above the horizon. Rather than get in the way in the kitchen—with Lucky, VJ, and Alex already in there doing their own cooking dance, Clair returned the chairs from the porch to the dining room.

"Clair, meet me out on the porch?" Jesse asked, on her way to the bathroom.

The offer unnerved Clair. *What did she want?*

From the moment Clair had seen her at the airport, Jesse was the person Clair felt the most resistance toward. Alex was kind and knowledgeable, VJ, open and motherly, even if she did smoke marijuana, but Jesse was threatening, challenging—the one person of Lucky's friends who stood out as the most unusual—and oddly, the most similar to Clair's daughter. Could that be why Clair felt so ill at ease, the way she felt so often with Cass? Maybe it was the tattoos, the ring in the navel and nostril, and the insolent way Jesse dismissed the rule of no cameras, doing as she pleased.

When Jesse returned to the porch she was carrying a couple of thick blankets from the bed tucked under one arm, and a couple of plastic squeeze bottles in her hand. She dropped everything onto the decking, then laid the blankets neatly, one on top of the other.

"I've been watching you, Clair, and I can tell you're in pain. Maybe I can help?"

I'm watching you.

"It's just my back … kind of a chronic thing. I've had it for years."

"I'm a licensed body worker. Come, lie down. I know I can help. Please take your shirt off."

"I've been told I need surgery."

"Shhh," Jesse said calmly, "Let me try."

"I was going to set the table."

"The others have that covered."

Reluctantly, Clair unbuttoned and took off her shirt, lying down on the blanket bed, resting her face on one cheek. She felt the soft wool of the blanket underneath her tickle her belly and face.

"If you don't mind I'm just going to straddle your back … it's easier since I don't have a massage table."

Clair recoiled at the familiarity of the gesture, but didn't say anything.

"Don't worry, nothing I'm going to do will hurt your back. I'll just unfasten your bra and tuck your panties down too. I don't want to get oil on them … they look expensive."

Clair felt pinned and uncomfortable, listening as Jesse rubbed her palms together, then gently but firmly, lay them on Clair's midback.

Clair almost moaned.

"Is this the place?" Jesse asked.

"Oh, yes," Clair whispered, feeling the warmth of Jesse's hands, and again noticing how long it had been since hands had been on her body.

"These are the kidney points," said Jesse. "Take some deep breaths, visualizing the air going to the area under my hands, and let each breath out slowly,"

"What do you mean, kidneys?"

"In Traditional Chinese Medicine, each organ is associated with a particular emotion. The kidneys relate to fear."

The rabbit, Clair thought.

Jesse held her hands in place for several minutes.

"Keep breathing slowly into my hands … ahh, you're doing nicely. I know that you fell recently and broke your wrist, but what I'm sensing feels old, like it's been around a while. Emotional armoring can be difficult to let go of. Have you seen anyone about the pain?"

"I saw a doctor years ago … he said I needed surgery."

"Uh-huh. That's always the first option in the medical model."

"I knew I didn't want to do that, so I guess I haven't done anything since then."

"Except learn to live with it."

"Yes, that, and he gave me painkillers."

"And you've been taking them?"

"On and off."

This was too close to one of Clair's secrets. The truth was she had been taking them steadily through the years until finally she was convinced that she was a drug addict but hadn't attempted to stop.

"Clair, I'm going to put some lotion on you that generates warmth."

Jesse put what felt like only a few drops onto various places on Clair's back and rubbed it in. "This is a blend of various essential oils."

Jesse's hands began to move on Clair's back in long, slow strokes, gliding up all the way to her shoulders and returning again to the small of her back, riding on the slippery surface of the oil. Sure enough, Clair began to feel a sudden warmth spreading.

She breathed in deeply. The fragrance wafted into her nostrils, smelling like a summer day in her garden, with her own hands plunged deeply into rich, dark soil.

Jesse's hands continued gliding up and down in the same slow rhythmic fashion until she stopped stroking and began sliding her thumb along Clair's spine. She moved with an even pressure, holding and releasing, holding and releasing, all the way up and back again. Clair could feel the sun's still-warm rays on her shoulders and the crown of her head, and Jesse's strong hands touching and kneading her body with alternating slow strokes. Once she was greatly relaxed, she felt the tips of Jesse's thumb going directly into the pain and releasing it. Her eyes started tearing with the ecstasy of it.

Jesse pushed a little deeper into the muscles and tissues, making Clair flinch.

"Don't resist, Clair. I'll back off a bit. Imagine a ball of golden light coming in through the top of your head, spreading healing light and heat throughout your entire body."

Clair inhaled again, trying to imagine the ball of light. Was it white or was it yellow?

"Good!" Jesse said quietly. "Now add some sound as you exhale."

"What?"

"I want to hear a big sigh as you exhale. Like this." Jesse, let out an open mouth sigh. "Ahhhh! Your turn."

Clair was soundless.

"Come on, you can do it."

Clair managed a small hesitant ahh.

"Good. Now let's do it together one last time. It's important to learn to vocalize … it releases tension that's stored in the muscles."

The heat was increasing, and Clair felt some tingling, a buzzing, under her skin.

"It's getting hot."

"That's okay, it won't burn you. Enjoy the warmth."

Beginning to trust, Clair relaxed into the heat and made some more "ahhh" sounds without being coaxed. Each time she did, Jesse praised her: "Good, Clair!" which encouraged more sighs. Jesse ended the massage just as they heard Lucky's voice.

"Dinner's up!"

"Take your time standing, Clair. Another couple of minutes won't delay dinner."

Quietly, Jesse left the porch. Clair lay there for a moment just breathing.

She felt both penetrated and expanded at the same time. It was oddly cooling, and yet there was heat underneath. With the oils and fragrances, and the sun warming the crown of her head, she felt utterly relaxed. It had been a long time since she'd felt this way without the help of a pill.

A foot below her under the wooden decking of the porch, a snake struggled to shed its skin.

CHAPTER 12

"C'mon, Clair Bear, get yourself in here."

Lucky's voice floated through the screen door, using an old nickname that only she and Patrick ever used for Clair. The affectionate moniker had always made Clair feel special. Loved, she supposed. Funny, that in all the years with Blake, he had never called her anything but Clair—and sometimes the ubiquitous "Darling," but that was mostly for others when they were in public, wasn't it?

"We're going to do a smudge ceremony before dinner," Lucky informed her, sticking her head out the door.

"I'm coming," Clair answered, but her body was deeply reluctant to move.

She could hear the others in conversation, every so often punctuated by abrupt gales of laughter. But urged on by Lucky's directive, she opened her eyes and managed to raise her head.

Jesse had really loosened something. My back feels so much better! Being mindful of the cast, Clair lifted herself up onto one elbow, bare breasts facing the setting sun. Kore was sitting close by, staring directly at her, tail arcing gracefully back and forth.

"Hey, Kore," Clair whispered, reaching a hand toward her, which Kore met with her head and an appreciative purr.

"Oh, you like that, do you? Well, we'll do some more later, but right now I've been summoned to a … smudging. Whatever that is."

Inside, the table was aglow with candlelight and the sun's last rosy rays. Paper towels were used as placemats, on which sat blue tin plates with matching salad bowls and wine and water glasses. The white anemones Alex brought stood loosely in a small glass bottle in the center of the table.

"Oh, it looks beautiful!" Clair exclaimed, eyeing the scene with appreciation.

"How do you feel," asked Lucky, "after Jesse's magic hands?"

"More relaxed than I have in years," Clair smiled. "And the pain in my back is actually gone." Then to Jesse: "Thank you so much, Jesse! That was a miracle!."

"Glad to have helped," nodded Jesse. "Just take it easy. I moved a lot of energy around."

Lucky held a small bundle of sage tied together with pink string while the others joined round her in a circle. Alex put a match to it, and the bundle smoked under Lucky's coaxing breath, releasing a pungent aroma into the room.

"We invite the presence of benevolence to join us, all for our highest good," chanted Jesse, as Lucky went around the circle waving her hand so that the cleansing smoke came to each of the women.

"Everyone, release all negativity in this moment," Jesse instructed.

Clair thought of Blake and her anger toward him. Her hate for him. She tried thinking words of forgiveness but couldn't quite form what those would be.

"Let go, surrender, and invite only the healing forces of love." Jesse put her hands in a prayer position held at her heart and bowed her head. "Namaste. The Divine Love in me bows to the Divine Love in you," Jesse concluded. Everyone copied her, repeating "Namaste," and head bowing to each other. Clair did it, too, but a few beats behind everyone. "And now," Jesse exclaimed, "let's eat!"

Along with the enchilada casserole, was a salad of fresh summer greens and avocados in a white ceramic bowl, a basket of tortillas, and two bottles of wine, red and white.

"I also put some Vidalias in the salad," Alex said.

"What's that?" asked Clair.

"Just about the sweetest onion in the world, right from my home state of Georgia," Alex answered in an exaggerated southern accent. "So sweet you can almost eat them like an apple."

"Who wants what?" Lucky asked, beginning to pour the wine.

"Red for me," Clair answered, holding her glass up.

When the glasses were filled, Alex raised hers up. "I'd like to make a little toast and share a story Kierkegaard once told about a man who went to heaven."

"It better be little," came VJ's voice. "We're hungry!" Everyone laughed.

Through the window, the sky was a palette of fading pastels with a darkened ridge of mountains in the west.

"Relax! It is," grinned Alex. "Ladies?" The women held their glasses in anticipation.

"When this man arrived in heaven, all the gods were lined up waiting for him. And by a special grace for the exemplary life he had led, the man was granted a wish. One wish for his next life."

Alex looked from person to person as she told the story, and Clair thought how lovely she looked in the pink light.

"Hermes asked him, 'Will you ask for beauty or youth or perhaps power?' But the man was clever and knew how this wish-thing worked. He didn't try to outwit the gods, for that would be hubris. What he said was, 'I wish for the laugh to always to be on my side.'"

Alex looked toward Lucky. "May you, Lucky, and the rest of you as well, always have the laugh on your side."

"To the laugh!" Lucky repeated, leaning forward to embrace Alex, as the women clinked their glasses, and repeated the wish. "And I want to thank you all for being here to make this birthday a special one, although I do have to admit turning fifty is harder than I thought it would be."

"What's harder?" asked Jesse, taking the casserole from Lucky.

"I've always been comfortable with my age, but I think the hormonal changes along with this one have gotten to me … night sweats, and I'm more emotional. Even Max has noticed it."

"You'll settle into it, Luck," assured VJ. "It's just another passage, but as the elder in the group, let me welcome you to the fabulous fifties."

"Not yet! Allow me to remind you that I have one more day of forty-nine!"

"Okay, small stay of execution," VJ laughed, "Menopause is an adjustment for sure, but you'll do fine. You're healthy and active."

"As the other person in the group over the fifty mark," said Alex, "I can relate to what you're saying. My period is still very irregular … comes, then it doesn't for a few months, then arrives again when I least expect it. Crazy-making!"

The casserole made its way around the table a second time, followed by the salad and tortillas.

"That's something I won't have to go through," Clair said, in a rare moment of sharing.

"That's right," Lucky agreed. "You had a hysterectomy."

"Me too," said Jesse. "Why did you have one, Clair? If you don't mind me asking."

"I'd had so many miscarriages, that after my daughter was born, they just decided to take everything out. How about you?"

"I had cancer," Jesse answered calmly.

Clair was shocked by the response and the matter-of-fact way it was delivered, but before she could think of a reply, Jesse said to all of them, "See, ladies, when you think of the alternative, aging is really a gift for which we should all be grateful."

"Here, here to that!" Lucky toasted, as they all raised their glasses a second time. "To the gift of age: May we all experience years and years of it."

"And we must respect that we're moving from one archetypal age to another," Alex added. "All women pass from Maiden and Mother to Crone. It's natural and inevitable. Menopause is an initiation experience, like puberty or childbirth. To ignore it or cover it up would rob us of a deepening experience."

"You're right, Alex," agreed VJ. "Thanks for the reminder of that."

"You're welcome, honey. So we don't want to look at it as being primarily one of loss."

"All well and good, although I must say I never liked the idea of being a Crone," VJ commented, taking a sip of wine. "It sounds like some bent-over old woman stirring the proverbial black pot."

"That's a witch," corrected Lucky. "Though witches too got a bad rap … burned at the stake and all. Oh, can you imagine!"

"Yes, and they were the healers of their day," Jesse observed.

"What many women don't realize is that menopause is a time when women can move away from being the caregiver and embrace their own lives," said Alex. "There can be much more autonomy and creativity, more opportunities. Actually, if you use the astrological system, it's not fifty, but the second Saturn return is the significant thing. And that doesn't happen until fifty-eight to sixty."

'What's that?" Clair asked.

She had been taking in what the women were talking about, ideas that were unfamiliar to her. The most talked about subject among the women she knew was when to get plastic surgery.

Alex turned to her, saying, "Saturn is Father Time, and also the great teacher. It rules hair, teeth, bones, things like that, associated with time and aging. When Saturn returns to the place in the Zodiac where it was when you were born, it coincides with stages of personal authority. The first one is at age twenty-eight or nine … a time to become an adult, take responsibility, and have inner authority, rather than outer as when we're children. The second return is late fifties … when we get to reap what we've sown and enter the stages of the elder years when it's beneficial to have a seriousness of purpose—time is foreshortened, so do what you came here to do—and yet at the same time, be able to cultivate a child's wonder and untroubled mind.

"I have my second Saturn return next year," said VJ thoughtfully.

"When is the third?" Clair asked.

"In our late eighties … when we give back to the world the gifts that make us who we are … assuming we've discovered them along the way. The elder years can be a most magical time as one is preparing to reenter 'the mystery from whence we came.'"

"But, here we are, at only fifty!" Lucky interrupted "So here's to fifty … the youth of old age!"

The meal was over and filling to the women in more ways than one. "Do you want more of this before I take it away, Clair?" Jesse was reaching for the casserole.

"Oh, no, thank you," Clair answered. "I've had plenty." She was not used to eating so much and felt stuffed.

As Jesse withdrew her hand, the bottom of the dish nicked the bottle of red wine, knocking it in Clair's direction. Clair watched the dark red liquid leave the throat of the bottle and inch towards her in a kind of dreamy slow motion. A red river heading toward her white shirt. No, pink. It made a pink streak as it bled onto the fibers of the weave.

"Oh, God!" Jesse yelled, grabbing a napkin. "I'm so sorry!"

"It's alright," Clair assured her, springing up. "It's torn anyway."

The others were instantly in motion, with napkins, mopping and blotting. VJ hurried to the kitchen for something she could wet and bring back.

"Really, it's all right," Clair repeated, as she leaned forward to reach for another napkin. When she did her, hair brushed ever so lightly across the flame of the candle. She smelled the singe before seeing an actual flame in her peripheral vision.

Cold water suddenly hit her in the face, making Clair gasp in surprise and shock. Her hands went to her head and her hair. The fire was out as quickly as it had started. Jesse was standing in front of her, an almost empty bottle of mineral water in her hand. The others had leapt to their feet, VJ running in from the kitchen. Everyone looked terrified.

"What happened? What happened?" VJ exclaimed.

Someone had knocked over a chair in the hustle; Clair remembered the crash-bang of it hitting the floor.

"She set her hair on fire," someone answered.

"What the fuck?" VJ exclaimed, confused.

Lucky came close to Clair, examining her, along with Alex.

"You're okay," Lucky said, bending down to look Clair directly in the eyes. She had hold of Clair's face. Clair realized Lucky was trying to get her attention, the way one would hold a child's face while telling them that things are under control..

Clair ran to the bathroom, Lucky close behind. Did she have hair left on the front of her head? Eyebrows? She wasn't feeling any pain, but maybe it would start any second or when her body came out of shock.

Oh, my god! They'd need to rouse Cleat on that radio thing or maybe airlift me to the nearest hospital.

She stared at herself, her face resembling the frightened rabbit. She pushed back her wet hair - at least there *was* hair. Lucky was beside her, the others in the doorway.

Reassured she wasn't burned, Clair began to breathe easier, until a moment later when the humiliation set in. *How stupid! I actually set myself on fire! In front of Lucky's friends yet.*

"It's just some wisps in the front … and side." Lucky lifted Clair's dark hair, examining the damage. "Jesse was like lightning with that bottle of water."

"Thank you again, Jesse," Clair said, turning toward the doorway.

"I can trim those ends for you tomorrow."

"Yeah, please … they'll need it."

The ramming speed of her heart slowed. Clair took her first deep breath of the evening. "I think I'd like to just sit outside for a few minutes." *Outside. Yes. That's where I need to be.*

Clair took the outstretched dishtowel from VJ's hand, and once on the porch, sighed deeply. The air was cool now, the sky glowing an emerald green. The sky was green! And glowing.

She put the dry side of the towel under her pink shirt to keep the dampness from her skin. When she did, she noticed that her bra, too, was splattered with wine; it looked as if she'd been shot in the heart. She rubbed her hair again with her fingers and pieces of it crumbled. In that moment, as her hair crushed to ash between her fingertips, the whole day came crashing in.

But it was more than just the day, wasn't it? It was her whole damn life.

She never should have come.

Why had she?

It was for Lucky. For her. To please her. She came for Lucky.

If she were home, she could have a really good cry. She'd put on sad music, La Traviata or Madame Butterfly, get in the bathtub and cry—about her failed marriage, the hurt and humiliation, Blake's child in another woman's body, her own broken and aging body, her isolation, her deep loneliness.

Oh, yes, she was adept at conjuring a good cry.

But that sad music was about to change.

An animal cried out in the darkened distance. Inside, the candlelight flickered, and she could hear the clinking dishes and muffled talking from the kitchen. The sun was now down. This strange day had ended. The sky changed color to a more midnight blue, the color it gets just before it turns black. It was probably close to eleven. A new moon, slim as a fingernail clipping, sat brightly in the sky, punctuated by a close bright star.

CHAPTER 13

After a few moments, there was a light tapping on the screen door.

"Feeling any better?" Clair heard Alex ask. "I brought some mint tea."

A tissue box appeared along with the tea, and Clair reached for one, then another, blowing her nose.

"Thank you," she said, looking up.

Alex's face was in shadow as she sat down and put an arm around Clair's shoulder. "You must feel like you've been assaulted."

Clair was quiet for a moment, then said quietly, "My husband left me six weeks ago." The statement surprised Clair even as it was coming out of her mouth. "His girlfriend is pregnant."

She felt Alex's body turn toward her.

"They're going to get married," Clair added with a sardonic laugh. "Sometimes I think I might go crazy."

Alex sat in the stillness, not speaking for a moment, then inhaled long and slow. "To be left in such a way can be crazy-making, for sure. I'm so sorry, Clair. Does Lucky know this?"

"I haven't had the chance to tell her yet. I will."

"Well, if it's any comfort … I can relate. Betrayal is the worst. Strips us down to the bone."

"It happen to you too?"

"Pretty much. The woman didn't get pregnant, but he did leave me for her. So, I know those feelings. I wanted to kill him."

"But you remarried him?"

"I did, years later."

"What's the whole story? I mean, if you want to tell me."

Heat lightning flashed for a millisecond, illuminating their faces.

"Well, Glen and I were high school sweethearts in this small town in Texas. Typical story … the football hero and the class president, the first girl ever to be elected. We were both National Merit Scholars and both planned to study pre-med, at Emory in Atlanta. We were stars. All was perfect … but also typical. I eventually gave up my plans for medical school and helped my husband financially, so one of us could finish. And I was pregnant at the time. A few years into his rising practice, he left me and our daughter for someone else."

Clair was listening intently, watching the changes of expression on Alex's face.

"That sounds like grounds for murder," Clair agreed, feeling her own pain, still so raw.

Alex took a sip of her tea. "Yep, that's what I thought."

"But you said you got back with him? How did that happen?"

Laughter from inside the cabin burst through the screen door, and the two women looked up for a moment and smiled.

"Lucky's enjoying this trip," Alex observed, with a small smile. She was so excited when you decided to come. It wouldn't have been the same for her if you hadn't."

"I'm glad I did."

In spite of everything that had happened, Clair realized in that moment that she actually *was* happy she had come.

"To finish the story," Alex continued, "I hadn't seen Glen for about ten years. He had divorced by that time, and I had finished my degree and become a psychotherapist. By that time, I understood from my training that it was just my ego that was so outraged. And that could be healed. I moved to Santa Fe and started my own life, and he did begin to step up as a father. Years later, at our daughter's high school graduation, well, basically Glen fell in love with me again."

"Did you too?"

"Hell, no. I was in a whole other place in my life. To me, Glen was a huge step backwards. I told him I wasn't interested, but he just kept at it … wearing me down," Alex laughed.

"Why did you take him back?"

"What convinced me was that he went into therapy. And then I knew he was serious. It took a long time … we began slowly

… and eventually it seemed like the right path to take. But, as I think I told you, I've never lived with him again."

"Why?" Clair asked, a bit confused.

"He still has a big practice in Atlanta. I live in Santa Fe. So, we just come together when we can. What can I say? It's worked … for us."

"Knock, knock!" It was Lucky at the screen door. "Mind if I join you?" she asked, stepping onto the porch.

"Oh, do," Alex replied. "I think I'm going to bed. Clair, I'll keep that little night light on for you." Standing, she hugged both of the women before disappearing inside.

"Walk with me," Lucky said, taking Clair by the hand.

"Where?"

"We haven't been out to the field yet … let's go before bed."

"But, Lucky, we can barely see."

"Behold!" Lucky exclaimed, producing a small flashlight and shining it into the darkness.

The other women called out their "good nights" as Lucky, leading Clair by the hand, headed toward the poles.

"See you in the morning," Lucky called back.

"Do snakes come out at night?" Clair asked, timidly.

"Only if they're hungry," Lucky quipped.

Clair was tired, worn out by the day, and so did not appreciate Lucky's humor. With just a new moon in the sky, the night was very dark, only a tunnel of rays shined from the flashlight beam, and the faint glow of the cabin was now getting more distant as they walked.

The illumination of the cabin reminded her of the lighthouses of Maine, beacons of hope on the horizon for lost mariners. "Did you know," she almost whispered, not wanting to break the spell of the absolute quiet, "that lighthouses have one-thousand-watt bulbs?"

"What?" Lucky asked. "Where in the world did that come from?"

"And on either side of them, top and bottom, are these kinds of dishes that reflect the light back into the center, compressing it, and that pushes the beam straight out—that's why it's so bright. The power of it is amplified so every bit of it goes out."

"Clair-bear, you know the craziest things."

"I was a tour guide for a few weeks one summer at a lighthouse: Perimeter Point. It was a beautiful little place, this grassy knob of a point jutting out into the sea. But I got bored repeating the same thing day after day, answering the same questions. So, I quit."

"I don't remember you working at a lighthouse."

"I think it was the summer you went to Europe with your roommate."

Clair knew very well that it was that summer, and how much she'd wanted to be included, to go to Europe … but there was no way her family could afford it, even if she'd been invited … which she wasn't.

The women continued, walking carefully over the uneven terrain, stopping when they reached their first pole.

Clair looked all around. They were surrounded in darkness, with only the tiny lighthouse of the cabin in the distance as a compass point. She wanted to tell Lucky about Blake and that he'd left, but didn't want to bring it up right before bed or she'd never sleep. Tomorrow. She'd tell Lucky about Blake tomorrow.

"Feel this," Lucky urged, encircling her hands around the slim pole.

Clair put her cast-free hand on the pole, feeling a slight buzzing in her palm, as she allowed her head to rest on the cool steel. The night smelled of sage. It occurred to Clair that she wanted to plant some when she returned home. "It's getting chilly." she said, feeling a nip in the dry desert air.

"There're no water molecules in the air to retain heat," stated Lucky. "That's why the temperature drops so much at night."

"And you think *I* know crazy things."

They smiled at each other, faces close, leaning in.

"It's so quiet here. You can't hear anything. At home I always hear the ocean, and it can be so loud at times."

A coyote laughed in the distance.

"Well, quiet except for that eerie creature," Clair added.

"Just a lost coyote calling out to his pack."

Clair hesitated, then asked, "Lucky, why did you like me when we were kids? I was so different from you."

"I liked our differences, Clair, and your sense of containment. I was all over the place, my energy so scattered … but you! You had this calmness, this reserve. Why, when you were focused on drawing, I was in awe of your ability to concentrate. You *became* the drawing you were making. And the results! Oh, Clair, you're such an artist, so creative. Frankly, I was envious."

Clair was shocked by Lucky's words, she had never in the least thought of herself in that way. To her, she'd always been scared and shy, always needing to be pushed by Lucky to do all the daring stunts Lucky was always proposing.

"Do you remember when we biked so far up into Maine that your parents had to come for us? You made us keep going … wouldn't turn back for the life of you."

"I was sure we could bike to the top of Maine and enter Canada!"

"And you wouldn't give up."

"Yeah, I was stubborn … and I always believed I could do anything. But truth be told, the other thing I liked about you, Clair, was that you were always more afraid, and that way I got to be the brave one, the Hero."

After a few moments, each reflecting on what had been revealed, Clair sighed and asked, "Shall we turn back?"

"Let's just walk to one more pole? Okay?"

Clair smiled—*same old Lucky!*—and began walking where her friend's beam was shining.

"Lucky, why did you never come back?"

"After Jim was killed, you mean?" Lucky began, already knowing the answer. "As you know, I did come back to New Hampshire to bury what was left of him. Until that moment in time, I'd always thought I had this charmed life … that I was, well, lucky. But Jim's death completely rocked me. I felt so vulnerable for the first time in my life and so unprepared for raising too small children on my own … so I ran home. I had no other options, but I also knew that New Hampshire was never really going to be home for me again."

1974

Clair's mother calls one evening during dinner. Faith never calls, and Clair can't imagine what's happened. It has to be bad.

"Your friend's husband has been killed. Heard it on Walter Cronkite. In Vietnam. His plane was," her voice cracks, "shot out of the air."

When Clair hears these words, her knees buckle like her bones have suddenly vanished, and she reaches for a kitchen chair to hold herself upright. This can't be true ... things like this don't happen to couples like Lucky and Jim. They'll find him alive. They will!

In the next few hours, she frantically tries to get through to Lucky, imagining the hell she must be going through. She opens a drawer where she keeps old photos and pulls them out a bunch at a time until she finds the one she wants, the rest scattered on the floor.

Lucky and Jim on their wedding day, walking under an arch of uplifted swords; Lucky, radiant in a white-satin sheath gown flared at her knees; Jim in his dress-white ensign uniform, so handsome and so in love.

But now she's being told by the Navy Chaplin that Lucky is under sedation. He will pass along her message. A few days later, along with Lucky's parents, Clair meets Lucky's flight at the airport, and stays with Lucky throughout the memorial service, helping with the twins, who are just two years old. Boys who would never know their father, his blonde good looks, his sense of humor, his love for their mother.

"Two years later," Lucky goes on, "I still had no plan, but thought at least I could go back to San Diego and get our things out of storage."

"But we did have a plan, Lucky, or so I thought … we'd talked about doing something together, a business, or something."

"Yeah, well, neither of us were making anything happen and it was time I took action. That was when I went back to California to pack up our things and then just drive, me and my boys, my little guys, my little pieces of Jim, was how I thought of them. We looked like something out of *The Grapes of Wrath*. Two boys and a stray puppy rescued from some highway in Arizona all piled into the '69 Ford station wagon."

"You told me one time you still have it out at your ranch."

"Yeah, I was so sentimental about the thing. It had brought us to our new life like some big white chariot. Both boys would learn to drive on it. I *couldn't* get rid of it. Would you believe that Max still uses it for ranch chores?" Lucky hesitated, recalling, then picked up her train of thought. "Anyway, I was trying to break up the trip with fun things for the boys; we'd been to the Grand Canyon, stuff like that."

"I remember getting a postcard from the Grand Canyon. I was excited that you were on your way back."

"I had heard of Santa Fe," Lucky continued, "its uniqueness: *"The City Different,"* it was called … so I stopped to take a look. It must have been written in the stars that I stayed, struck by the physical beauty of the place, even the loneliness of it. I think I needed the land to reflect my own grief. Clair, I was a mess, holding myself together with a fine thread for my sons. So, this emptiness," she spread her arms wide and turned in a slow circle, "became the place that could contain all my tears and the rage I felt that my 'lucky' life had been taken away. I was robbed of my husband, my beloved … and my sons wouldn't have that wonderful man in their lives because of some stupid war that we had no business being in."

Clair could feel Lucky's outrage still simmering.

"I had some money from Jim's death, and without giving it much thought, I bought the ranch and some horses, and me and my boys began our healing together. They actually thrived, though I know they missed having a father … and that's when Max showed up with his movie-star cowboy looks, art supplies, a toolbox, and never left. He became a great father to my boys and, well, in the process, we all fell in love with him. I had been lucky after all, even after a great tragedy."

"I hear you, honey … and I'm so sorry you were hurting so horribly. I can see that I had pinned so much hope on you to make me happy that I was in limbo, waiting for you. You had told me you were coming back."

"I know. I'm sorry, Clair. I knew I was disappointing you. But, also, Clair, honestly, I was afraid of you."

"Afraid of me?" Clair was stunned by this statement. "Why? How? I helped put you back together."

"I know, I know, and this is hard to say … but, oh, Clair, as much as you helped me—and you did—so much! I needed you, and you were there, despite your own difficulties. You were there but, also, Clair, you were this big dark hole … so unhappy that it radiated from you. Without wanting to, Clair, you had become your mother."

Clair felt her friend's words like a slap. "But I helped you," she insisted.

"And I'll always be grateful."

"I never wanted your gratitude, Lucky. I wanted you."

"I kept inviting you out here. I thought in the way the light here lit me up that maybe it would do the same for you … bring you some lightness."

They stopped and stood in the dark night, hardly able to see each other's faces, which was good, for Clair couldn't hide her tears.

"Clair, I hadn't planned on staying away when I went to get my things. I got captured, kidnapped, fell in love … with the land, the light, and eventually the man. I adore Max. He's just the right person for me, and he loves me and my boys. He's even patient with my manic nature … he just laughs. And that's exactly it: He has the laugh on his side."

⚡

Several candles stood in jars, so Clair lit them instead of putting on the bathroom light. The candles smelled strongly of lavender, good for sleeping. There was a nightgown hanging across the small wooden chair. It seemed intentional and Clair thought it must be for her. These lovely friends of Lucky's were really taking care of her and she felt it so deeply. She thought about what Lucky had told her and, though she had felt hurt at first, she knew Lucky was right.

I was a black hole … still am to some degree. No wonder Blake left; I don't think we ever shared a laugh.

Standing at the small white porcelain sink, Clair tied her hair back with a covered elastic band from one of the open cosmetic bags on the shelf. Dipping her fingers into a jar of cleansing cream, she rubbed it over her face in smooth, practiced strokes, watching as black formed under her eyes from the mascara she had applied almost a whole day ago.

She knew she hadn't visited because she was angry with Lucky for abandoning her. All these years she'd been hoping to punish her, but never would have been able to speak the truth of it. Maybe their frank conversation was good. It had gone on long enough that they hadn't admitted what was keeping them apart.

She soaked a washcloth in hot water, bringing it to her face, then watched as her naked face revealed itself from the steamed mirror.

Lucky's door was closed tight as Clair tiptoed past, feeling her way into the semi-dark of the bedroom she was sharing with Alex. She took a quick peek in the window wondering about the spider, but it must have wedged itself along the windowsill for the night. The bed was turned down for her, and she snuggled into the fresh cotton sheets and fell asleep immediately, without the sleeping medication she depended on every night at home.

Before she'd closed her eyes, flashes of light lit the landscape, the mountains in the distance, the little shed down the road, the four hundred stainless steel poles, the sage, the cactus, the stealth coyote out hunting for food. Once her eyelids had dropped their curtain, lightning flashed in her mind, too, illuminating her dreams, lighting the dark corners and recesses, as well as the vague figures who recoiled at the sudden exposure, horrified they should be seen.

CHAPTER 14

When Clair woke, it was dawn, a red-rose blush just beginning to wash the room with pale light. A dream floated through her mind, but disappeared before she could grab the fragile pieces. Alex was snoring softly, more of a purr, and Clair wondered if *she* snored. Blake did, loudly, especially if he'd been drinking. Did he drink because he'd been so unhappy with her? That's what her father used to say to her mother.

You crazy woman, it's because of you I drink. By that time, he'd be hollering, and Clair would crawl under her bed and cover her ears, only daring to come out once she'd heard the slam of the front door and the sobs of her mother. The sobs were less dangerous than the yelling, though it filled the child with sadness and an empty feeling of being helpless to do anything about it.

But none of that mattered anymore. Her parents were long dead, and Blake was long gone.

Clair slipped out from under the covers, and tiptoed across the room, checking on the spider as she passed the window. *Oh, my!* she thought, seeing the poles with their tips lit from the rising sun, looking like a giant birthday cake.

In the kitchen she found a variety of teas in the lift-up cabinet. She put the kettle on to make "a nice cuppa," something her mother used to say. Waiting for the water to boil, she opened the back door and stepped out onto the porch. What did the others call it? *Por-TAL.* Yes, that was it. Must be Spanish. VJ was impressive with her fluency in the language.

The air was still, but a million birds were active. *Where did they live with no trees around?* The environment was empty. Desolate. Like Lucky had said, it felt lonely … a good place to grieve.

The first whistling of the tea kettle brought her back to the task at hand.

Kore was now sitting on the counter, startling Clair, appearing as she had, out of thin air.

"Hey, Beautiful! Guess you're an early riser too. Shall we go sit on the portal?" On the way out, hot cup of tea in one hand, Clair grabbed the sketchpad and pencil from the dining room table, glad that the cast didn't hinder simple hand movements.

The field was breathtaking in the morning light, the sky streaked with pink clouds, each pole visible and in its place like a silent army awaiting orders. As she sketched the gorgeous emptiness, she thought of the artist who put this here in the middle of nowhere to get people to come to this very place, to experience this very thing, this very moment. Be here. Look at this. Listen to the silence. And to use Lucky's word: *Behold!*

At home, the morning news would be on and might stay on all day in the background. The newspaper would be on the *porch*, not the *portal*. The phone might ring, and even if it was a solicitor, these were the interruptions of daily life, away from this silent place.

This really is a holy place, like an open-air church. What a vision this Walter DeMaria had! It must have blown his mind when he thought of it, how he would do it, where it would be. Who would come.

At home she could be just as isolated, living on the seacoast as she did, so why did she have to leave there in order to hear her own voice? She thought about Ben and ran her fingertips over the drawing on her cast. As an architect, he would love this place. She wished she could tell him about it, bring him here.

There is no way he took her bag! she stated to herself emphatically.

High in the sky, she saw a flock of birds swooping and diving, playing in the blue air.

I'm happy, she thought suddenly, astounded.

Kore was rolling in the dirt out beyond the portal, prompting Clair to smile, it seems Miss K is done with the beauty routine. The tea was steaming, so she began taking very small sips so as not to burn her tongue. It was good—Earl Grey—perfume-like, a favorite of her father's. At home Clair usually drank English Breakfast, but thought that when she returned home, she'd branch out and have some Earl Grey or maybe a Chai? All of a sudden, her heart jumped to her throat in one strong beat, and she stood bolt upright, spilling her tea onto Alex's nightgown and through to her thigh, making her yelp.

But she had seen something … no, a person! … running in the field. She started to head inside and alert the others, but then recognized that it was Jesse, running like a gazelle, with a light easy stride through the small bushes. She looked like a fairy creature from a storybook. *The Dance of the Elves* or something like that.

Relieved that it wasn't some stranger running through the field, Clair sat back down and watched as Jesse grew progressively larger. Perspective: a revolutionary idea when it was introduced back in the 15th century. A new way of seeing.

Clair wondered how Lucky and this sprite of a woman, with her tattoos and piercings, came to be friends because, judging by appearances, they seemed so different. In fact, each of Lucky's friends seemed different from one another. Back east, the women Clair knew all seemed the same—tailored clothing, silk-wrapped nails, hair that was cut and styled at trendy salons, gold jewelry, expensive shoes and bags. But, really, since she'd left Boston, it was the knitting ladies who were her friends. And now, the psychic, Grace. Not a one was interested in Gucci.

"Hey, there!" Jesse called, in a whisper, as she got closer. "I thought I was the only one up so early."

She was wearing bicycle shorts, a halter top, and a baseball cap sitting backwards on her head.

"Good morning," Clair greeted her, matching Jesse's whisper. "… it's actually two hours later for me, so I got up a while ago. I don't think anyone else is up yet."

"Well, we'll give 'em a little more time before I ring the rise-and-shine bell."

Jesse began doing a series of stretches—bending side to side, grabbing the toe of her shoe and holding it out in front of her while balancing on one leg. Lean and muscular, her body responded like elastic, apparently happy to be pushed and pulled in every direction. Her running shoes were dusted with red earth, and when Jesse bent over from the waist, putting her head to her knees, Clair saw another tattoo peeking from her sacrum, but since it was upside down, couldn't decipher what it was.

"My daughter Cassidy would like you," Clair said as Jesse sat down on the step. "She fought us for a year about getting a tattoo, then showed up in a bikini at a pool party we hosted sporting one on her belly. Her father nearly killed her."

"What kind of image did she choose?"

"A pomegranate, dripping blood … or seeds, as Cass informed us."

"Holy shit! The girl knows how to provoke!"

"She was thirteen and had just got her period. But, yes, she likes to shock."

"She actually sounds like quite an interesting young woman."

"I thought she was just trying to make us mad more than be interesting."

Jesse laughed. "I drove my parents crazy too. Maybe it's healthier than kids who never do, but what do I know? I've never had kids and, well, I never will."

Clair detected sadness in her voice.

"How did you and Lucky meet?" she asked, changing the subject instead of diving into a subject where she knew there was pain.

"VJ came to my exotic dance classes, and one day invited Lucky to come along. It wasn't really Lucky's thing, but she was a good sport."

"So, you're a dancer?"

"Actually, a lawyer by education, but the past few years I've been moving into a whole new life. I've left 'The Law,' as they say. Now I teach dance and yoga and meditation and, as I think you can testify, do massage."

"What made you leave your practice?"

"I told you earlier that I'd had my innards removed from cancer. Well, it was then that I decided I'm done with this stressful life and found a new way of being. And I've been healthier and happier ever since. Having cancer gave me just what I needed: courage. And a boost into a life that was much more suited to the lifestyle I wanted to create."

Yes, Clair thought, *a new life that I actually create. Grace had said, "Tell him goodbye and thank you." Could Blake's leaving actually be an opportunity for a life of her own?*

Jesse continued. "I got the tattoos to mark certain significant moments … they're a rite of passage … something your daughter seems to understand. And at such a young age. What's she up to now?"

Clair was surprised Jesse was so interested. "She's in Europe for the summer. It was her high school graduation gift."

"She'll come back having discovered much about herself. What a fortunate girl!"

"So, what are your tattoos?"

"This ankh on the back of my neck … it's for Sekhmet, the Egyptian Goddess of Rage."

"I know her," Clair interrupted, pleased with herself, "I saw her at the museum in London.

"Well, I had much to learn about releasing rage and figured she'd be a good reminder. And on my sacrum," she twisted her body, as if trying to see," is a symbol for the Chakra system, the 'energy centers' along the spine. I'm giving Lucky a tattoo for her birthday. I've made her an appointment with my guy … Bodhi's such an artist."

"I didn't know Lucky wanted a tattoo."

"I figured it was about time she had one," Jesse laughed. "And speak of the devil! Shall we have a little round of 'Happy Birthday to You?'"

Lucky sprung out of the door and stuck the landing, arms raised. "Ta Da! Please don't. I know there's a cake lurking in my future, so let's save it." Then she exclaimed, "Holy shit! Those poles are still there! I thought they might disappear in the night!"

Alex and VJ followed her out, carrying trays with coffee pot, cups, cream and sugar, and found their places along the wall and step. Clair was thinking of Cass with new respect. Could it be that her daughter knew more than Clair gave her credit for?

"Let's be here now for a moment," Lucky said, head turning, taking in the field. "This is magnificent."

"Ooo, I better get my camera," Jesse said, hurrying into the house.

Once they were all seated with coffee, VJ stated, "Well, Lucky, today's your day … so how do you want to spend it?"

"Hmmmm," Lucky said, finger tapping her head, "Okay, I know … after we finish luxuriating here with our coffee, I'd like to begin with a yoga class … Jesse? Would you be so kind?"

"Would be my pleasure, Ms. Birthday Girl."

Clair froze a moment, then confessed, "I've never done yoga."

"Only seen it on TV?" VJ asked, jokingly.

"Don't worry, Clair Bear … Jesse is a wonderful teacher … you'll love it. Like you did the massage."

"Okay, I'm game," Clair said, thinking '*I'm game*' is not a response she often gave.

"Good, then after we finish here, let's take fifteen, change, and then meet back here," Jesse suggested, rising up to a seated position like she was levitating. Her body just rose up with seemingly no effort at all. Clair was impressed.

While Alex took a quick shower, Clair went to the bedroom, made both beds and changed into the pair of bike shorts and a striped short top that Jesse had lent her, pulling down on the top so, with any luck, it would reach her waist. She pulled back her hair, pleased that she had some at all and that the ends weren't too badly singed.

The room looked as if it might exist in another century: rough-hewn walls, iron headboard, simple-wooden nightstand with candlestick, a bare bulb sticking out of a wall unit. No curtains in the window … why would there be? … just flies beginning to buzz in the growing heat. The spider was out of hiding and holding court at the very top of her web, ready to pounce at the first movement of any victim who flew too close.

Excerpts from her conversation with Jess kept coming to mind—along with thoughts of Cassidy. She'd been hard on her daughter, trying to make her into her own idea of what a daughter should be. There was always a battle between her ideal and who Cass really was. She remembered Cass at ten, dressed like Madonna, while Clair was struggling to keep her in plaid skirts and Oxfords. What a waste of time and emotion! All the fighting, the battles, the tears and door-slamming. She had repeated her own history with her mother without realizing it.

⚡

"Just follow along," advised Jesse, looking at Clair once they were assembled on the portal. "Do what you can and don't worry about the rest. We're not in a contest; this is strictly for our own benefit. And that's why we mostly keep our eyes closed during the poses."

The five women were arranged on staggered yoga mats, Jesse facing the others, framed by the blue of the sky and the distant mountain range, and sitting very erect, legs crossed Buddha-style in front of her. Behind her, clouds were swelling and darkening. She explained that yoga meant union—the divine union of body, mind and spirit—and that this particular form of yoga was called Kundalini, the purpose of which was to "raise the life energy, which lies coiled like a sleeping serpent at the base of the spine." Jesse went on to explain that there were centers of energy along the spine, each representing a higher level of consciousness, and they were called "chakras" or "wheels."

"Let's begin in Easy Pose," Jesse guided. "Legs crossed in front, if you can, with hands in Prayer Pose, palms together and placed in front of the sternum. Just do the best you can, Clair, with your cast. Now, close your eyes and focus your attention at the brow, a quarter inch inside the skull."

Clair rolled her eyes upwards as if she were going unconscious, trying to locate that place.

"Now take a deep breath and hold it."

The muscles of Clair's back and chest, her diaphragm and lungs as well, resisted the inhalation, unaccustomed as they were to deep breathing, and she quickly grew dizzy.

"Kundalini is a way of living … it takes you from the concerns of controlling survival to the experience of the heart, connected and free."

Just as Clair was about to burst, Jesse said, "And now release the breath."

Clair opened her eyes for a moment to keep from falling over, as another wave of dizziness struck her. She noticed the poles had shifted in formation.

"The breath is life. Prana. You'll find in time that long bouts of deep breathing will calm the mind, balance the emotions, and harmonize body, mind, and spirit. We'll now sing the opening chant. Clair, you can just hum along."

Clair opened her eyes again to respond, but Jesse's were closed.

Evidently familiar with this, Jesse and the others began to sing in a language Clair didn't understand. Jesse's voice was louder than the rest, a beautiful voice, clear and harmonious. On the third repetition of the chant, Clair joined in, mouthing the final words … something like "na-mo."

When it was over, Jesse said, "That mantra aligns us with the Divine Teacher within."

The clouds disappeared along with some of the poles, and the sun grew warmer and brighter as they continued a series of cleansing exercises that Jesse called "Kriyas."

She guided them to keep their eyes closed, to "keep the awareness inside."

"When you inhale, vibrate to the sound of "Sat." When you exhale, vibrate to the sound of "Nam." Inhale Sat, exhale Nam. Sat Nam means true identity, the identity of your soul, not your personality. When you say it for the first time, a seed is planted for transformation."

The sleeping serpent opened its eyes.

CHAPTER 15

Breakfast was a feast. VJ made huevos rancheros with green chiles—and fresh herbs she had grown herself. Alex fried potatoes with Vidalia onions, along with thick crispy bacon, adding warm tortillas, local honey, and more coffee to the menu. Jesse photographed the entire production, while Clair busied herself arranging the portal, removing the yoga mats and setting up blankets and cushions. She brought out the flowers and a blue-and-white checkered tablecloth for the narrow bench that would serve as the buffet table, placing the cheerful white anemones in the center.

The women sat, plates in their laps, Kore going from plate to plate, enjoying anything given to her … but especially the bacon.

A flock of crows circled overhead, black streaks cawing from an azure sky.

"Yoga takes a lot of concentration," Clair ventured, between bites.

"It does," agreed Jesse. "That's why it's called a practice … though it flows more once you're familiar with the postures and poses."

"Maybe I'll find a class when I get back home." Clair said, surprising herself.

Clouds began forming on the far side of the field, changing the field's shape once again.

"Looks like a storm this afternoon," Lucky observed, pointing to clouds rising thousands of feet high.

"I love the storms this time of year," Alex stated "You know, when you can be standing in the sun and see storms all around. Sometimes rain can be falling, but the air is so dry that the drops don't make it to the ground. They just evaporate on the way down.

"It's called 'virga,'" Lucky informed them, "or 'male rain,' for some reason."

"You don't know? It's because 'verga' … with an 'e' … also refers to the slang way of saying 'penis' in Spanish," stated VJ, with a grin. "They're spelled differently but sound the same. Believe me, you gotta watch how you use the word."

⚡

Satiated, the group kicked back on blankets and chairs and did what they returned to all through the three days: continuous heart-to-heart talking, one to all, one to one, in various combinations of dyads and triads. And while they talked, Clair thought about rain not making it to the ground. Rain that had formed high in the sky, deep within the thunderclouds. Rain falling and drying up before reaching its intended destination. Rain, on its way to a parched earth. Rain, a god itself, prayed for, but evaporating before it can satisfy the flowers, replenish the reservoirs, and fill the oceans and rivers and streams.

⚡

"Blake has left me, Lucky." It was while doing kitchen cleanup together, Lucky washing and Clair drying, that Clair found the courage to finally utter her truth.

"What? Oh Clair, I'm so sorry! And so sorry I pushed you about coming."

"No, it's alright … I'm glad I came. It's good that I did. I needed to."

"What happened? Tell me," Lucky urged.

"Simple. He has a girlfriend. She's pregnant, and," Clair added in a contemptuous voice and a tired shake of the head, "he wants to marry her."

"That bastard!" Lucky spit out. "I never really liked that man."

"And would you believe that his baby *and* Carl's are due around the same time? Christmas. On New Year's. It's kind of freaky."

"How are you managing, Clair? That's a lot to process."

Clair held up her arm in the cast. "I'm broken, in multiple ways apparently. Somehow in the last twenty-four hours, I'm feeling better. Being with you and your friends, I haven't thought about Blake at all. At home I was obsessed … my mind couldn't let go, but here? I don't know, I just feel lighter about the whole damn thing." She smiled shyly. "And, Lucky, you'll laugh at me, but the day it happened I was so desperate, I ended up going to a psychic who told me to tell him goodbye and to thank him."

"Oh, but I'm not laughing," Lucky assured her, hugging her friend. "It's wise advice. I want to hear all about it."

Laughter and sounds echoed through from the others in the living room.

"Yes, I want to tell you. Grace—the psychic—she's wonderful. We've become real friends. And, Lucky … she knew about Patrick, said he was with me." Clair's eyes went moist, but she was smiling. "I want you and your friends to meet her."

"We'll plan a trip!" Lucky exclaimed.

"Shower's empty! Who's next?" Alex announced, coming into the kitchen, hair a little damp.

"You go, Lucky," Clair urged. "I'll finish up in here."

"Thanks, I will," Lucky accepted. "Hey, Alex, guess what? Clair's going to be a grandmother! You should tell her about being present for your grandchild's birth."

"Congratulations, Clair! You hadn't mentioned that."

"Yes, I wanted to tell Lucky first," Clair smiled apologetically. "And, also that my grandchild with my soon-to-be ex-husband Blake—and Blake's *own* child with his girlfriend—will be arriving around the same time. How's that for a headline?"

"Wow! This is really an extraordinary time for you, Clair. It would be interesting to check out your astrology."

"I've never done that," Clair replied, thinking, *I've never done most of what I'm doing now.* "But, Alex, tell me about your grandchild."

"Happily," she beamed. "I've mentioned, I think, that I'm very close to my daughter, my only child, so from the moment she told me she was pregnant, I entered this kind of bliss-state knowing *she,* because I just knew it was a girl, was on her way. I talked to her throughout my daughter's pregnancy. I even dreamed of her."

Clair had been happy, too, hearing of her Carl's child, but then the day got mixed up with Blake's news, which took over her feelings and robbed her of the joy of that moment.

Alex continued. "One wonderful thing was that my daughter Erica and one of my best friend's sons were the parents, so it was like our whole families had joined together on a DNA level. We were all delirious! It was a home 'water' birth, and we were all invited to attend."

What would it feel like if Cassidy were to marry one of Lucky's sons?

"The lights were subdued, music played softly in the background, and the pool was set up and filled with warm water. Her husband was present as her coach, of course, and though Glen and the other grandfather were there, they were mostly content to stay in the background. My friend, Laurie, her mother, and I served as support, holding her hand, breathing with her, and feeding her ice chips. Oh, Clair, if you get the chance to be present for your grandchild's birth, do it! It's the most amazing spiritual experience!"

Clair hadn't even given any thought to the possibility of attending the birth, but suddenly she did. Births had been so horrible for her, alone and in pain, that hearing that it actually could be joyful was rather a shock to Clair's system.

"I was so proud of Erica, so present, so conscious throughout her labor … inviting the baby to come out with every push, to find the strength, the courage, to be born. The world was waiting for her. Everyone in the room was crying by the time she made her entrance."

"A girl." Clair stated the obvious.

"Miss Angelica Belle Hollingsworth. Angel or Tinker Bell to me, her doting grandmother."

The water pressure in the shower was surprisingly strong. Clair stood under it with her eyes closed, enjoying the individual jet streams pinging off her scalp. She was long past even trying to keep her cast dry, which was due to come off in a couple of weeks anyway. She looked again at Ben's drawing, and pushed away the thought that he might have stolen her bag. *Why would he?*

Out of the shower, she reached for a towel, dried off, and wrapped it around her head. The others had placed their toiletries on the small wooden table under the window for her use: several make-up bags, hairbrushes, toothpaste. Fortunately, Alex's make-up bag had an unopened toothbrush. Clair picked up one of the jars of moisturizer and spread it across her face. A larger squirt bottle held body lotion that she spread over her body, noticing that her skin was unusually dry. The cream smelled of vanilla, a pleasing fragrance.

The light was on over the sink and she looked at herself in the mirror as she toweled her hair, nearly laughing out loud to see herself in this strange environment, like being awake in a dream. She imagined a scene of seeing a psychiatrist and telling him: *I was standing in a little bathroom with a built-in wooden tub, tiny sink, and bare light bulb. Beyond the curtainless window, alive with flies, was space, totally empty space. I could see nothing. No houses, no buildings of any kind, just clumpy grasses and mountains in the distance. Oh, and Doctor, I had lost all my clothes and was naked except for a cast on my arm.*

She then imagined the doctor looking at her without emotion and asking, *"Which arm?"* and she threw her head back and laughed out loud.

Before bed last night, she had washed out her underwear and was surprised they were completely dry. The women were going to find clothes for her, and Jesse had offered to trim off the burnt ends of her poor hair. Clair shuddered at that memory of her hair catching fire. If Jesse hadn't been as quick with the water, it could have been a disaster. She thought she might blow it dry, try to give it some shape at least. But as she picked up the hair dryer, all of a sudden the bathroom light snapped off. So there she stood in the cloud-dimmed light from the window, in her underwear, dark hair springing into unruly and untamable loops.

"Hey, the electricity is off!" Clair shouted to the others as she walked to her room's doorway, holding a towel around herself.

"Clete said that could happen," Lucky called out from the living room.

"But I was just about to dry my hair!"

"Not to worry, Clair," Lucky laughed from the other room, "it will dry."

Alex opened the screen door, sticking her head just inside. "Hey, c'mon out here! We've got clothes for you, Clair, so we're going to play 'runway model.' And Jesse is here with scissors, looking pretty eager to snip."

The temperature was hot now. Hot in the house. Hot on the portal. Clair was almost glad to be without much clothes on, though she felt awkward standing there.

"My clothes would be far too big for you," said VJ, "but I have accessories!"

"Wait!" Jesse exclaimed, "I want to start by trimming her hair while it's still a little damp."

Clair sat on the bench, towel now across her shoulders, pretending she was in a two-piece bathing suit so she didn't feel so uncomfortable about being in her underwear with strangers. Jesse first sprayed Clair's hair with a pleasant smelling liquid. "This will encourage your natural curl."

In an act of faith, Clair relinquished all control of hair she generally tried desperately to tame and focused on the field, the growing clouds hovering above. Noticing Jesse's beaded bracelets, she thought of Ben.

No, he couldn't have.

"The man I met on the plane had some similar bracelets," she observed.

"It's called a *mala* ... used to keep track of prayers. He's probably a Buddhist," Jesse informed her.

"Or a thief," Lucky added, teasingly.

"Okay, done! Clair, bend over," instructed Jesse, "and give your head a shake."

Clair did as she was told.

The women had brought several choices of clothing for Clair: shorts, capris, T-shirts and jeans, dressing her up like a paper doll. "Strike a pose," they exclaimed, with every new combination. But the outfit that got the most votes was, as it turned out, from Alex: a pale-blue peasant dress, V-neck, sleeveless, mid-calf length, that had attached fabric ties so it could be easily tightened, if needed.

"Hands down, that's the one," Lucky caroled. "Go look. There's a mirror in my room."

Standing in front of the mirror, Clair had the amusing thought that the only thing that looked familiar was the cast. Her hair had a different shape and texture, and she never wore clothes that looked like this—the self who she knew was tailored, conservative, smooth-haired—who was this barefooted, curly-haired, woman in a peasant dress staring back at her?

"Well," Lucky said, when Clair came back outside. "What do you think?"

"Yes, I like it … very much," Clair answered, gathering the fabric in her hand. "I hardly recognize myself, but I like the way I feel."

She wondered what Blake might say, seeing her like this … or even the ladies in the knitting shop. Grace, she thought, would probably say, *Now will you tell him goodbye and thank him?*

⚡

All five women were in agreement that they take an hour or so for some alone time, and then come back together for some afternoon activities, or non-activities, yet to be determined. Lucky and Alex wanted to write in their journals; VJ had a book to read; Jesse, a meditation practice; and Clair? She wished she had her knitting, missing the one sure way she had of occupying her mind and hands. Old habits were hard to break.

"Idle hands are the devil's playground," her mother used to say, if Clair hadn't completed at least six or more inches in an hour of knitting. "You're not focusing, Clair *Sinead*," her mother would chide, always adding Clair's middle name, after her grandmother, when scolding her.

I was never really allowed to daydream, to fantasize, to play. It used to be that I could retreat into drawing and painting, but all that came to an end when Trick died.

Clair picked up the sketchbook and pencil she had brought out yesterday, leaned back against the wall of the cabin, and let her hand take flight. By the time the women reconvened, she was putting down the pencil and holding out the drawing for her own scrutiny.

"Wow, Clair, that's amazing!" exclaimed VJ, coming up alongside her. "You captured the field as it is, but also you've expanded the dimension somehow. Made it more."

Clair looked at the simple rendition, lines and shading, and yes, there was something more—the sky blended with the earth, the poles were appearing and disappearing on the page, even as one looked. It was all one interactive, synthesized, vibration. That's what she saw, that was her gift, and what terrified her all those years ago about her brother's death. She had seen things when she was a child, saw too much that she didn't understand, and when it came out on paper, it was terrifying. After that, she willed herself not to see and not to draw. To keep her head down and her eyes firmly closed.

CHAPTER 16

"Hey, guys, I brought craft things I used to do with my children," announced VJ, beginning to take things out of a canvas bag. "That is, if you guys feel like doing it."

"Whatcha got?" Lucky asked, watching with curiosity as a jar of Vaseline, several pairs of scissors, rolls of white tape, artificial flowers, leafy greens and fruit, sequins and small bags of glitter and glue all spilled onto the floor.

They had moved off the portal to get out of the afternoon heat and were seated in a circle on the living room floor.

"Mask-making," answered VJ. "I thought it would be both interesting and entertaining."

"I love this idea!" Alex cried out with delight.

"Why am I not surprised?" commented Jesse, "But I vote yes too," then added in a theatrical and mysterious voice, "It might show us our true hidden inner selves."

"Oh, no! Not that!" Alex played along in mock horror.

VJ had them pair up: Lucky and Clair, Alex and Jesse. As a demonstration, she'd brought a mask she'd made at home. Holding it up to her face, it changed her utterly, as the mask was quite wild-looking, painted black, with green leaves and purple grapes hanging off one side.

"Choose which of the two will go first," VJ directed, "and whoever is the helper smears Vaseline on her partner's face … don't over-goop … just enough to keep the plaster from sticking. And here're some headbands to keep your hair out of the way. So, one of you just needs to lie down and relax."

Clair and Alex laid on the floor, heads on towels, while Lucky and Jesse began the smearing process. Kore sat watching with feigned interest.

"Lay the strips of cloth into this plaster I'm mixing up. You can choose to make a full or half mask. Keep in mind that if you choose the full mask, your mouth will have to be covered too."

Both Clair and Alex immediately exclaimed, "Half!" in accidental unison, cracking up the others.

Next came laying the gauzy strips full of paste goo across the women's faces, causing exclamations of "Ooooo!" and "Yuck!" from the women.

"This is very quick-drying plaster, so get it on before it starts setting up," VJ advised.

As Clair lay still, cool plaster tightening across the top of her face, the mask she would create leapt fully formed in her mind's eye, and she gasped.

"Everything alright, Clair? It won't be much longer if you're getting claustrophobic."

"I'm okay," she murmured, but still felt a little shaken by what she had seen.

The process didn't last long, and they completed all four women with four half-masks, now drying in the sun.

"We can decorate them later," VJ said, "once they're fully dried."

Lucky brought out five Negro Modelo's with a wedge of lime on each bottle neck as they settled outside once again. "This, my friends, is going to taste like the best thing you ever had."

In the heat, lolling on the deck, Clair had to admit VJ was absolutely right. *I need to buy beer when I get home!*

"Mask-making is very Dionysian," Alex declared, after taking a long swallow of beer.

"I knew you were going to bring him up," teased Lucky. "Alex has a god for every occasion," she said to Clair in a stage whisper.

"I know, I know!" Alex laughed, "But hearing the story of the gods always adds depth to a children's activity."

"So tell us about Dionysus, Alex," Clair urged. "I'd like to know more about this god," to whom she lifted her beer glass in salute.

"Well, if you insist," grinned Alex, settling into her storytelling self. "Dionysus was the Greek god of wine and ecstasy. Son of Zeus. Also known as the god of madness, as in wildness. His women followers, who were many, were known as *maenads*, and they would lapse into rapture whenever he was around. During their wild orgies, the maenads wore masks depicting him, allowing themselves to become the god. That's the magic these sacred ceremonies invited. It was other worldly; psychedelic. In fact, history confirms that everyone who participated in these sacred mystery rites was in an altered state of consciousness. Not very different from our present day worship of rock stars, and the drug enhanced attendance at their concerts."

In the distance, thunder rumbled while a hot breeze blew across the blanket where Clair sat. Drawing in quick strokes, she was trying to capture the image that had entered her mind willy-nilly while the plaster was drying on her face.

Lucky had called for the women to take another "break in the action." "I'm getting old, you know," she'd said. "I'm fifty now." It seemed that the beer and heat had made her and the others sleepy.

All but Clair.

She was energized, buzzing as if a switch had been turned on.

She thought about these women. What they had talked about, what they knew, how supportive and loving they were with each other. They teased, yes, but good-naturedly, and Clair never detected any underlying tension. And she was a master at detecting underlying anything.

She thought about VJ's early years, being arrested at Kent State. Drug trips. Famous lovers. Clair's own life seemed so boring, so straight and narrow—not to say, there wasn't value in choosing that way of life, but hers was a shotgun marriage. Did she ever really love Blake? Did he, her? They married because of circumstances, namely that she was pregnant. Choices were few and far between in those days. He was upstanding; she appeared to come from a good family. They got married and Clair wasn't shamed or stoned.

She heard Grace's voice in her mind: *I see six golden lionesses in the desert.*

Grace had a vision. She *sees* in her visions. Clair was struck by the simple realization of that.

I used to have visions, she remembered.

Until she squeezed them out of existence.

She was alone on the deck. The others—gone to their rooms.

The white bird came back. Aiming itself at the eaves, as it had the last time they'd seen it, wings spread wide like fingers, but it took many tries before it managed to land. Then it took off again quickly and flew away as if it had forgotten something.

On the bench was VJ's pipe and lighter. Clair found herself picking it up, an unbidden action, and holding it to her lips. She flicked the lighter, taking a small drag and immediately coughing as she did. Undaunted, she tried again. Only once had she smoked pot, and that was in college. Bringing the pipe to her lips again, she took a deep inhale and held her breath.

On the exhale, a relaxed sensation flooded her body and mind, past the sturdily built and tightly controlled floodgates.

Me? she thought. *Did I see in the same way as Grace? All my drawings and paintings as a child, is that what I was painting? Did my ability to draw give me access to some split-off inner world of visions?*

Clair flipped through her scattered sketches on the drawing tablet. It was happening again. The images from deep inside were resurfacing. She was losing her grip. That thought of losing control, like stepping into an aircraft, used to frighten her, terrorize her. But she wasn't feeling fear this time.

In a moment of confidence, she stood up, tied the hem of her dress in a knot to make it easier for walking, tucked the small binoculars into her pocket, and stepped off the portal, wearing Alex's straw hat and Lucky's cowboy boots.

I will walk in the field to the end of a row. It couldn't be that far, and the cabin will always be in sight. Tucking her hair behind her ears, she positioned the hat down low on her forehead. She strolled, taking her time, watching each step, her breath heavy just from the walking.

Must be the altitude? It was true she didn't do much exercise, but could her lung capacity be this diminished? Determined, she kept up her slow but steady pace, stopping only at a cactus—big bright green pads with a forest of impenetrable and lethal six-inch needles surrounding it.

First pole. She looked back at the cabin with an inflated sense of pride—an unfamiliar feeling for Clair, whose embers had almost been extinguished. But now she breathed on them.

The cabin looked small, a tiny matchbox in the vastness.

The sun came in and out as clouds raced across the sky. When the sun was out, the rays were so intense that she could feel it burning her skin, grateful for the sunscreen she'd put on before leaving the cabin. The clouds were low now, weighted, almost pressing down on her, and filled with low rumbles like bowling balls colliding. She noticed one in the shape of a spaceship and thought of George, who must be UFO-ing in Roswell now. She wondered if Ben was with his daughters.

The ground was covered with highlights and shadows, just like the puzzle pieces she had seen from the air. Now she was in one of the puzzle pieces. Which one, she wondered, and how did it fit into her life?

At the second pole sat a pile of stones, one on top of another, largest at the bottom, gradually getting smaller as the pile rose. Noticing a small piece of green glass, Clair placed it on the top of the cairn.

Where had the glass come from way out here? What had been the life-course of that strange piece of green glass?

At pole number three, the ground started to descend gradually, and the cabin disappeared from sight. She passed a tiny bush that looked as if it had been groomed by a bonsai master. At a low point, the ground was wet from yesterday's rain. There was a small amount of standing water out of which stood bright green bushes surrounded by an oasis of clover. As she got closer, she could hear the plant alive with honey bees.

What an ecstatic experience for bees, flying through such intoxicating air! Maenad bees.

As she watched, she saw something she couldn't quite believe. A white bee. Pure white. Were her eyes playing tricks? No. There it was—a pure white honey bee, feet yellow with pollen.

The pole where the ground dipped was much taller than the others, another few feet or so; she had lost sight of the cabin in her descent. Smooth tan mud like mocha frosting surrounded a puddle where alongside it other visitors had created yet another shrine, using fragments of rocks all in the shape of diamonds— twenty or so—marking the four directions.

Hundreds or thousands of people had come here and made this gesture, this offering. What was it that compelled people to make shrines? To say, "I'm here? I exist now." The shape of the cairn reminded Clair of an old gravestone she'd come across in one of the cemeteries in town. It displayed a little etched poem that read: "As you are now, so once was I. As I am now, you, too, will be."

In other words, we're all on the same bus.

At the fourth pole, she reached out and held on to it tightly, leaning back, looking up to its pointed tip and the sky beyond. "Hello!" she called out, just to test how her voice sounded, but the sound disappeared, absorbed by the wind and the space. Suddenly, she felt a mild ringing in her ears.

And then a thought flashed. *Oh, my God, Grace was right! I saw my brother's death before it happened. And that's when my visions stopped. I never let myself see anything more after that. I was too terrified of what I might see next. Now, I wonder ...could I let them in again?*

Fifth pole. Then Clair noticed that the cabin was now very far away. She tried counting the number of poles left in the row, but the heat waves distorted her vision and she kept losing track. The sun was now a furnace; she could almost feel her skin blistering. Breathing hard, mouth dry as the dusty ground, she thought, *Enough!* driven now by an image of an ice cold glass of water. Or perhaps another beer?

Time to head back.

As she turned, a prairie dog jumped out of its hole, and tiny arms dangling at its waist, began barking at her sudden invasion of its territory. The animal was no threat, she knew, but it surprised Clair, and as she leaped backward, her feet twisted in Lucky's too-big boots and she fell, barely missing a small, but lethal-looking cactus. She winced as the needles grazed her upper arm on the way down to the hard ground, but she did manage to keep her cast safely aloft. When she landed, Alex's straw hat bounced off her head, and Clair's eyes followed its rolling motion, landing six feet from where she lay. At the hat's resting place, she suddenly noticed the snake curled under a bush. The hat upturned several feet closer to the snake as if Clair was offering it as a new home.

At first she couldn't quite distinguish the snake from the lower branches, but when its black eyes and distinctive pattern came into focus, she knew. Not only had she disturbed the cute prairie dog, but also a diamondback rattlesnake. And it had noticed her as well.

Adrenaline filled her body in one massive pump of her heart, which contracted hard, then released. The dust from the ground had flown into her eyes, but she dared not blink, fearing the snake might misinterpret the movement.

Even in this predicament, she couldn't help but notice, the snake was beautiful: tan-colored with a black-and-rust diamond pattern. Studying the small scales of its skin and the thick muscles of its body, Clair counted five rattles on the tip of its tail. As she lay in the red dirt, she abruptly remembered that rattlesnakes could jump their own length.

The sun baked down and the wind blew in small twisters, dust adhering to her face, which had finally broken into a sweat. Details became crystal clear in her mind. The shrill bark of the prairie dog, its blond coat and tiny fingernails. The smell of the red clay of the earth. A rainstorm in the distance. Everything in her wanted to run and scream, but her mind screamed louder: *Don't move a muscle!*

The snake and Clair watched each other with curiosity. *Maybe it's a female? Do they lay their eggs in bushes or in lairs underground?* Then the pink tongue flashed, darting toward her several times. A little pink fork. Was it trying to get her scent? Did it smell her morning shower, Lucky's body lotion, Alex's hat and dress? What did it taste of her in the hot afternoon air?

I have to move, eventually, she thought, and began very slowly pulling her arms in. As she inched backward, she remembered a game she and the neighborhood kids played long ago, called *Statue,* the object of which was to move, but not get caught doing so. She moved, slow as a glacier, finally getting to her feet in movements so incrementally small that her muscles ached trying to hold her frozen positions.

Her heart was still pounding but had at least slowed from the heart-attack speed it had first clocked. She tried to wet her lips with her own pink tongue, but her mouth was devoid of any moisture. The prairie dog came out of its hole again, barking, but she didn't flinch. She glanced for a moment over her shoulder, making sure there was no other bush to fall over, entertaining a moment of horror, picturing multiple coiled snakes with beady eyes watching her from under every bush. Once on her feet, and having made sure nothing was behind her, she turned quickly, abandoning Alex's hat, and began to run, boots flapping.

It was then that she began to scream.

She ran, huffing and puffing past the poles, holding the dress high on her thighs. She didn't feel frightened, the screaming was mostly a release from being so still, an impulse, an explosion of all that had been trapped inside. Past the third pole and the second was a volcano of repressed energy, spewing and spurting. She ran until she reached the beginning pole, then stopped. Holding onto it with one hand, she heaved and coughed. Her chest hurt, her mouth like cotton. She looked up and could see the cabin clearly now, the others on the porch, beginning to rise up, one or two stepping down and coming toward her. Had they heard her screams?

And then she doubled over and began to laugh. At first just a chuckle, as she glimpsed herself in her mind's eye lying in front of that snake. Then she laughed at herself, running and screaming through the desert, and the women, now enthusiastically running toward her. For the first time in a long while, Clair felt fully alive.

CHAPTER 17

With glasses perched on the end of her nose, Lucky poured liquid from a triangular tequila bottle over Clair's shoulder and upper arm. A large red scrape was visible from which fine cactus hairs protruded.

"You'll have to hold still," she told Clair, picking up the tweezers.

"It doesn't hurt," Clair said bravely.

"Yeah, 'cause you're so pumped up with adrenaline. Hold still now."

"Those will sting later," observed VJ. "Let Lucky get them out."

Flushed and animated, Clair had told them the story of her encounter with the snake, as they walked her back to the cabin. Now they surrounded her under the portal, tending to her wounds, mostly her upper right arm from her brush with the cactus. Dark clouds were gathering in the sky, promising an evening storm.

"I'm sorry about your hat, Alex. I didn't dare try to get it."

"I don't blame you! I wouldn't have either," Alex laughed. "I can get it in the morning."

"I'll run and get it now, Alex," Jesse volunteered, "The wind may take it who knows where. Did you say at the fifth pole, Clair?"

"No, don't go," Clair exclaimed. "The snake might still be there."

But Jesse was already sprinting toward the poles, camera in tow.

"I think I've gotten most of them out." Lucky was running her fingers over Clair's arm. "There might still be some hidden, but it's looking good."

"Oh, and Clair," Alex added, "I packed a jar of calendula cream … it's on the shelf in the bathroom … rub some on. It's an anti-inflammatory and will help with the irritation."

Clair took a face cloth from the linen closet, turned on the water at the sink and, gazing at herself in the mirror, saw a reflection she hardly recognized. She wasn't wearing any makeup and her hair, uncombed since Jesse had cut it that morning, was in waves around her face. The afternoon light from the window created a luster in her cheeks—or was it that a fire had been ignited from within? Her eyes burned brightly, intense, alive. "Who are you?" she asked out loud of the Clair looking back at her.

Holding the steaming cloth to her face, Clair wondered, *Is this what Grace saw on that rainy afternoon? She had described lionesses and Africa, but said the images were symbolic. Am I now in the scene she imagined? But she'd said, "six lionesses." She must have included Kore! In this strange land, with these women, she said I would find my pride. Will I?*

"Hey, Clair!" Lucky knocked. "C'mon! Jesse's back. We're waiting for you."

"Be right there!" Clair called out, hanging the cloth on the towel holder but still pondering so many questions.

Alex was pouring shots from the tequila bottle into five small juice glasses as Clair returned to the portal. A blue plate of cut limes and a mound of salt sat nearby.

"Your hat!" Clair exclaimed to Alex, seeing it on one of the chairs. "Oh, Jesse, thank you for finding it. Did you see the snake?"

"The hat had blown away from the pole and into the field by the time I got there," Jesse answered, "so I didn't have to get near the snake pit."

"Clair, we're going to teach you how to drink tequila like a native," announced Lucky, handing her one of the juice glasses. "Just remember the formula: Lick, Shoot, Suck! First, you lick the stretchy part of your hand between your thumb and index finger, sprinkle some salt there, lick it off, 'shoot,' meaning you drink, and then bite the lime and suck."

"Okay," Clair agreed, "a lick, a dip, another lick …?"

"A drink and a bite," Lucky prompted. "Like this." She demonstrated, with a shake of her head and a small grimace. "Now you try."

The others joined in with her as Clair got the rhythm. *A lick, a dip, another lick, a drink, a bite!*

Clair shivered as she downed the shot in one gulp and bit into the lime.

"Holy Jesus!" she howled, with delight.

"Okay, another round all together!" VJ cried gleefully, filling the glasses.

As the women continued in their relaxed merriment, the snake whose home was a foot below them, could feel the constriction of her too-tight skin, and began inching herself forward, body swelling and contracting, as she loosed and freed herself from skin that no longer fit, leaving it behind in the dirt as she slithered toward the light.

⚡

Clair sat on the floor next to VJ while VJ was organizing the things needed to create the henna tattoo she had promised—a washcloth, towel, and the henna paste in a tube-shaped object. The women moved inside when the wind picked up and the sky darkened. Now grateful that the power had returned, VJ and Clair were seated under the one lamp in the living room, the others, lounging and gabbing on Lucky's double bed.

"Decide what you want?" VJ asked Clair, whose eyes had been focused on the graduated silver rings along VJ's ear, seven in all, gracefully hugging the pale curve.

"Oh, I'm not sure, VJ. Maybe you can surprise me? But I do want it on my arm."

"To balance out the wounded one … good choice."

Clair leaned back against a pillow, thinking about piercing her ears.

"This will take me a little time," VJ told her, "so just relax."

VJ began by lifting Clair's arm and washing it with cool water.

Clair inhaled deeply, enjoying the opportunity to rest. She felt tired, though the others had told her she might feel that way from the lower oxygen levels in the high altitude. *I'm pretty sure the tequila had something to do with it,* she thought, with amusement.

"I'm going to keep my eyes closed so I'll be surprised," she informed VJ, so she would not think Clair was being rude. "Tell me how you learned how to do this," she asked, curious as to how someone acquires this strange skill.

"My youngest daughter spent a lot of time in India," VJ answered. "Mehndi is a part of the culture, practiced for certain festivals, like weddings. The drawings are highly symbolic, and I have something in mind for you that I hope you'll like … unless you've changed your mind about me surprising you and have thought of something?"

"Nope, surprise me." Clair took another deep breath, remembering that Jesse had instructed her that it would bring calmness. "I told you all about my daughter, Cass. So now tell me … how old are your daughters?"

"Twenty-five. Stella is the youngest of my biological daughters. My oldest is Pax … she's thirty, same age as my adopted daughter Lulu, who's Vietnamese."

Clair's eyes popped open, but she avoided looking at her arm. "How did that happen, if you don't mind me asking."

"It's pretty simple really. It was after the war and my partner and I heard there was a child in need. So, we adopted her."

"That's lovely, VJ," Clair said, closing her eyes, "that you offered her a home and a life with more opportunities."

"We feel she chose us … like we were meant to be her family. And sadly, there's still prejudice against Vietnamese people, so her opportunities were limited."

"And you have a son too?"

"Yes. Oliver is twenty. He and Stella have the same father. Pax's father was from my hippie days."

"What was Stella doing in India?"

"Exploring, searching—hoping to find a spiritual teacher."

"Did she find one?"

"No, but she did come back with a girlfriend, so maybe she's her spiritual teacher. Partners often are our greatest teachers. They'd like to marry but of course a same sex couple in India's not possible yet … hopefully that will change at some point. It must. And they're fighting for it, for themselves and others."

Clair was surprised by VJ's casual mention of her daughter partnered with a woman. She knew no one in a gay relationship. At least not openly. *But why shouldn't everyone have the right to love who they love?*

"My daughter Cassidy is in Europe now. I guess she's searching too, but I'm not sure for what. Probably sex and drugs, with a little art thrown in so she has something she can tell to her father and me."

"Well, I can relate," VJ grinned. "I was majorly into sex, drugs, and rock and roll." She began to draw along the skin of Clair's hand and arm. VJ had a throaty, soothing voice. "It's a great time for these young ones to explore and be out and free in the world and to see something other than this fucked-up culture."

Clair thought VJ's assessment of the culture was harsh, but didn't want to challenge it. She leaned back further on the pillow, closed her eyes, and asked, "Do you draw everything freehand?"

"Yep. I went to art school before I became a revolutionary," VJ laughed, enjoying her description of herself. "I'm drawing out the design with a white-tipped pen, so I have a pattern to follow with the henna."

Clair was so curious about Lucky's friends, so unlike any women she'd known during the past thirty years. But now back home she'd met Grace, who was also unusual—moving to another country, married to an artist, immersed in something most people would find a joke—reading tea leaves, being psychic, seeing symbolic images.

"Where did you go to art school?"

"CalArts in Santa Clarita."

"My daughter will begin her first year at the School of the Museum of Fine Arts in Boston this fall."

"Ahh, yes, you live on the opposite coast. The Museum School is a great choice."

"Are you from California?"

"Born and bred. Actually, both my parents were in the movie industry. My father was a director, my mother an actress. VJ named them, both dead now, and Clair remembered reading about them in movie magazines of the past.

VJ continued. "My dad wanted me to become a director, but my art was in another direction, so to speak. Then the Vietnam protests took precedence over everything else, and I left school … and never went back. Instead, I went to protests and Woodstock, hooked up with a guy, got pregnant, left him and came to New Mexico, where I lived in the shadow of the Indian drum and the place where the atomic bomb was conceived, created, and detonated. It was here in the land of opposites that my revolutionary nature was replaced with a maternal one."

If Grace had taken Clair one step along the way of opening up, Lucky and her friends had cracked the door wider. Suddenly, everything was just so different. She had no reference points: the women and their lives; cowboys and tequila; a landscape like an African savannah; even the very air itself, creating hard-edged clouds, so close you thought you could touch them. Clair was loosed from her moorings, like a boat sprung free in a storm. Not used to such a lack of boundaries, she felt darn right dizzy.

Occasional bursts of laughter from the other women punctured Clair and VJ's more focused space, and they both smiled, listening. "They're having a great time," VJ observed, even as she focused on the drawing. "Lucky's been so looking forward to this and to you coming here, Clair."

"Yes, Alex told me the same thing," Clair said, pleased.

Kore came to nuzzle next to Clair on the blanket as the air turned noticeably cooler.

"Storm's coming," Alex announced, coming around the corner. Then seeing VJ's artful drawing on Clair's arm, opened her mouth to cry out with delight.

"Shhhhh," said VJ quickly. "No hints! Clair doesn't know what I'm branding her with."

"I can hardly wait!" Clair blurted.

"You'll see soon enough. I'm almost finished."

"I'm going to put the casserole in the oven before the electricity goes off again," Alex said, heading toward the kitchen. "We'll want to eat at some point."

"Hey, I'm hungry now!" VJ called after her. "Let's all snack and drink … I just need another couple of minutes more."

Lucky and Jesse wandered into the room, closing windows ahead of the rain as they moved through. And both had a similar reaction to Alex's when they saw what VJ was tattooing with the henna on Clair's hand and arm.

"VJ, I'm getting a little curious—and worried, frankly—hearing how everyone is reacting." *Maybe I should have decided on something myself,* she thought.

"Oh, no, Clair, don't worry—it's astounding," Lucky chimed in, attempting to calm Clair's concerns.

"Okay, madame! Your artwork is complete," VJ crowed. "You can look now."

CHAPTER 18

Black clouds darkened the sky, turning the day into a chilly and premature evening. Most of the light now was from the woodstove and candles that were positioned around the living room, glittering from Mason jars. Drawn in that inexorable way, a few moths flicked around the flames, enraptured.

Clair sat on a blanket with VJ's soft yellow pashmina over her shoulders. The glow from the open woodstove cast her shadow, enlarged and dancing on the wall behind her. She had been studying VJ's work: the slim henna snake that began with rattles at her fingers, ascending in graceful undulating curves, along hand and arm, ending with a forked tongue aimed up her forearm. In the flickering firelight, the snake looked as if it was moving … as if it was alive.

"VJ, this drawing is, well," Clair hesitated, trying to find the word, "perfect! I never would have thought of a snake. I would have chosen a flower or something equally predictable, but this … is so … right. And wild!" Clair enthused, her eyes wide in disbelief.

"After your encounter in the field today, a snake seemed like the obvious choice," VJ said, pleased with her effort and Clair's response.

The others lay on the rolled-up blankets, pillows under their chests, faces making a semicircle toward the stove while the wind banged in erratic fits at the windows like one who is desperate for shelter.

"Alex, what is snake energy?" Clair asked. "In the animal cards?"

"The snake is about transformation because it sheds its skin. It's about releasing the old ways and patterns that no longer serve. It can mean a whole spiritual healing, an awakening. Very powerful, Clair. And as you've told us, you are in a time of transformation—maybe the biggest of your life."

Clair looked at each of the women. "I wouldn't have been able to call it that … a transformation … before being here with all of you. Blake leaving me seemed more of a personal tragedy, but it's helpful to think of it as an opportunity for transformation and happiness."

Cedar logs sizzled and popped in the metal stove, filling the room with the remembered aroma inside her mother's old cedar chest, where woolen coats and sweaters were stored to keep the moths from eating holes in them. She was feeling more akin to these women now, more accepted, like they had scraped aside their differences of experience as easily as they scraped the dinner plates and arrived at a comfortable place where they were just … women.

Lucky took a sip of the tequila and asked, "Doesn't hanging out by the fire all wrapped up in blankets remind you of pajama parties from when we were teenagers?"

"Yeah and sneaking in whatever liquor had the most in the bottle," VJ added, with a mischievous grin. "In fact, it was the first place I got drunk … *and* threw up. In Doris Day's toilet, would you believe it?"

"What???" The women exclaimed in unison.

"I was friends with her son, Terry. Oh my God, I never wanted another drink after that! But fortunately," VJ chuckled, "I outgrew that phase."

"I am jealous that you had boys at pajama parties!" Lucky stated emphatically.

"Yes, indeed. Remember, it was Hollywood after all."

"It's kind of interesting, when you think about it," Alex said, "that as those teenage girls of long ago, we helped each other when our bodies were changing, hormones on a rampage. Now, here we are again, helping each other—bodies changing, hormones dimming. Just another passage."

"Yeah, but watching ourselves decay," smirked VJ, filling the glasses, "isn't nearly as exhilarating as growing tits!"

"Oh, sure it is!" Alex, joined in. "You just have an attitude problem, not seeing the humor and utter fascination in watching everything melt, sag, and wrinkle."

"Oh, you're just at the beginning of it," VJ rebutted, "Me? Why, I have gray hair in my pubes! I'm seriously thinking about getting some hair dye."

"Just pluck those babies right out," encouraged Lucky. "That's what I do."

"Yeah, when you just have a couple, but if I did that, I'd be bald down there. And I'm not ready for a Mr. Clean *mons pubis* just yet."

They were all laughing hard, collectively lapsed into a shared humor that was accelerated by each other's irreverence and delight, the alcohol, an illegal drug, and pheromones coursing through their bloodstreams. Clair, whose facial muscles were untrained for such a workout, laughed until her sides ached and her eyes ran with tears. It took a while, but they all finally settled down into collapsed heaps.

"But, ladies," offered Alex, "think of the silver lining of age."

VJ cracked, "You mean that we're turning silver and getting more lines?" They all laughed again.

Undeterred, Alex went on. "Well, yes … but also, think of all the amazing wisdom we're acquiring as we move to this more venerable stage of life."

"If we can remember it!" cracked Jesse, bending over double in a fit of laughter that ignited the others, until the laughter finally subsided. Then they were quiet for a moment, just listening to their own breathing and the whistling wind as it picked up speed across the wide open land.

"But, you know," Alex broke the silence, "whether toddlers, teenagers, or seniors, women are almost always looking for connection. It's how we're built, what we value: relationships, connection, intimacy."

"Sometimes to our detriment," VJ pointed out, as she bit the lime.

"Yes, some women sacrifice all that they are," pondered Alex, "not even knowing who or what that might be, for a life that isn't even satisfying. But, no doubt, it feels safer than going out on their own." She reached her hand to her mouth, "Oh, I'm sorry, Clair, if that hit too close to home right now."

"It's alright," Clair acknowledged. "It's true. I stayed because I thought I was safe, had an identity … and because I didn't have the courage to face life alone."

"But, you know, relationships aside," Jesse added, sitting up. "I gotta say—I really enjoyed my alone time these last couple of years, having to rely on my own wits and creativity. And I haven't even missed sex, although I thought that would be the hardest part."

Clair licked the salt from her hand. "It's been more than two years for me, and I've been married!" she laughed.

They all joined the laugh, Lucky adding, "Well, then, girl, it's about time you got yourself well laid."

In a more pensive voice, Jesse mulled, "We all know relationships can be just the best … *if* you're with the right person, of course. I, however, have decided that it's time for me to build my own ship this time—before trying to build a *relation*ship."

Everyone groaned. "Well, good for you, honey," encouraged Alex, patting Jesse's leg. "That's the right order of things." With a grin, Jesse slapped Alex's hand away.

Alex chuckled. "But, you know, ladies, there is an image called a *mandorla.*" Made when two circles overlap. As I tell my clients, it's the image that illustrates a healthy relationship. But first the individual circles have to have their own integrity, like an individual person … like what you said, Jesse, your own 'ship.' If the circles don't have good boundaries, they blur and smudge and make a mess when they try to merge. When they're strong in themselves, they can merge with another strong circle, and instead of making a mess, they create the *mandorla*. It's a beautiful almond shape, amazingly like a vulva, ladies, which represents the relationship. But these circles never merge all the way in a healthy coupling. They remain themselves but, at the same time, create the special center that holds them together."

"That's quite beautiful, Alex. I wish I had known about the mandorla. But I'm glad I know about it now … for future reference."

"Say, Clair, why don't you tell us a bit more about the man from the plane that drew on your cast?" Lucky asked, her eyes twinkling.

"Oh, there's not much to say." Clair began, thinking to avoid Lucky's question, but then stopped herself. *There's actually a lot to say, isn't there? I* have *been thinking about him.* So, instead, she took a quick breath and plunged in. "Well, the thing that struck me the most was that his eyes were direct when he looked at me, and they never wavered. Blake never really looked at me, not in the eyes. So, at first Ben made me nervous, but then instead of feeling threatened or penetrated in a scary way, I realized that his eyes were simply inviting me to be myself, a person he wanted to know. And then I realized that I wanted that too."

The women were silent, giving her their full attention. All were sitting up, cross-legged or leaning against the cushions. Kore had nestled in VJ's lap.

"He's divorced," she continued, "and was traveling to Dallas to visit his daughters before going off on an adventure of his own."

"Well, that's cool," Jesse observed with approval. "He takes care of business, and himself."

"He's an architect. I've actually been in a museum addition he designed. The space is lovely, filled with light where the light doesn't just enter but dwells. It's funny because, at one point, I wanted to become an architect … but it was only for my brother because that was what he wanted to do."

"Why didn't you?" Alex asked.

"My family wanted me to get a 'practical' education, which means what they thought of as a woman's education. You know that old thinking: a teacher or a nurse or a nun, for God's sake." The group burst into laughter.

"There were so few choices for women," Jesse said, wiping her eyes from laughter-tears.

"Well, of those three choices," Clair continued, "I chose teaching, but then had to drop out anyway when I got pregnant."

"There went your career as a nun!" VJ joked. There were more giggles.

"But I did design the house I'm living in, so I had somewhat of an interest."

"Clair Bear," responded Lucky, "you have an interest in all things creative, but you're a natural painter, an artist. I see you. I've always seen you."

"Thank you for the reminder, Lucky. I've actually enjoyed getting back to drawing while I've been here."

"We all need reminders," said Alex. "And we can always change our minds."

"Ironically, Ben told me he's thinking of leaving his profession, that he chose it to please his architect father, which many men do, it seems. You know, follow in the footsteps of their fathers, my own son being one of them."

Silently, she considered for the first time what her son might have done had he not followed Blake into law. *I could tell it never really suited Carl. He could do it, he was capable, but he didn't love the law. What might he have chosen if it was from his heart?*

She went on. "Ben said he wants to get back to sculpting, something he'd studied before architecture. I liked that he didn't feel like he had to have all the answers. And he admitted that he's made some mistakes. Blake always had all the answers. The only "right' answers."

"That's quite an intimate conversation for a few hours on an airplane," Lucky commented, eyebrows raised.

"I haven't traveled very much lately, but it was, wasn't it? And I told him about Blake and me. I hadn't told anyone that except my psychic friend. But Ben seemed to understand and relate."

"An empathetic and vulnerable man," Alex summarized. "How lovely when they come along."

"I can show you him," Clair rose quickly, disappearing into the bedroom for a moment. "I've just about filled this up …" she said, returning, holding the drawing tablet. "Hope no one minds."

"Let's see those, Clair." Lucky reached for the book, opened it to the first page and kept turning. She saw a hasty sketch of the field from the portal, the poles mere scratches on the page; one of the white bird a moment before landing on its nest, flapping wings filling the page in a frenzy; there was a regal portrait of Kore after her bath; another of ominous-looking clouds; and one of each of the women, where Chair had managed in quick strokes to capture something of the essence of them all.

Lucky looked up. "I knew you'd been drawing, but when did you do all these?"

"Five or ten minutes here and there … they don't take long."

"No snake?" Lucky questioned.

"Haven't had the time yet, but now I don't have to." Clair rotated her wrist, appreciating the beauty of the henna drawing.

The last one in the tablet turned out to be the one she wanted to show them—the man who Lucky had wanted to convince her had stolen her luggage. The sketch was in profile, high chiseled nose descending in a straight line from the full eyebrow, then making a distinct right angle to the philtrum, the vertical indentation in the center of the upper lip that creates the Cupid's Bow. She knew odd terms like *philtrum* from the anatomy book given to her by her brother and had taken more care drawing that lovely prominence as well as Ben's sensual mouth. His hair, in contrast, was an edgy salt-and-pepper buzz cut. His grey eyes, which she remembered the most, were not visible in the drawing, that little detail remaining for now in her memory.

"Now I ask you," Lucky joked, holding up the drawing to the rest of the women, "is this the profile of a lover or a thief?"

⚡

After a dinner of lasagna and salad, the star of the night was VJ's homemade angel food cake, topped with whipped cream and strawberries.

"The strawberries are from my garden, frozen especially for this occasion for you, Angel, on your birthday."

"Thank you, VJ," Lucky said warmly with affection as she got up from the table to hug VJ. "I love you, dear friend, and always feel nourished, body and soul, by your food."

"De nada, my love! There's no one I'd rather cook for than my family—and, you, my dear, are family and have been for a long time now."

"And just so you know," VJ, handed Lucky an envelope, "we, your three amigas, are getting you a series of Watsu massages."

"And I'm throwing in a tattoo of your choosing," added Jesse, "'cause it's about time you got one."

"Oh, you guys! Thank you!"

"Lucky," Clair reached for Lucky's hands, "I have no gift to give you tonight, but hopefully it will show up with the rest of my things at the airport tomorrow."

"Oh, you dear friend … don't you know that your being here is my gift?" And the two embraced to the cheers of the others.

"To women's friendships!" exclaimed VJ. And they all toasted.

Once seated, Clair leaned in toward Alex, "What's Watsu?"

"It's a special kind of water massage done with your body in a weightless state. It's marvelous! You'll have to have one when you come back."

And I am coming back, Clair thought, and with the decision made, smiled.

Jesse took pictures of Lucky with the dessert, Lucky's face aglow with happiness and a fair amount of Patron Silver. Then setting the camera's timer, she jumped into the shot, behind Lucky's chair, yelling, "Lean in if you want to be in the picture!" Lucky couldn't help but make a silly face, jokester that she was.

The whipped cream on the cake top wouldn't hold a candle in its soft texture, so after the traditional "Happy Birthday" song, sang with gusto and much misguided harmonizing, Lucky blew out the candle in the mason jar nearest to her, then rose and went around the table blowing out the rest until the room was lit only by the occasional lightning flash.

Sitting back down at the head of the table, Lucky reached for the hands of the women alongside her, saying, "Let's all hold hands and feel the loving and creative energy connecting us. I am so happy to have my sisters around me. I love you all so much!"

The five joined hands and closed their eyes, each feeling the warmth of the others as a wave of energy traveled in a stream, enveloping them. No separation—rather, the felt-experience that *all are one.*

Leaving the dishes on the table, the women reconvened on the floor. Clair recognized her growing regard for these four women, the easy way they teased each other, playfully provoking, and yet without any meanness or defensiveness. On some level, they might as well have been playful eight year olds—only now, with licenses, PhD's, and credit cards, loose in the world without adult supervision. Clair had always thought of herself as the bathroom-monitor type—so eager to please the adults that she didn't get to play with the other children. In some ways, these women reminded her of the knitting women, in their ease of banter. And it reminded her that she hardly ever played. Well, never, really.

The henna serpent on her wrist tightened its grip.

"By the way, Clair, the dye will flake off after it fully dries," VJ explained. "Then it'll go through a series of odd shades, darkening over the course of a week before fading away."

Clair picked off a couple of the flakes, then, being fastidious, swept up the pieces into a tissue. "I'll miss it when it's gone," she said, leaving the room to toss the tissue in the trash. She chuckled to herself, feeling strangely proud when she thought about wearing the henna tattoo in public tomorrow. The very idea of having a tattoo on her body was insane! She knew it wasn't a real tattoo with ink needled into her skin, but still, it looked quite striking, and she smiled an enigmatic smile.

What would my friends in Boston think? Well, I never see any of them anymore, do I? Not after being away so long. They really aren't friends anyway, are they? More like acquaintances. Lucky is my only real friend, although now I feel like I also have Grace, as well as Alex and VJ and Jesse. And perhaps even Ben.

Her world was expanding in the loveliest way, with human connections, with heart, with no barriers and no walls.

Once Clair was seated again, Lucky looked at each of them, from face to face, saying, "And I have a gift for each of *you*." She leaned down to a little basket that was under her chair and withdrew four small boxes, handing them out to the women. "It's so special to me that each of you could be here to celebrate this grand occasion of mine." She laughed. "Please, go ahead— unwrap them."

Clair untied the ribbon and lifted the lid off the box. On the cotton bedding inside was a thin sliver of silver in the shape of a tiny lightning bolt. She sucked in her breath. It was so beautiful in its simplicity!

Lucky stood up and raised her glass. "DeMaria, the artist who brought us all to this magical place, said that the lightning strikes are more apt to be psychological than physical. So even though we haven't seen lightning strike the poles, I hope you have all been struck … in the best way possible."

Undressing for bed later that night, Clair took a closer look at Lucky's gift. "I hope you have been struck," Lucky had said.

I have been struck. But what exactly does that mean?"

A few hours later, a loud crash of lightning hit somewhere close by, shaking the windows and awakening the women, causing them to all shriek at once.

"Did it hit a pole?" Lucky's voice was heard throughout the cabin.

The five converged in the living room all heading toward the door.

"Be careful!" someone said.

The clouds were black and threatening, visible only for lingering seconds when distant flashes lit the sky like a bad fluorescent bulb.

"Well, we can't really tell if anything was hit," said Jesse, peering into the darkness, "but the temperature is wonderful, and we're awake now. Shall we sit for a while?"

"We can't forget to pack these!" said Lucky, having spotted the masks they left to dry earlier in the day. She picked hers up, tying it on with the attached strings.

"Whoa-a-a! Wow!" the women all chorused.

"Let's all wear our new personas," cried Alex, putting her mask on, with the others following in turn. Gleefully checking out each other's masks, eyes peering from behind, they "oooed" and "ahhhed" as they saw their individual creations. Then, spontaneously, one by one, the women took to the field and began moving, turning, laughing—touching the ground and raising their arms up to the sky, where the lightning flashed like a strobe and thunder rumbled.

Then, a gift!

Drops of rain joined the dance.

The earth was warm underneath Clair's bare feet, the rain cool on her skin. The sky opened a big crack that hung for a moment like a door swinging wide open. She thought if she could just see past the bright light that she'd know everything.

Lucky's hair came out of its braid, falling in wet strands as the rain went from drops to deluge. Without a thought, she shed herself of her white cotton pajamas, dropping them along the ground. Seeing her, the others followed suit, even Clair, who at first couldn't believe what was happening, watching the wet women become wild, naked maenads, dancing.

In the house, the golden orb spider dropped down for a kill, stopping while she watched the show in the field, letting the fly consider its fate. The eagle circled above in the stormy sky; the coyote stopped his prowl and sat down, transfixed; the serpent coiled in a bush for a better view; the prairie dog sat up with tiny dangling feet; the lions arrived from the astral field. All watched. Kore sat on the portal in her cat wisdom, out of the rain, long ears alert on her regal head, eyes glowing golden with every flash as she watched with equanimity, long tail in slow undulation.

Clair raised her arms to the heavens, hesitating at first, shyly, for she hadn't praised God in a while. Seeing her raised cast, she thought, *That's done, I'm done with the past.* The snake along her right arm waved in the air. *That's my future, and whatever it might hold.* She lifted her face and let the rain cleanse her of the dust and debris of her life.

During the flashes she saw the others: VJ, voluptuous, with heavier, older breasts that had nourished three children; Jesse, the wounded warrior, with noble scars across her body; Alex, the woman's scar of birth smiling across her lower abdomen; Lucky, her friend and initiator, with a bandaged heart; they all danced. These women, all different, each perfect, struggling in their own way—living with and growing from the life events that had shaped them, making them who they were in this moment.

They were women who had failed and succeeded, who had shed many tears and screamed at injustice, and who ultimately were learning to forgive others and themselves and live on courageously. The maenads in their masks, mad with love for Dionysus, danced on, joining hands, bodies coming together in a tight circle, naked, slippery, ecstatic, free, until the whole world was dancing ... dancing.

A luminous flash and a sound like a tree falling caused them to halt their dance in a single step and look toward the field. A strike! A strike! One pole was hit that was straight in front of them, but at the farthest edge of the field. The blinding arc traveled down the slim length of the pole, rendering it ablaze with colored light. The contact hovered at the tip—a sky god's finger touching the pointed tip of the pole—divinity in direct contact with the earth. A holy sight. At the same time, an arc formed across the top plane of the poles like writhing snakes, and the women felt a prickling on their feet and heads, as if touched by pine branch needles.

And they danced on.

CHAPTER 19

The sun was up, soft rays streaming into the room when Clair opened her eyes. For a moment she watched vacantly as the floating dust particles were suspended in the light. The air was more humid after the rain, although she could already feel the day's growing heat. She breathed in deeply to a count of eight, as Jesse had taught her, held it, then relaxed into a long slow exhale. As she did, she closed her eyes to the brightness, while images from the pre-dawn hours flooded her mind—the rain, the firestorm in the sky, the dancing.

What had happened last night? Or was it this morning? Only hours ago? And, did it even happen? It seems more like a dream.

At that moment, she remembered the dream that she'd been just having. *Charlton Heston! What was he doing there?* She rolled onto her side to reach for the drawing tablet on the floor. Alex was still sleeping, blonde hair in a halo on the pillow, arm extended out in a welcoming gesture. And naked, as far as Clair could tell.

And as Clair's own arm reached out, she realized to her surprise that so was she. Her watch was on the floor next to the tablet, showing that the time was 8:15—alongside tracks of muddy footprints that still looked like they were dancing.

On the tablet, she wrote, "Charlton Heston?"

"Good morning," Clair heard a yawning voice say.

Alex sat up in the bed, pulling the sheet up with her. Her hair remained in the pillow-caused halo that extended around her head.

Clair laughed. "Your hair!"

Alex laughed too. "Does it look like yours?"

Clair reached up and felt her own frizzed-out locks.

"I think we got touched by the gods," Alex chuckled. "Clearly, Zeus was throwing lightning bolts around."

"What's that about Zeus?" It was Lucky. She leaned into the room with just a long T-shirt on and flashed them one breast.

Clair and Alex both hooted out loud. Not only at Lucky's exposed breast, but also at Lucky's long hair that was nearly flying around her head like serpents.

"Hey, Lucky! You look like Medusa," commented Alex, grinning.

"Well, I'm not the only one who got zapped," Lucky shot back, pointing at them. "Fuck, we were lucky we weren't killed!"

"Yeah," agreed Alex. "Talk about bad publicity."

"There goes the neighborhood!" cracked Lucky as she continued to the bathroom.

Hearing the latch on the bathroom door catch, Clair announced, "I remember a piece of a dream I had."

Alex sat more upright, immediately attentive.

"Want to share?"

"Yes, I'd like to … but I can't imagine what it's about."

"What do you remember?"

"Only that I was with, um, well, Charlton Heston. How do I find meaning in him?"

"So," began Alex, doing what she was born to do, "tell me about Charlton Heston."

"Well, he's an actor in Hollywood. Also, a political figure, president of the Rifle Association."

"But what about him is personal to you?"

"He played Moses in *The Ten Commandments*."

"Go on …" Alex smiled encouragingly.

Clair pondered the question. "Catholics that we were, my school got to see the film long after it came out, but our parish actually sponsored a showing of it at the local theater. I was young, maybe seven or eight—and it was a rare thing for my parents to take me to anything. But what stayed with me about the movie was when Moses had been cast out of Egypt by his brother Ramses. Moses was crawling through the desert, squeezing out the last drop of water from his pouch. The narrator says, in this deep holy voice: 'The clay is ready for the Maker's hand.'"

"What about that very long movie caused you to remember that part?"

"I think it was because I understood it somehow, young as I was, being a good little Catholic girl. Moses was as low as he had ever been, about to die from thirst, but it was only then that he was ready for the hand of God."

"Well, there are various ways to interpret a dream, but I think you've nailed it. Moses is at rock bottom, banished from his homeland, the self he knows … being an Egyptian prince … dead. He's thirsty, spiritually dry, and about to begin the search for his true identity, his deeper self."

Alex stood up, wrapping the sheet around her. "Clair, if the shoe fits, wear it."

"Hey, everybody!" yelled Lucky, exiting the bathroom. "Let's get a move-on! We'll meet in the kitchen for coffee in ten minutes; we need time to do that ceremony before Clete arrives."

"We can talk more about this later," Alex nodded to Clair, heading toward the empty bathroom. "And anytime you have a question about a dream or something else, you can always call me. We're sisters now."

Clair felt the sincerity of the remark and the warmth in her heart that followed.

"Anybody up over there?" Lucky banged on the wall to the other bedroom.

"Our hair!" VJ yelled through the wall.

"Nobody touch theirs," Jesse commanded. "I want to take pictures!"

"Someone please make me a vanilla latte," VJ pleaded.

The kitchen was a train wreck when Clair entered the room: dishes everywhere, food still on them, dried and stuck. The bright red color of the lasagna had turned brown on the edges. The once crisp salad was now only limp leaves and tomato pieces scattered in the sink.

"Oh, yeah," Lucky observed, standing there damp from the shower, wrapped in a towel, hair not as wild, "we forgot to do this last night."

Clair nodded. "Well, you could say we had other things on our minds."

"Well, I for one don't care about eating this morning," Lucky added, looking around at the mess.

"Me either," VJ said, coming in. "Just my vanilla latte."

"Where are Jesse and Alex?" Lucky asked.

"I'm here," Alex strolled in all dressed.

"How did you get the frizz out of your hair?" Clair asked.

"I just ran my wet fingers through it. That takes the electrical charge right out. Oh, and Clair, I want you to wear my dress home. You cannot go out in public in your disreputable suit! I don't think they'd even let you board."

"Oh, Alex, thank you!" Clair responded warmly. "When I looked at my suit this morning, I thought, what a mess I'd be … but I'd love to wear your dress. I'll send it back to you once I get home."

"Absolutely not—I want you to have it. It was never the right colors for me, however, it looks beautiful on you. Oh, and Lucky, to answer your question, Jesse went for a quick run and will be back pronto."

"VJ, how about you make the coffee," Clair suggested, "and I'll start this cleanup. It won't take long at all." In the chaos of the kitchen, Clair knew what to do. And she enjoyed a good cleanup, resulting in a pristine space, no clutter or mess.

Once all were seated on the portal, cups in hand, and the kitchen in good enough shape, Lucky began sharing her plan for the final ceremony before they left.

"So, I had asked that you all bring something to bury … something in your life you're ready to leave behind that no longer serves you or the direction you want to go in."

Clair had thought about Lucky's request ever since she'd read the invitation, but she hadn't known until this moment what she would choose.

"And," Lucky continued, "I asked that you plant a seed for what you want to grow. Now, I know that planting in the desert doesn't guarantee the growth of anything, but I've brought sunflower seeds, and who knows! Maybe the rain and sun gods will be kind."

The women followed Lucky single file, each with a digging spoon and their own thoughts. Carrying a pitcher of water, Lucky brought them out to a new spot in the field not near any of the poles, but rather on a lower plot of ground, still moist from last night's rain. The fragrance was different too; fresher, cleaner, and a few flowers were in bloom that weren't blooming yesterday.

"Let's spread out!" she shouted into the wind, "so this can be a private matter. Dig two holes, a foot or two away from each other, and it's there you'll bury what you brought to leave behind and plant the seeds I gave you. I'll leave the water in the center here, so you can each water your planted seeds."

It seemed a solemn occasion to be taken seriously and executed with intention. Clair did that. Digging two holes a foot apart, she could sense the others doing the same, although she didn't look at any of them. This was a private moment. If she thought back to childhood, it was like deciding what to give up for Lent—except with Lent you were giving up something you liked, something that would deny yourself, a sacrifice to offer God. This occasion was different in that one task was about giving up and burying something you were ready to release.

Without hesitation, Clair twisted off her gold wedding ring. She held it in both hands raised close to her mouth, so she could whisper what she had to say to it. She had known that when Ben had noticed her ring, he'd assumed she was married. But she actually hadn't been married for a long time now. She was completely ready to let go of this symbol of two lives joined. Not so others would know, but because it was the truth. She and Blake were not together, and he was getting ready to marry another woman and welcome their child.

So, what meaning does this ring have? None, it seemed. She whispered, "Here is where I leave you, Blake."

Clair let go, placing the golden ring in the hole. She whispered, "I let go of the promises we made to each other. Neither of us kept them, anyway. You, more blatantly, with your affairs, but me, too, with my coldness toward you. I wasn't ever meeting you halfway, but I liked being able to blame you so I could be the victim. I leave behind the sadness and anger that I've been carrying. And I thank you for our children."

Then she squeezed her eyes shut, focusing on what she wanted for her future. She took the seeds and dropped them into their separate hole, whispering over them, "*And I plant these seeds for my own growth, for my own life, my own passions, and for joy!*"

What a concept! she thought. *I'm ready to know myself. I'm ready to live full-tilt. And I'm ready to follow a new script.*

Squatting in the sandy New Mexican soil, Clair reached her *ultima thule*—the farthest she'd ever been from herself, at least the self she'd known her whole life. Here, now, in the heat of this day, was someone she was just discovering. This moment, her fingers covered in dirt, a false hope discarded, a seed planted, she vowed to harvest that new self, the one she was always meant to be and always had been, deep inside. This was the opportunity to claim more territory and—with it—more truth.

The Fool has left the Cave and the journey has begun.

CHAPTER 20

The Albuquerque Sunport was a hive of activity that evening two hours before Clair's red-eye flight back to Boston. The five women linked arms as they walked toward the terminal.

"So, who has the next birthday?" Lucky asked, already knowing the answer.

"Mine is in a couple of months," Clair answered without missing a beat.

"We're in! Sure! I'll be there!" the others chimed.

Arriving at the ticket counter, after dodging a stream of tourists eager to enter the Land of Enchantment, Clair found it disorienting to be back in such a chaos of people and activity after the stillness of the field. But knew she carried a piece of that "New Mexico quiet" in her now—like the thin, clear air, deep in her lungs.

Returning to Maine now seemed like a haven where she could assimilate these new feelings and ideas, rather than it being a last desperate handhold before a final slide into the Atlantic Ocean of depression. She put the plastic bag with her clothes in it on the floor, leaned her elbows on the counter, and waited until *Greg*, as his badge announced, looked her way. Lucky was beside her too, the others standing a distance from them, out of the way.

"Can I help you, Miss?" the bespeckled young man asked.

"Yes, Greg, I hope so. I'm Clair McKendrick. I had my luggage taken the other day on a flight from Dallas to Albuquerque ... know anything about that?"

Greg began hitting keys on his computer..

"I reported it when I left and was told it would be taken care of, but I'm not sure what that means. I have a reservation back to Boston leaving later tonight. A first class ticket."

"Oh, Mrs. McKendrick, yes, here it is," Greg said nodding, suddenly engaged. "Wait just one quick minute."

Clair turned to Lucky and shrugged. "They said this wouldn't be a problem."

"He does seem to know something," observed Lucky, when suddenly she gasped. "Clair, your wedding ring!"

Clair looked back at her with such perfect calm that Lucky knew right away.

"You didn't," she admonished, sliding her sunglasses up onto her head, eyes wide open.

"I did," Clair grinned, like it was no big deal.. "But not the diamond band … I'm not crazy … that's in here," she said, pointing to the plastic bag carrying her linen suit. She'd left behind the torn blouse. "Thought I should save that ring for Cassidy. But, yep, I buried the wedding ring in our bury-and-plant ceremony. it's living in the field now. Hope it doesn't poison the plants," she laughed. "I followed Grace's advice and finally said goodbye—and thank you."

"I think the lightning knocked some sense into you, my friend." Lucky put an arm around Clair's shoulder.

Just then, Greg returned, a big smile on his round face, pulling Clair's bag behind him.

"Oh, my God!" Clair cried out. "You found it!" The others gathered round and cheered, nearly frightening Greg, who took a step back, not quite trusting the energy of this pack.

"We're very sorry for the inconvenience, Mrs. McKendrick … and we're pleased to return your luggage to you. Do you want to take a look inside, make sure everything is there? And I hate to ask, but do you have some I.D. to prove you're who you say you are."

Comically, like a Greek chorus, five women sang out in unison, "She is!"

"I can tell you the contents of the bag and show you my driver's license … which happens to be inside the bag."

"That would be fine," he said, formally. His dark hair had small points of blonde on the front.

As she reached in the bag, searching for her wallet, she asked, "Do you know what happened to it? How it got off the plane?"

"I don't," Greg answered, "but I think there was a letter that came with the bag … taped on the side. Hmmm, not there. Let me see if it fell off in the back room."

While Greg was gone, Clair knelt down and unzipped her bag. She felt oddly happy to see it, this thing of her own. It was familiar, and it felt good to have it back. Opening it, she glanced at all the things she'd thought she'd need: clothes she had planned on wearing, but didn't; make-up she would have applied, but didn't; vials of pills she would have taken. These were all based on tenets upon which she'd based her life, costumes she had worn back home, and might have worn still, had she not had the good fortune to set her hair on fire, face-down a snake, and dress in strangers' clothing.

Reaching further inside, Clair found what she was looking for: Lucky's gift. The ribbon was a little skewed, but it was still decorative enough for a special present.

"This is for you, Lucky, my dear and forever friend. I love you so much."

Lucky put her hands over her heart, tears exposing deep feelings, which words would not express any better. She unwrapped the tiny box, smiling all the while, until her eyes fell upon a gold locket nestled on a white silken pillow.

"Oh, Clair!" she exclaimed, reaching for her friend. "It's just like the one I lost!"

"Yes," Clair nodded. "I didn't know what to get you for your birthday, but wandering in a little antique shop one day, I saw this and knew. Open it."

The other women moved in closer to see.

As the gold heart opened, it revealed the wide-grinning faces of two young girls, one wearing a locket—as those girls, now women, clutched each other, confirming in this moment what the great spiritual sages and quantum physicists alike attested: The past, the present, and the future co-exist.

"Found that letter—here it is." Greg was back, holding up an envelope.

"And here's my license to prove who I am," Clair said, taking it out of her now-recovered purse and handing it to him after tucking the plastic bag into the case.

Greg looked at Clair, then at the license picture. "Changed your hair," he commented. "Looks fabulous."

"Um … thank you?"

Stepping away from the counter, the mysterious envelope in hand, Clair joined the women, who formed a circle around her, all curious about the contents of the letter. Clair expected that it would be an apology from the airline, but the heading began: "Dear Clair." Her eyes shot immediately down to the closing and then up at the four faces looking back at her.

"What's it say?" Lucky asked, impatiently.

"It's from Ben," Clair answered. She took a deep breath and began reading it out loud.

> "I know you'll be happy to get this back. I
> have quite a story to tell."

She lifted her eyes from the page in disbelief, then continued.

> "While I was waiting for a limo outside the
> airport, I noticed a man standing near me
> who I recognized from our flight. He had a
> familiar-looking bag, and then I
> remembered yours, which I'd seen you open.
> It didn't match his other bags, so when he
> was busy hailing a cab, I looked at the
> nametag."

"Gutsy move," Jesse said emphatically.

> "I picked it up and said, 'Excuse me, sir, but
> I think you've taken the wrong bag.'"

"Yes!" Jesse cheered.

> "With that he began to run."

"Oh, my God!" Clair exclaimed, eyes growing ever wider.

> "It was quite a scene, Clair. Airport security
> and police. All a pretty exciting way to
> begin my wild west adventure."

"Oh, my God," Clair intoned again. "Can you believe this?"

Clair's face was flushed, mouth agape as she faced Lucky and the others.

"Well, isn't that just the coolest thing!" Alex exclaimed.

"A real live hero," VJ agreed.

As the women were talking about the letter and Ben, Lucky, who was staring off into the distance, said, "It's Ben."

"Yes," Clair affirmed, "he wrote the letter." She wondered why Lucky was sounding confused.

"I don't mean the letter," Lucky clarified. "I mean there's the man from your drawing pad. There's Ben." She pointed outside.

Clair followed the direction of Lucky's finger and saw a man having just stepped out of a black jeep attached to a silver Airstream, two lounge chairs tied on the back.

The man had on cargo shorts, shirttail out, a baseball cap on his head.

"That *is* Ben." Clair spoke as if in a dream.

"He has great legs," VJ weighed in.

"What's he doing here?" Clair asked, but inside she already felt the answer.

"He's going to get a parking ticket, leaving his rig there," worried Alex.

"Honey, I don't think the man cares." Lucky rolled her eyes, then watched as Ben jogged alongside the panes of glass, slowing as he passed through the automatic doors. Then crossing the threshold, he turned his head toward the airline counters, where the women all stood in disbelief.

Clair saw recognition and relief flash in his eyes as he spotted her, his pace slowing as he came forward, whole face smiling. His eyes were the same as she remembered; they never wavered.

"You got your bag, I see," he called out, then approached her, slowing his pace. "I was hoping you would."

"I was just reading your note," Clair held it up along with the new ticket Greg had issued. "Thank you, Ben … so much! What a story."

"My pleasure. Made me feel like James Bond for a moment," he laughed, reaching to shake her hand. "Wow, you look different … I mean, great … but yeah, different."

When his warm hand wrapped itself around hers, Clair touched her hair self-consciously. "Had an impromptu haircut, but Ben, these are my friends." She indicated the others.

"Who's the birthday girl?"

"I am," said Lucky, stepping toward him, hand extended. "And this is Alex, VJ, and Jesse. And speaking for all of us, you are quite the hero, though I admit I thought you might have been the thief."

Ben laughed out loud. A rowdy full laugh. "Yes! The notorious ladies-luggage burglar!"

Turning to the others he shook their hands in turn, eyes crinkling into well-worn grooves exposing the truth of his face.

"I got in from Dallas a couple of hours ago," he explained to Clair, hand to his chest as if he'd been rushing and was trying to slow his heart rate. "Just picked up the Jeep and Airstream, and when I checked the time of the last flight to Boston, I hoped I might catch you. See if the suitcase got back to you."

At that moment, she read his mind about another reason.

The group of six had moved out of the way of others waiting to check their luggage. Outside a policewoman with a scowling face was moving toward the jeep. Alex saw this and went running outside, Jesse behind her.

"Clair, do you want to do something crazy?" he asked suddenly. He looked as if he thought about it any longer, he wouldn't have the courage to get it out. "I mean crazy besides the snake that I'm seeing crawling up your arm … which I hope you'll tell me about sometime." His gaze had darted to the henna snake, but now focused on her face, hoping it might reveal what was still unknown to him. Her answer.

She looked up and met his gaze.

"Come with me," he said, prompting her.

She could barely form a thought, her mind was jumping in a staccato fashion. She held up the letter he had written. "You asked me to have dinner in a few weeks."

"You're right. I did but then I thought why wait, so I'm asking something different now."

Clair pried her eyes away from Ben and looked at Lucky, who was close enough to overhear their conversation. *What did Clair seek from her? Permission? Encouragement?* Lucky uttered no words, but her answer was crystal clear.

VJ stood still as a statue alongside Lucky. Both were wide-eyed with suspense as they all waited for Clair's answer.

"Come with me, Clair," Ben coaxed in a whisper. "Listen to that voice inside that's ready to jump on board. Think of the best that could happen." His dark eyebrows raised. "That we have an adventure, that we see incredible wonders, that we ... continue our conversation?" His voice trailed off.

Clair looked at her surroundings, at how there were people everywhere leading their suitcases like small animals. She looked at Ben, noticing his beaded bracelet again. *I must ask him if he's a Buddhist.*

She remembered back to that rainy day in Maine. That terrible day when her world collapsed and left her under the rubble in the darkness, certain it would crush her. But it hadn't. With a little help from her friends, she'd climbed out. She longed to break through the lonely facade she had lived behind, crack the plaster, take off that mask and her old clothes, dance in the rain more, discover something more of her real self. She felt that that person would want an adventure after all those years. All those years.

Possible images of the future flashed through her mind of high red cliffs, rushing river water, nights under the stars sitting on two lounge chairs. Ben had brought a lounge chair for her, for goodness sakes. She noticed that beyond the large plate-glass windows, Alex was using all her skills as a therapist to convince the policewoman not to tow the vehicle. And Jesse, gesticulating wildly, was reassuring the officer that the jeep and the trailer would be moved any minute now.

"I have a trailer full of art supplies, books, maps, and food," Ben enticed, hoping that would sweeten the deal.

"Before I give my answer, I have one serious question for you."

"Anything."

"Do you have Tequila?" Clair asked, looking up at him in wonder.

He grinned widely. "Not only that, but limes and salt as well."

Clair glanced out of the window again. The camper was sitting there. No ticket yet. Curtains hung in the windows. What would it mean to go with him? Anything was possible. Everything was possible. She felt her voice, the one stilled from years of being ignored, now back, and it was saying "Yes, yes, yes!" to Ben, to adventure, to life, to what the hell, to letting in all she could, all she hadn't, all that was possible. Every fiber of her being, every molecule in her that was dancing the dance of the universe, Shiva's Dance, stepped forward.

She waved the newly-issued first class ticket in the air.

"Anyone want a free ticket to Boston?"

⚡

EPILOGUE

Clair stands on the rocky beach, enjoying the mild air for a mid-September day. She wears loose white cotton pants rolled up to her calves, drawstring cord dangling, yellow T-shirt hugging small breasts and slim body. The fairy-stone talisman encircles her neck, but now there is also Lucky's gift of the lightning bolt pinned to the ribbing of her cotton T-shirt. Her hair is dark, wavy, unbound.

Sunlight dances on blue-green water. She checks the Baume & Mercier watch with a leather band on her left wrist—all healed—and heads for the house. Along the way, she admires the fall-blooming red rhododendrons that she nursed back to health after a particularly cold winter.

In the bedroom beset with bouquets of feverfew, chamomile, asters, and Queen Anne's lace, she looks around one last time and smiles at three twin-sized Euro beds, made up with white throws over soft yellow linens, identical in all but size to the king-sized bed holding court in the center of the room. On the wall above the bed hangs one of her old paintings, an abstract, in shades of pale yellows and orange, with touches of light blue and a rounded white shape that could be a helium balloon that has escaped or even a shimmering autumn moon.

Since she's returned, Clair has been going through boxes that haven't been opened in years. One day she finds a whole collection of her paintings that her mother had carefully stored away.

Oh, Mom, I wish I'd known that they mattered to you ... that I mattered to you.

The French doors to the patio are wide open, gauzy curtains fluttering at the hemline. She moves through the house, picks up a straw basket in the kitchen, exits, then enters the garage. It's dark there and cool, she observes, before opening the car door and sliding onto the soft leather seat.

Clair drives under a scroll of metal letters at the end of the driveway—"Harbor House" in reverse: "esuoH robraH"—where a Sotheby's sign sits by a stone pillar, announcing: "For Sale. Shown by Appointment." The air through the open window tosses her hair wildly. She allows it. Her left arm, gaining muscle from her physical therapy program, rests on the car door. It's the day before her forty-eighth birthday. She feels young, though she's not blind to some recent gray hairs that have threaded through the others.

After a ten-minute drive along the Maine coastline, she pulls up at a smaller clapboard house with green shutters where a sign in front offers, "Tea Leaves. Readings." Opening the gate, Clair follows a pebbled path to the backyard, passing a row of Rosa rugosa, a prevalent plant here, whose fall fruit is bursting with Vitamin C, just perfect for a cuppa like her Irish grandmother might have brewed. She pauses, eyes searching.

"Hello!" she cries out, seeing Grace bending over a ground-level vegetable bed.

"Hullo, yourself!" Grace waves then rises, holding her lower back, and heads stiffly toward her friend. She laughs ruefully and says in her lilting English accent, "I've got to hire someone to raise these beds … they are just too low for me now."

"Here, let me take that basket, Grace," Clair offers the older woman, "and I'll ask Geraldine for her grandson's name and number. He does that kind of work and I know would be grateful for the job."

Beyond Grace's Garden of Eden, the channel is busy with boats. It is well-attended by flocks of seagulls fighting for airspace above them and diving for chum tossed overboard by tanned-faced fishermen in oilskins and tall rubber boots.

The two women embrace warmly. Grace takes off her gloves to hold Clair's face in her two hands, and observes, "You look happy, my girl … got some friends arriving tonight, do ya?"

Clair loves Grace's warm motherly way and her wisdom, which Grace shares as freely as she does the bounty of her garden. The two have become close since Clair's return from New Mexico, with Clair willingly taking on the role of helpful daughter as well as that of friend.

"I'm picking them up at the airport at seven," Clair grins. "I've made clam chowder, to which I've added the green chile that Lucky sent—a little taste of New Mexico. And because it's Maine, a lobster salad for a second course."

"Very well thought out."

"The beds are made up for Alex, VJ, and Jesse. Lucky and I will sleep together like we did as girls."

The garden is a picture of abundance—Monet's Garden at Giverny—flowers showing off their fall colors, fruit trees heavy with apples, pears, and peaches, branches slumping, ready to give them up. Vegetables had been in neat rows, but now are meandering everywhere, Morning Glories climb the old vegetable vines without any fear of heights—all beautiful, bountiful, bursting with life and labor.

"Well, as you can see, there's no need for you to shop for any veggies; I've been filling a couple of baskets for you."

"Thank you for all this, Grace. We will eat like queens! And you're coming for dinner on Wednesday, right?"

"Wouldn't miss meeting The Pride … not after the stories I've heard," she laughs, rolling her eyes. "I'm also sending with you a basket of veggies for The Knitters. Do you mind dropping it off for them?"

Clair and Grace used a verbal shortcut with each other when speaking of Geraldine, Flora, and Millie, collectively and lovingly referring to them as "The Knitters" just as Lucky, Alex, VJ, and Jesse were "The Pride."

"No, of course I don't mind, and they'll be delighted … though they do all complain about too much roughage."

"Oh, Lord!" Grace shivers. "Spare us from that!"

Clair laughs then stops and sighs, looking concerned. "Actually, they've been having a hard time. Everyone's a bit worried but trying not to show it. Flora has another medical test scheduled for next week."

"Oh, dear. Let me put a bouquet of sunflowers together before you leave. Flowers make everyone feel better. But I have a feeling that there's no need to worry. And give Flora my love."

Clair nods gratefully. "Yes, I will."

"Come. Follow me, Clair. I've made tea for us," invites Grace, and leads Clair to a tray with two empty China cups and a clay teapot covered by a tea cozy. Grace removes the cozy and takes the pot. As if it's choreography, Clair promptly takes the two empty cups from the tray and follows Grace to the bench where they like to sit and look out toward the sea. The bench is one Grace's husband had made, and through the years has acquired a fine patina.

"By the way," Grace says, setting the teapot on a small table, "I love using VJ's clay teapot. Thank you for it. It's just the right size and the spout doesn't drip, the mark of a well-made pot."

"As VJ would say, 'De nada!'" Clair smiles, pleased that she will be seeing the women again and especially that they are coming out for her birthday.

"I'm looking forward to meeting her and the others, but especially Lucky, of course. I've heard so much more about her as she's so intertwined in your early life."

"They're excited to meet you too … and they all want tea-leaf readings."

"How jolly! Well, then, I'll get out my appointment book."

The air feels warm on Clair's skin, and she can hear the snap-snap sound of flags on the masts of boats.

"So how are you feeling about your birthday?" Grace asks.

Clair pauses a moment, considering the question. "Marvelous," she says. "Optimistic, hopeful … things I never could have imagined feeling. You were so right when you told me, 'Tell him goodbye and thank him.'"

"And the divorce? How's that coming along?"

"It's happening," Clair shrugs. "After my initial reaction of shock and fury."

"Perfectly understandable, dear." Grace reaches out and pats Clair's hand.

"Well, I'm in favor. I'm ready, even eager. I know now it should have happened years ago. It'll be quick. I have the house, which is worth quite a lot. And I have my art collection, also more than I expected. I don't want anything more from him. I've had a good eye through the years, taking risks on new artists, and it's paid off. I'm lucky." Saying that stops her. "Did you hear that, Grace? I'm lucky too. Lucky's not the only one." And she laughs.

Grace pours more tea into their cups, smiling as enigmatically as a Cheshire cat. "Tell me more, dear."

"I've realized that the best part about this whole separation and divorce thing is my communication with Blake—it's so much better! I talked to him on the phone the other day about Cassidy and her art program. We actually had a pleasant conversation. We even shared a laugh. The animosity between us is diminished. I find I feel neutral. He's not the bad guy; we got ourselves here together."

A flash of sunlight reflects off the silver lightning bolt on Clair's shirt. A fisherman on his boat sees a sparkle from shore as he hauls up a lobster trap, and he wonders momentarily what the flash could be. The piece of jewelry that Lucky had given each of the women had become Clair's constant—every day she took it off the previous day's clothing and pinned it onto the present day's attire.

She had begun wearing it that day at the Lightning Field and kept wearing it during the week with Ben as they traveled through the desert southwest in the rented land yacht. It became part of her daily attire as they got to know each other, which happens pretty fast, it turns out, when you're living in a two-hundred-square-foot space. They did, of course, have the great outdoors, to cook over an open fire, drink a Negro Modela or down a shot of tequila, all while gaping at scenery that made them both gasp. Ben read poetry to her and turned out to be a gentleman, giving Clair the bed for herself since they'd had no time for a proper courtship.

Clair laughs to herself, thinking about it. *That arrangement lasted two nights.* Then he joined her in the bed and in her arms, leaving them both breathless and ravenous. To Clair, the pin of the lightning bolt had become a talisman that brought her immeasurable good luck.

"Oh, and did I tell you? I'm legally taking back my maiden name. Once the papers are signed, I'm Clair Cassidy again."

"Well, let me extend my congratulations to you on becoming yourself."

"And, in other news, they did an ultrasound on Carl's baby."

"And it's a ...?"

"Girl!" Clair sang. "And Grace, I knew it, I just knew it."

"Double congratulations!" came Grace's musical voice, which then took on a more serious tone. "I am so happy for you, Clair."

"Look!" Clair pulls an envelope from her straw basket and hands it to Grace, who opens it and reads the card out loud.

"Happy Birthday, Grammy." Inside the envelope is a paper that Grace unfolds.

"That's her," Clair exclaims, pointing to a bubble of hard-to-distinguish black and white. "My granddaughter. I'm calling her 'My Little Mermaid' and sometimes "Guppy," because she's swimming inside her mom."

Grace studies the blurred image. "Why, I think she favors you."

"A mini-me of my own," Clair says with delight, holding the image to her heart. "Carl made it for me on his computer. And I got something from Cass too … one of her first works of art at school–a stunning mixed-media scene from her time in Italy that's so creatively constructed. I remember when I used to put her artwork up on the refrigerator. Now she's studying art for real. I'm so proud of her. She grew up quite a bit traveling in Europe and did some growing as well, so it's been much easier for us when we're together."

Suddenly, one of the cats leaps out of nowhere and sprints across the yard.

"They're getting so big!" laughs Clair. "I can't tell the kittens from the mom anymore."

"And they're wild. I wish you'd take one home with you."

"I might. I'd love one, but I have to decide how much traveling I might be doing."

"I can always babysit," Grace offers. "Comes with the deal."

"Then, yes, sure I will once Lucky leaves."

"I don't mean to force you into a decision, Clair darling."

"You're not. I'd love to have another feline after living with one in New Mexico. Oh, and speaking of …. I have another picture to show you," she says, rummaging in her basket.

"Now, isn't Kore the regal queen!" Grace remarks, looking at the picture Clair hands her. "And formidable. I would say she certainly has grown into Persephone."

"Yes, you're right, I can't wait to show this picture to The Pride … Clete sent it," Clair smiles, looking at it, "along with some information on the field that I'd asked for. That was so dear of him. I was worried about Kore when we left. And Clete sent this picture too." Clair hands it to Grace.

"Lovely! A big circle of bright yellow sunflowers," Grace observes with pleasure.

"They're the flowers we planted in the final ceremony at the field," Clair smiles. "I've made a framed picture of it for each of The Pride to take home, my birthday present to them: pictures of their intentions flowering."

In the distance, the sound of children's blissful squealing echoes across the water. Grace and Clair look at each other, grinning at the playful sounds.

"I had dinner with Ben again a few nights ago."

"And …?"

"Nice. Very nice," Clair admits. "I met him in Boston, and we had dinner at this charming little neighborhood bistro in the Back Bay. It's wonderful spending time in Boston again. It's been a while, and I'd forgotten how much I love the city and all it offers. Then we walked to the esplanade along the Charles River and listened to a concert at the Hatch Shell. Ben brought a blanket to spread out on the grass. It was a lovely night. For my birthday, he wants me to go to the Cape for a weekend after Lucky leaves."

"It's sounding serious."

Clair's brow furrows in contemplation. "No, it's really not. I know I'm not ready for serious yet … nor is he. We're both beginning our new lives. It's more like we're becoming really good friends who support each other in this time of transition. Is there romance? Sure, which is quite exciting since I haven't had any, maybe ever. But Ben's rented a studio loft on Beacon Street and has begun sculpting again, a longing he's had for years. And The Knitters have offered me wall space in their shop for some of the drawings I made at the field. When you come for dinner on Wednesday, I'd like you and The Pride to help me choose which drawing to frame."

"That will be hard … I love them all."

"Jesse said something while we were at the field. She said she's building her own ship before building a *relation*ship. We groaned at the corniness at the time, but I've been thinking about it. Grace, I need to do that. I want to do that!"

"You get to do that!"

"That's right," Clair agrees, toasting her cup of tea to Grace's. "And it's official today: The sign is up and the house is officially on the market."

"Good for you! Are you still keeping the acre you showed me?"

"Yes, the one at the furthest edge of the property with that private cove on the beach. I'm excited about designing another house there, something small for me, with a light-filled studio and a couple of extra bedrooms for the kids and grandkids and my friends … and who knows, maybe even Blake's child?"

"You've made some remarkable changes, Clair. I hope you're proud of yourself."

"I do feel good about the steps I've taken in the last few months. I know I have a ways to go … and every once in a while, I do feel the fear come up."

"What does the fear say?"

"Oh, that this happiness I feel is not real and will disappear. Or that I won't be able to paint anything, that the images that used to show up in my mind that inspired me won't come anymore. I had a frightening dream the other day."

"Tell me."

"Well, I was in my house and, as I was walking through it, looking out at the ocean, everything became dark, ominous, frightening, and then the floor started collapsing under me, each step disintegrating as I began to run through the rooms."

"I'm sure that was terrifying, Clair, but perhaps it's an image of your old world disintegrating. There's an order to things, first disintegration then building the new. We all feel fear occasionally and it's healthy to acknowledge that, but don't let it stop you from doing what you feel called to do."

"Grace, you always help me look at things in a more comprehensive way."

"I'm glad I can. The best part of aging is being able to offer a hand to others."

"I did show Ben the acre the last time he was here. He encouraged me to, 'have at it,' as he put it. I like that he has confidence in me, that he believes I can do it." Clair puts her hand to her chest. "He sees a strong me. He promised he'd step in if my design gets too unruly, but on one condition: I have to ask."

"He's a good man, Ben … reminds me a bit of my late husband. So creative."

"He is. I love that about him." Clair puts her hand over her mouth as if she'd revealed a secret. "Oh, dear! Did I say love?" The two women share a chuckle before Clair continues. "So, I'll draw up the plans for my new home during the winter and be ready to build next spring and summer." Then, she adds with a wry grin, "Aren't I lucky to have a friend on standby, willing to offer his expertise?"

Grace smiles and reaches toward Clair, patting her hand in a supportive gesture. "You're doing fine, my girl … remember, there's no rush, with anything or anyone. You're defining who you are and what you want in your life with every choice you make. Dream as big as you dare and let your imagination soar. Become yourself, Clair Cassidy. And then let it all go—and just be."

Clair stands up, hands on hips, unknowingly striking a Wonder Woman pose as she looks out toward the horizon and the deep blue of the ocean, which had contained such a tragic memory. She admires the cerulean blue of the sky—not New Mexico blue—but lovely all the same and, with a great sense of peace, remarks, "It's all so clear."

ACKNOWLEDGMENTS

Deep Bow ...

... to my *second* sister, **Mae Bradshaw**, the Alpha to my Omega, who can reminisce with me all the way back to four years old. And to our parents, **Jo and Frank, and Jo and Frank**—yes, that's right, our parents all had the same names. They raised us with love and laughter, lots of friends around, and, best of all, with each other.

... to lifelong "prom date" **Gale Kunkle**. Yay! *The girls of OLN! We are the best of friends*—they got that right—sixty-eight years and counting. Why is it that more often than not we regress in a flash to being thirteen?

My Gemini Pals:

... to **Maureen Curran**, friend of fifty-one years, who invited me out of my shell by asking me a million questions that made me reflect, which in turn created my need to write. And she always said, "Yes," even to the outrageous idea of renting a rundown Winnebago and taking off on a cross-country trip that changed our lives forever!

... to **Deanne Newman**, friend of thirty-nine years, Jungian analyst, who dives deep with me daily into the Unconscious, or is equally up to the task of binge-watching 121 episodes of *Lost,* which is how we spent our covid "vacation." DeeDee and I met at a gym, of all places, and after meeting, quit our careers as weightlifters and never joined another gym. We got what we came for, not muscles but an enduring friendship as we "walk each other home." Thanks, Ram Dass.

Both of these women believed in me long before I believed in myself. They were first in line to read the seedling sprouts of this story more than twenty-five years ago; they are the first ones I called in my deepest tragedy; they are the ones I call when I want to laugh the loudest or bare my most shameful secrets. I am truly at "home" with each of them.

My "Soul Guides":

… to Sister Fish, **Leana Melat**, who swam in her home territory of the dreamworld with me, showed me the neighborhood, both the castles and the scary places. Every Thursday I could sit in the comforting green leather chair and expose my most hidden places and still feel loved and welcomed. Such is her heart.

… to awesome **Csara Shubin**, who told me I could leave, which changed everything. She enlarges my understanding of, well, everything. With Csara, I stand bedazzled as if I'm looking at pictures of the universe captured by the James Webb Space Telescope.

… to **Arielle Guttman**, brilliant astrologer, friend of thirty years, who kicked open another door of understanding—the map of my present existence on a piece of paper—and taught me the symbolic language of the stars. Here is where you are. Here is what's coming up. Here is where you're going.

… to **Linda Leonard**, Jungian Analyst, writer, hiking pal, your books, and our deep, meandering, conversations, woke up a sleeping part of my soul and led me to a deeper layer of my own journey into the unconscious. I am so grateful.

My Pals:

… to **Chris Spanovich**, bunny-love, creative artist, master builder, mighty warrior! The first woman I met in New Mexico, who showed me a whole different breed of womanhood; those early morning raku firings and building with mud bricks. Chris, we always close the place down, don't we?

… to **Micki Lando-Brown**, gone too soon, who said, "You can do that!"

… to Sister Fish **Elizabeth Ann Dugan**, neighbor, and Bama girl, who gave me the means to begin!

… to Sister Fish **Paddy Keen**, dear neighbor, chef extraordinaire, who feeds and nourishes me in all kinds of ways.

… to Sister Fish **Patricia Sheppard,** neighbor, who's keeping the flame alive at 1330.

… to **Eva Schwartz**, also a neighbor, who coaxes me out to walk, and can lift heavy objects!

… to **Julianne Burton-Carvajal**, yet another neighbor, whose early editing expertise made me think this story might be worth another look.

… to **Lynn Zell**, baby cousin, remembering our summers in the muggy heat of Alabama where the Bruce clan gathered at 1920 Rocky Hollow, and how you cried because, no matter what, my dress was always bigger than yours.

… to **Susan Eartheart**, for the miles through the mountains and arroyos, and the conversations!

… to **Mary Beckman and Kim Anderson**, who together with me, became The Three Amigas! *"Bulletin! Three senior citizens and four dogs were last seen cross-country skiing in a snowstorm though the forests of Northern New Mexico high on gummies bought illegally from the state to the north. If you see them, let them be. They look scary but are harmless."* Amigas, I will carry that riotous moment with me forever. And so many more. Thank you!

… to Sister Fish, **Tina Sheffield**, who offered a port in a storm, which has now become my haven by the sea, while Tina, an English lass, with the bawdiest laugh ever, has become my dear friend.

… to Sister Fish, **Joan Bloomgarden**. We met while going for PhD's; she got her doctorate. I got her! We created our way through thirty years of a multitude of art projects and travels with our guys through the wild west.

… to "brother" and fellow writer, **Nathan Leblang**, who read and encouraged.

… to **Deanne Jameson**, who sat in a little boat with me and talked through an early version of the story.

My Santa Fe Writing Group:

… to Joan Brooks Baker, Felice Gonzales, Peter Goodwin, and Anna Jastrzembski, who listened to scenes and asked, "What happened next?"

My Writing Midwives:

… to the late **Linna Thomas**, my own personal Glinda the Good Witch, co-founder of Coalesce Books in Morro Bay, California, who, twenty years ago, offered me a job in her magical bookstore and reflected back to me a new image of myself. "Fare Forward, Voyager!"

… To **Sherri Hereford** and **Joanne Hand**, the keepers of the flame at Coalesce Books who read a version of this story twenty years ago, I thank you. I've loved books all my life and to get to work at a bookstore that's right out of a fairy tale was my joy, and these two women made it so!

… to **Brian Schwartz** and his team, who made my dream of publishing a book a reality and who has afforded me yet another incarnation of myself. Thank you, Brian, for guiding me along this untraveled path. You made it exciting and you made it happen.

… to **Patricia Alexander**, my editor, par excellence! I'm so grateful for your expertise in helping me to tell my story more clearly, for making the editing process actually fun, and for pointing out, very gently, that perhaps I didn't need all those ellipses. Now, let's go have lunch!

… and I raise a shot glass of tequila to **Steve Holzer**, visionary artist, gone way too early, who kidnapped me and brought me willingly into the Underworld for fifteen extraordinary years. I was with Steve when I began doing my early research for this book in Maine, 1997. Together during several trips to the Lightning Field, along with our third musketeer, Big Boy, our "hairy dolphin,"

Steve, playmate extraordinaire, gave me the great love story of my life. And he had "the laugh—in fact, he was infamous for it! He's laughing now. I can hear him, as he is *not* one to rest in peace. 'Til our next hot date in the quantum, Steve O!

My Family:

… to my parents, **Jo Bruce and Frank Garfi**, a confederate and a yankee, who met in another war, but whose love for each other would help heal any divide. My mother taught me that to have a friend you must be a friend. As an only child, with no sisters, I've been gathering them ever since. My father taught me kindness and showed me an artist's lens of the world.

… to the late **Dick Sanborn**, my one and only legal marriage, the small town boy with big ambition and lifeguard good looks who enticed me at nineteen to marry him and go down his yellow brick road … and I did. I thank him for the best of us, our two beautiful sons, Eric and Matthew.

… to my beloved firstborn, **Eric**. While his father was learning to land jets on aircraft carriers. I was learning to "Mother," my job being the more terrifying; Dick at least had an instructor and a manual. I hope I've done a few things right. Eric is a lifelong adventurer, photographer, filmmaker, soccer referee, born to travel and teach. He's taken me to places I never would have even considered going … like Antarctica! Seeing him as a father is what makes me the most proud of him. And to his wife **Kendre**, kindhearted, loving, center of their home, yet a modern woman with her own life path. These two have given me the crowning jewels of my life: my grandchildren, **Andrew, Emily, and Claira**, who brought me to a whole new dimension of love. I feel so honored to have a front-row seat as they enter today's world as kind and contributing adults, each in a profession perfectly matched to their talents. And they are fun, and funny, a joy to be with.

… and in memory of my tender-hearted, freedom-loving son Matt with his dazzling smile: **Matthew Bruce Sanborn, 5/3/69 to 1/31/12.** You were the Feeling expression of our family, Matty. I'll love you forever. And I understand—you had to go. *"Skiing through the trees, Mom, is like my church!"* See you next time, Beautiful Son, on the mountaintops you love so much.

BOOK CLUB QUESTIONS

1. The book begins with a quote "The Invisible is Real." How do invisible realms show up in the story?

2. Why was *The Lightning Field* the right title for this novel? What did it mean to you?

3. How does the experience of losing her brother Patrick impact both Clair and her family?

4. Patrick, another victim of the family of origin, couldn't bear it any longer and set himself on fire—why would he choose such a painful death?

5. What is Grace's contribution to the story?

6. Why did Clair stay so long in her marriage?

7. Clair was a victim of childhood abuse through the alcohol addiction of her father and the household dominance of her mother's depression—how did you feel about Clair when she herself was repeating her family's patterns?

8. What is the significance of Clair's meeting with Ben? What was his impact on the story?

9. Why did the author deliberately have Clair arrive at the Lightning Field stripped of all her possessions?

10. What part do Lucky and the other women play in Clair's awakening?

11. Did you have a favorite character? If so, who? Least favorite character?

12. Which of the characters would you want to have as a friend?

13. The book is about women's friendships—do the characters remind you of any of your own friends?

14. Do you have these kinds of frank discussions with your friends? If not, would you like to?

15. What particular scenes stand out as significant to you and why?

16. The story uses many symbols, like the snake, and myths, such as Persephone. What did that add to or subtract from the story for you?

17. How does Clair's character and her perception of herself change over the course of the story?

18. What acts of courage did Clair take on her own behalf?

19. Do you (or someone you know) receive powerful nudges from your intuition? Have you had any psychic experiences?

20. Do you feel you learned something new by reading *The Lightning Field*? If so, what?

21. Do you have any favorite quotes or passages you would like to share?

22. Has there ever been a catalyst like the Lightning Field in your own life that sparked a new way of thinking or a transition for you?

ABOUT COALESCE PRESS

"Coalesce" reflects the mission of Morro Bay's beloved bookstore: *to grow together and unite*. Coalesce Press was established to extend the voices and stories that bring communities closer.

In Memory of Linna Thomas

Linna Thomas embodied the very essence of what made Coalesce Press a beacon for literary voices on the Central Coast, bringing to her publishing endeavors the same gracious spirit, unwavering support, and keen literary instincts that defined her 52 years as the heart of Coalesce Bookstore and Garden Chapel in Morro Bay.

Coalesce Press reflects Linna's deeper understanding that books are not mere commodities but vessels for the "spiritual magic that only occurs when one reads," and she dedicated herself to nurturing that magic by providing authors with not just a publisher, but a friend and advocate who believed in the transformative power of words. *Steeped* would have strongly resonated with Linna.

Learn more at CoalescePress.com